"So what's up? Did you call to check up on me?"

Paige laughed. "I'm looking for a youth hockey league in the area."

"You're in luck. I happen to have a buddy who's a hockey fan, and he's coach, commissioner and sponsor of the local youth league all rolled into one."

"You call it lucky. I call it blessed. You, Grady Jones, are a blessing."

For moments he literally floundered over the phone. Finally he sputtered, "Uh, n-no one, th-that is, what I mean… I take it this is for your son."

"Who else? I know it's an imposition, but my son wants to play hockey. It won't make him happy, but I thought it might improve his attitude."

Grady imagined that she seemed as reluctant to end the conversation as he was. He promised to talk to his buddy and get back to her soon. A moment of silence followed, then Paige spoke softly.

"I meant what I said, Grady. You've been an answer to prayer for me more than once, and I thank God for that."

"Makes me wish I believed in prayer."

Books by Arlene James

Love Inspired

*Everyday Miracles

ARLENE JAMES

says, "Camp meetings, mission work and the church where my parents and grandparents were prominent members permeate my Oklahoma childhood memories. It was a golden time, which sustains me yet. However, only as a young, widowed mother did I truly begin growing in my personal relationship with the Lord. Through adversity He blessed me in countless ways, one of which is a second marriage so loving and romantic it still feels like courtship!"

The author of over sixty novels, Arlene James now resides outside Dallas, Texas, with her husband. Arlene says, "The rewards of motherhood have indeed been extraordinary for me. Yet I've looked forward to this new stage of my life." Her need to write is greater than ever, a fact that frankly amazes her, as she's been at it since the eighth grade!

When Love Comes Home

Arlene James

Steeple
Hill®

Published by Steeple Hill Books™

STEEPLE HILL BOOKS

Steeple
Hill®

ISBN-13: 978-0-373-81295-0
ISBN-10: 0-373-81295-7

WHEN LOVE COMES HOME

www.SteepleHill.com

Printed in U.S.A.

Therefore, let those also who suffer according to the will of God entrust their souls to a faithful Creator in doing what is right.
—*I Peter* 4:19

Victoria, I know you are too small to read or even understand this yet, but the place you hold in my heart is immense, and it's never too early to say, "I love you." Granna

Chapter One

 ❧

Grady frowned across the desk at his older brother and fought the urge to fold his arms in an act of pure defiance. It wasn't just that Dan expected Grady to spend Thanksgiving traveling for business but that he expected him to do it with Paige Ellis.

Pretty, petite Paige made Grady feel even more hulking and awkward than usual. It didn't help that Dan might have just stepped out of the pages of a men's fashion magazine. Slender and sleek, his dark hair having long since gone to silver, Dan served as a perfect contrast to his much larger—and much less dapper—younger brother. Dan was elegant, glittering silver compared to Grady's dull-as-sand brown.

Dan's white shirt looked as if it had just come off the ironing board, while Grady's might have just come off the floor. The navy pinstripes in Dan's expertly knotted burgundy tie perfectly matched his hand-tailored suit. Grady's chocolate-brown neckwear, on the other hand, somehow clashed with a suit that he'd once thought brown but now seemed a dark, muddy green.

The only thing the Jones brothers seemed to share, besides their parents and a law practice, were eyes the vibrant blue of a perfect spring sky. Grady considered them wasted in the heavily featured expanse of his own square-jawed face.

"It's not as if you'd enjoy the holiday anyway," Dan was saying.

Grady grimaced, conceding the point. Okay, he wasn't eagerly anticipating another chaotic feast at Dan's place in Bentonville. Why would he? A fellow couldn't even watch a good football game without one of his three nieces or sister-in-law interrupting every other minute.

"I didn't say I wouldn't do it," he grumbled. "I said the timing stinks."

No one wanted to spend a major holiday flying from Arkansas to South Carolina, but for Grady the task seemed especially disagreeable because it involved a woman and a kid.

Grady did not relate well to women, as his ex-wife had been fond of pointing out. She had contended that it had to do with losing his mother at such a young age, and no doubt she was right about that. He always felt inept and stupid in female company, never quite knowing what to say. As for children, well, he hadn't known any, except for his nieces, and he'd pretty much kept his distance from them. These days their adolescent behavior made him feel as if he'd stumbled into an alternate universe.

Besides, family law was Dan's forte, not Grady's. Give him a good old bare-knuckle brawl of a lawsuit or a complicated legal trust to craft. Even criminal defense work was preferable to prenups, divorces and custody cases, though he hadn't done much criminal defense since he'd left Little Rock. After his marriage had failed he'd come back home to Fayetteville and the general practice established by his and Dan's father, Howard.

"The timing could be better," Dan agreed, "but it is what it is."

Grady made a face and propped his feet on the corner of his brother's expansive cherrywood desk with a nonchalance he definitely was not feeling. "You're the attorney of record," he pointed out. "You should do this."

Dan had worked every angle on this case from day one. By rights, he ought to be there at the moment of fruition. But Dan had a family who wanted him at the dinner table on Thanksgiving. And Grady had no feasible excuse for not stepping in, even at the last minute.

"Trust me," Dan said, "Paige isn't going to complain."

Paige Ellis had doggedly pursued her ex after he'd disappeared with her son nearly three and a half years ago. Now the boy had been found and was waiting in custody of the state of South Carolina to be reunited with his mother.

Grady was glad for her. He just wished he didn't have to be the one to shepherd her through this reunion. The petite, big-eyed blonde made Grady especially uncomfortable, despite the fact that they hadn't exchanged half a dozen words in the three years or so that she'd been a client of their law firm.

"You'll want to look this over," Dan went on, plopping a file folder a good two inches thick onto the desk next to Grady's feet. "All the pertinent paperwork is ready. You should probably take it with you when you inform Paige about her son."

Grady bolted up straight in his chair, his feet hitting the floor. "Now hold on! The least you can do is deliver the news."

Dan turned up both hands in a gesture of helplessness and rocked back in his burgundy leather chair. "Look, I'd love to deliver the good news, but this needs to be done in person ASAP, and Chloe has a jazz band program at three."

Grady knew without even looking at his watch that it was at least half past two in the afternoon now. No way could Dan get to Nobb, where Paige Ellis lived, and back to Bentonville, where his daughters went to school, by three o'clock. If he skipped out on Chloe's performance, Dan's wife, Katie, was liable to skin him alive. Katie wasn't shy about demanding that Dan make his family a priority. Grady didn't understand how his brother could be so disgustingly happy in his marriage, but he was fond enough of Dan to be glad that it was so.

After a few more minutes of discussion, Grady sighed in resignation, gathered up the file folder and strode back to his office, grumbling under his breath. Just thinking about Paige Ellis made him feel even more hulking and plodding than usual.

Thanks to an expensively outfitted home gym, he was in better shape than most thirty-nine-year-olds, but that didn't keep him from feeling too big and too clumsy. Standing a bare inch past six feet in his size twelve shoes, his square, blocky frame hard packed with two hundred pounds of pure muscle, he wasn't exactly a giant, but he'd felt huge and oafish since puberty, when he'd dwarfed the other boys. In the company of some delicate, feminine little creature like Paige Ellis, he felt like a lumbering monster.

Entering his office, Grady turned down the lights, crossed the thick, moss-green carpet, dropped the folder onto his desk and switched on a lamp. He sat down in his oversize brown leather chair, tilted the bronze shade just so and opened the folder. He began thumbing through the notes and documents, scanning the material and jotting down notes as he went.

His ability to read quickly and comprehend completely was his greatest asset and brought in a considerable amount of income in consulting fees. Other attorneys knew that Grady by himself could accomplish more in the way of research than a roomful of clerks. Consequently he spent a good deal of his time alone at his desk.

Grady reached the end of the last page in the file.

After making a copy of his notes for the folder, he tucked it into the file and carried the whole thing to the office of Dan's terribly efficient personal secretary.

Janet was none too fond of Grady. She stared at the file that he placed on her desk, then looked up at him, her pale pink frown seeming to take issue with his very existence.

"What is this?"

"Case file."

She blinked at him, her lashes too black and clumped together. "I can see that it's a case file, but why are you giving it to *me*?"

"You're Dan's secretary."

She let out a long-suffering sigh and narrowed her eyes at him, her lips compressed into a flat line.

Janet had given up complaining that Grady didn't have his own personal secretary, but she made her displeasure known by grudgingly performing those tasks which he did not perform for himself or push off on the young receptionist. Grady had made a half-hearted attempt to find a male secretary at one point, but without success. He'd gotten by with a part-time male law clerk from the University of Arkansas School of Law. Having no personal secretary was an inconvenience, but he had no desire to stutter and stammer his way around a strange female.

Janet flipped open the file folder and checked the contents for herself. "Ah. The Ellis file."

Grady's face heated.

Without a word the secretary handed over the necessary warrants and writs that would be required to prove identities and custody assignments to the South Carolina authorities. She also passed Grady a map and a pair of printed sheets showing the next day's available flights to and from South Carolina via the regional airport and Tulsa, some ninety minutes away. Then she immediately rose and carried the folder into the back room, where it would be swiftly and efficiently filed.

Donning a camel tan cashmere coat that reached midcalf, Grady took the elevator down to the parking lot and a cold, drizzling rain, briefcase in tow. He slung the briefcase on to the seat of his Mercedes and followed it, resisting the urge to huddle inside his coat until the heater started blowing warm air.

While navigating the forty-some miles between Fayetteville, Arkansas, and the tiny community of Nobb tucked into the foothills of the Ozarks to the northwest, Grady mulled over what he would say to Paige Ellis, much as he would have thought out an opening statement. He found the Ellis place on the edge of the village just past a pair of silos and a big, weathered barn. A dirt lane snaked upward slightly between gnarled hickories and majestic oaks, past tumbledown fencing and rusting farm implements to a small, white clapboard house.

After parking his sedan next to a midsize, seven-year-old SUV in dire need of a good washing, Grady stepped out of the car. A scruffy, well-fed black lab got up from a rug on the porch and lumbered lazily down the steep front steps to greet Grady with a sniff.

Dan had judged it best not to call before arriving, and Grady hadn't questioned that decision. Paige Ellis worked from her home as a medical transcriptionist and kept regular hours, so she was apt to be available on any given weekday. Suddenly, though, Grady wondered if it was too late to warn her that he was about to descend upon her. Then the dog abruptly opened its yap and did that for him.

The seemingly placid dog howled an alarm that could have put the entire nation on alert. The lab couldn't have been more vociferous if Grady had shown up wearing a black mask and hauling a crate full of hissing cats.

Feeling like a felon, Grady hotfooted it to the house, practically leapt the steps leading up to the porch and skidded to a halt in front of the door, which needed a coat of white paint. He saw no bell, but a brass knocker with a cross-shaped base had been attached to the door at eye level and engraved with the words, As for me and my house, we shall serve the Lord.

Somehow Grady was not surprised to find this evidence that Paige Ellis was a believer. Dan and his family were Christians, active in their local church and given to praying about matters, as was his father, but Grady himself was something of a secret skeptic. He didn't see any point in arguing about it, but he privately wondered if God even existed. If so, why would He let so many bad things happen, like his mother's death and Paige Ellis's son being abducted by her ex-husband?

With the dog still barking to beat the band, Grady reached for the knocker, but before his hand touched the cool metal, the door yanked open. There stood an old fellow with more balding head than sooty, graying hair. Slightly stooped and dressed in a plaid shirt, khakis, suspenders and laced boots, his potbellied weight supported on one side by a battered cane, he swept Grady with faded brown eyes recessed deeply behind a hooked nose that had been broken at least once. Apparently satisfied, he looked past Grady to yell at the dog.

"Shut up, Howler!"

To Grady's relief, the aptly named dog seemed to swallow his last bark, then calmly padded toward the porch.

"Matthias Porter," the old man said, stacking his gnarled hands atop the curved head of his cane. "Who're you?"

Grady had at least four inches and fifty pounds on Porter, and that cane wasn't for show, but the way the old fellow held himself told Grady that he was a scrapper and the self-appointed protector of this place. Grady put out his hand, aware of the dog moving toward the rug on one end of the porch.

"Grady Jones. I'm here to see—"

"Jones," the older man interrupted, "you're Paige's attorney, ain't you?"

Grady nodded. "Actually, my brother, Dan—"

Porter didn't wait to hear about Dan or anything else. Backing up, he waved Grady into the house, saying, "I don't shake. Too painful. Arthritis in my hands. And you're letting in cold air."

His ears still ringing from the dog's howling, Grady stepped forward and found himself in a small living room. He took in at a glance the braided rag rug on the dull wood floor, the old-fashioned sofa covered in a worn quilt, the yellowed shade on the spotted brass lamp next to a broken-down recliner and a wood-burning stove that filled a corner between two doors. A shelving unit stood against one wall at an angle to the recliner and couch. In its center, surrounded by books and numerous photos of a young boy, sat a combination television-set-and-VCR.

Grady knew that the search for Paige Ellis's son had been expensive. If the condition of this house and its furnishings were any indication, the search had required every spare cent that she could scrape together. Feeling out of place and too big for the space, Grady watched Matthias Porter hobble through a door and disappear into a hallway. He had no idea who Matthias Porter was, but it didn't matter. Standing there like an overgrown houseplant, the handle of his briefcase gripped in one fist, he waited with a strange combination of dread and anticipation for Paige Ellis to show herself.

Paige looked up from the computer screen as Matthias entered the room, her fingers automatically typing out the words that continued to drone into her ears. The interruption was sufficiently unusual, however, to have her shutting off the recording a moment later.

Matthias had been a great comfort since he'd moved in nearly two years ago, and he never interrupted her work with anything trivial. Beneath his gruff, somewhat aloof exterior, he was really very sweet and considerate, not to mention protective. She tossed the headphones onto the desk.

"What's wrong?"

"Dunno. But something's up. You got company."

"Who is it?"

The answer knocked her back down into her chair. "Jones."

Her heart thudded heavily. Vaughn. This could only be about Vaughn. Why else would her attorney arrive here unannounced? *"Lord, please let this be good news,"* she prayed, gulping. She looked up at Matthias. "Did Dan Jones say why he's here?"

Matthias shook his head. "Not Dan. Big fella. Says his name's Grady."

Grady Jones was Dan's brother and law partner. She could see even less reason for *his* presence. As curious as she was shaken now, she stood up to her full five feet height and moved woodenly around the desk that occupied almost all of her tiny office.

The room was really nothing more than a screened-in back porch roughly converted with plywood, batts of insulation and plastic sheeting. When Matthias had moved in, she'd refused to even consider taking over Vaughn's bedroom, so this had become her only option.

Paige tugged at the cardigan that she wore with jeans and a flannel shirt and led the way down the hall to the living room, smoothing her fine, yellow blond hair en route. The last cut had been a bit too short and shaggy for her taste, but the stylist had insisted that the wispy ends feathering about her triangular face made her chin look less sharp and brought out the soft green of her eyes. Since her large, tip-tilted eyes already dominated her slender face, Paige wasn't so sure that was a good thing, but it was too late now to worry about it.

Matthias skirted the stove and went into the kitchen as Paige greeted Grady Jones, offering her hand.

"Mr. Jones."

He backed up a step, before slowly reaching out to briefly close his large, square palm around her small hand. Her heart flip-flopped. She'd seen him often around the office in Fayetteville when consulting with Dan, but they'd rarely spoken. A big man with even, masculine features, he reminded her of a bear standing there in that expensive tan overcoat, a wary bear with electric-blue eyes.

"Can I take your coat?"

"Oh, uh, that's all right," he said, shucking the long, supple length of it and draping it over one arm.

"Won't you have a seat then?" She gestured toward the sofa.

Nodding, he backed up to the couch and gingerly folded himself down onto it as if worried he might break the thing. For some reason she found that endearing. She perched next to him, crossing her ankles, and waited until he placed his briefcase at his feet and dropped his coat onto the cushion beside him.

"What's going on?" she asked warily.

"First of all," he said, his voice deep and rumbling, "I want you to know that Dan would have come himself if possible."

She swallowed and nodded her understanding, afraid to ask what was so important that her attorney's partner and brother would come in his stead. Fortunately, Grady Jones didn't keep her in suspense.

"It's good news," he stated flatly. "We've found your son."

She heard the words, even understood that her prayers had finally been answered, but for so long she'd accepted disappointment after disappointment, while trusting that this day would eventually come. Now suddenly it had, and she sat there too stunned to shift from faith to realization.

Then Grady Jones began to explain that Vaughn had been picked up from school by child welfare officials in South Carolina, where his father was being held under arrest after an alert state trooper conducting a routine traffic stop, had recognized him from one of the many electronic flyers they'd distributed to law enforcement agencies around the country. Finally, the realization sank in.

Vaughn was safe and waiting for her to come for him! At last, at long last, her son was coming home!

Clasping her hands together, Paige did the only

thing she could think to do. She closed her eyes, turned her face toward the ceiling and thanked God.

"Oh, Father! I praise Your holy name. Thank You. Thank You! Vaughn's coming home!" She began to laugh, tears rolling down her face. "He's coming home. My son is coming home!"

Grady Jones cleared his throat. Paige beamed at him. With two bright spots of color flying high in his cheeks, he looked down. That was when she realized that she was gripping his hand with both of hers.

She was crying and laughing at the same time. How was a man supposed to react to that? Grady wondered. Displays of emotion always unnerved him. He'd been uncomfortable before; now he wanted to crawl into a cave somewhere. Racking his brain for something, anything, to say, he came up blank, which left him feeling even more hopelessly inadequate than usual.

She suddenly released him, jerking her hands back into her own lap as if he'd snapped at them with his teeth. He felt a fresh flush of embarrassment, but at least his brain began to work again. After a few moments he realized that certain matters had to be addressed. He opened his briefcase and extracted documents, explaining each in detail.

The first would allow the Carolina authorities to release information which would help prove the boy's identity and had already been faxed to the appropriate party. The next proved her identity. Another granted her custody in the state of Arkansas. The fourth proved that such a grant both superseded and complied with Carolina law, and so on. The last document was a charge filed against Nolan Vaughn Ellis for interference with the lawful physical custody of a minor, allowing the state of South Carolina to hold him until such time as the issue of jurisdiction could be settled. Finally came the flight schedules.

"We assumed you wouldn't want to wait until after the holiday to be reunited with your son," Grady told her matter-of-factly.

"I'd go right this minute if I could!" she declared, wiping at her eyes with delicate, trembling fingertips.

He thought of the fresh, lightly starched handkerchief in his pocket, then he looked into her eyes and promptly forgot it again. Those enormous eyes, sparkling now with happy tears, were a soft, muted sea green. He was vaguely aware of the perfect cupid's bow of her dusky pink lips and the adorable button of her nose, but up close like this he couldn't get past those big eyes. Her long, brown lashes, spiked now with her tears, seemed gloriously unadorned. She put him in mind of a sprite or a fairy, her sunny yellow hair wisping at the nape of her neck and around her face. The delicate arch of her pale brows proved that the blond shade was completely natural.

Grady gulped and forced his mind back to the issue at hand.

"Uh, that's, uh, why I'm here instead of Dan. Th- the holiday, I mean. Dan has to consider his family, you understand, but I have no obligations of that sort."

She tilted her head as if trying to figure out why that should be the case. After a long moment she said, "I see."

He winced inwardly, feeling as if she'd looked him over and found the reason why he, unlike his brother, was alone and unattached.

"You, um, you just tell me which of these times works best for you," he mumbled, flushing with embarrassment yet again.

Smiling slightly, she took the printed flight schedules into her small hands and bent her head over them. The edges of the paper trembled. Realizing that she was very likely in shock, he felt duty-bound to point out that the flights leaving from Tulsa were considerably cheaper than those leaving the regional airport.

She nodded and after several seconds said breathlessly, "Early would be best, wouldn't it?"

"If we hope to get there and back in the same day, yes, I'd say so. Plus, they're an hour ahead of us on the East Coast, and we could have lots of legal hurdles to jump before we can bring a minor back across the state lines."

"Well, then, the 5:58 a.m. flight is probably best."

Grady nodded, mentally cringing at how early he'd have to get up to have her at the airport in Tulsa before five o'clock in the morning as security rules dictated. Might as well not even go to bed. Except, of course, that he had to be alert enough for a two-hour drive to the airport in Oklahoma.

"Can you be ready to leave by three in the morning?" he asked apologetically.

She nodded with unadulterated enthusiasm, handing over the papers. "Oh, yes. I doubt I'll sleep at all, frankly."

"I'll be here for you at three, then."

"No, wait," she muttered thoughtfully, drawing those fine brows together. "You'll be coming from Fayetteville, won't you?"

"Yes."

She smiled, and he caught his breath. She literally glowed with happiness.

"Then I'll come to you," she told him. "It'll save time."

Grady frowned. "I couldn't let you do that."

Her tinkling laughter put him in mind of sleigh bells and crisp winter mornings.

"You forget, Mr. Jones," she said with mock seriousness, "that you work for me. Shall we meet at your office? Say, three-thirty? That's cutting it fine, I know, but I can't imagine we'll encounter much traffic along the way."

Her plan would save him over an hour all told, but he just couldn't handle the thought of her being out on the road alone at that hour.

"I'll pick you up here," he insisted.

She blinked, then she smiled. "I guess I'll see you here at three in the morning."

Only then did it occur to him that he might have explained his reasoning instead of just growling at her. Confounded, he snapped the papers inside his briefcase once more and got to his feet, muttering that he had to go.

She popped up next to him, asking, "How can I thank you?" Then next thing he knew, she'd thrown her arms around him in a hug.

"N-no need," he rumbled, his face hot enough to incinerate.

"Please thank your brother for me, too," she went on, tucking her hands behind her and skittering toward the door.

Grady had heard the term "dancing on air" all his life; this was the first time he'd actually witnessed it.

He ducked his head in a nod and stuffed one arm down a sleeve, groping for his briefcase. Getting a grip on the handle, he headed for the door, still trying to find the other armhole of his coat.

"Mr. Jones," called a rusty voice behind him.

He froze, looking back warily over one shoulder, his coat trailing on the floor. Matthias Porter stood next to the stove, beaming, his eyes suspiciously moist. Grady lifted his eyebrows in query.

"I'll see she gets some rest," the old man promised. "Don't you worry none about that."

"Very good," Grady muttered.

Paige opened the door, and he charged out onto the porch. The dog pushed itself up on to all fours and assaulted his eardrums with howling, multioctave barks, the top end of which ought to have shattered glass.

"Howler, hush up!" Matthias Porter bawled from inside the house, and the fat black thing dropped back down onto its belly as if it had been felled with a hammer.

"Thank you again!" Paige called. "Try to get some rest."

Grady scrambled for his car in silence, desperate to get away, but once he was behind the wheel and headed back down the rutted drive, he found that the day was not so gray as it had seemed before. He thought of the happy glow that had all but pulsed from Paige Ellis's serene eyes, and he couldn't help smiling to himself.

He suspected that he'd never again think of Thanksgiving as merely a turkey dinner and a football game.

Chapter Two

Paige sighed with pure delight and settled comfortably onto the leather seat of the Mercedes. She couldn't stop smiling. She suspected, in fact, that she'd smiled in her sleep, what little of it she'd managed to get.

Matthias had insisted that she retire to her bed immediately after dinner, and she had done so simply to humor him. Surprisingly, she'd actually slept a few hours. When the alarm had gone off in the dead of night, she'd awakened instantly to dress in a tailored, olive-green knit pantsuit, her excitement quietly but steadily building.

Her parting with Matthias, who had insisted on getting up to see her off, had been predictably unemotional. He, more than anyone else, knew what this meant to her, but his pride didn't allow for overt displays. Paige understood completely. For a man with nothing and no one, pride was a valuable thing, a last, dear possession.

When they'd heard the vehicle pull up in the yard, Matthias had practically shoved her out the door, rasping that she'd better call if she was going to be returning later than expected. After almost falling over Howler, Paige had climbed into Grady's sumptuous car, where a welcome warmth blew gently from the air vents.

Excitement percolating in her veins, Paige unbuttoned her yellow-gold wool coat and removed her polyester scarf before securing her seat belt. Grady Jones had been right to insist that she not drive herself to his office. She was much too anxious to manage it safely.

"Coffee?" Grady offered as he got them moving. He nodded toward a tall foam cup in the drink holder nearest her.

His voice and manner were gruff, but she didn't mind. Even if it had been a decent hour and she hadn't been on her way—at last!—to her son, Matthias had taught her that gruff was often just a protective mannerism. Besides, it had been thoughtful of Grady to provide the coffee, so even though she rarely drank the stuff, she put on her sweetest smile and thanked him.

"There's sugar and cream in the bag," he said, indicating the white paper sack between them.

"Black's fine," she assured him, unwilling to risk trying to add anything to a cup of hot coffee in a moving vehicle. Saluting him with the drink, she bade him a happy Thanksgiving.

He inclined his head but said nothing, concentrating on his driving. She noticed that his drink holder contained a metal travel cup emblazoned with the logo of a Texas hockey team. She'd seen the same logo on a framed pennant in Dan Jones's office. The brothers apparently shared an interest in the game. They seemed to share little else, other than their occupation.

Besides the obvious physical differences, Dan was friendly and chatty with a quick, open smile, while Grady struck her as the strong, silent type. She felt oddly comfortable with him, safe, though she sensed that he did not feel the same ease in her company. Perhaps he was a loner, then, but a capable one judging by the way he handled the car, and a thoughtful one, too. He'd brought her coffee, after all.

Smiling, she sipped carefully from her cup and found that the beverage was much less bitter than Matthias's brew. Then again, what could possibly be bitter on this most thankful of Thanksgivings?

They traveled for some time in silence while she nursed her coffee and stared out the window. Unsurprisingly, she looked fresh and eager, her big, tilted eyes glowing. That just made Grady feel even more worn and rumpled than usual and did nothing to improve his mood. He knew he ought to say something, but as usual he couldn't think of anything that seemed to make sense.

Somewhere along the turnpike southwest of Siloam Springs, she pointed out across the dark hills and valleys, exclaiming, "Oh, look! Christmas lights."

Grady turned his head and saw a two-story house outlined in brilliant red. "Little early," he rumbled without thinking.

"It is," she agreed, "but aren't they pretty?"

He didn't say anything. Red lights were red lights, so far as he was concerned. He suggested that she might want to get some sleep. "It's still an hour or more to Tulsa."

"I'll sleep once my son's tucked in his own bed again," she commented softly, and they fell back into silence.

After a few minutes, he reached for his coffee and was surprised when she said, "So you're a hockey fan?"

"Hmm?"

"It's on your travel mug."

He glanced at the item in question, drank and set the travel cup aside. "Right. Yeah, I like most sports."

"Me, too."

That surprised him. "Yeah?"

"Uh-huh, I'm really hopeful about the Hogs's basketball season, aren't you?"

Surprised again. "Football's more my thing."

"Oh, that's right. You played corner for the Hogs football team, didn't you?"

Surprised didn't cover it this time. "How did you know?"

"I looked you up on the computer right after my first appointment with your brother."

"You looked me—" His gaping mouth must have

appeared comical, for she laughed, and the sound of it brightened the interior of the night-darkened car.

"I have a propensity for trivia, sports trivia in particular. The name sounded familiar to me, so I looked it up."

Grady worked at shutting his mouth before he could mutter, "I don't think that's ever happened before."

"Oh, you might be surprised," she told him. "There are some big sports fans around. My father was one of them, you see, and having only daughters, he literally pined for someone to discuss statistics with. My older sister, Carol, wasn't interested. She lives in Colorado now."

"And you were? Interested, I mean."

"Very. I much preferred sitting in the living room with Dad discussing RBIs and pass completion rates to washing dishes with Mom in the kitchen." She laughed again.

"So it was more an attempt to get out of your chores than a real interest in sports," he surmised.

She shook her head. "No one got out of chores in our household. I just like knowing things. Information is powerful, don't you think?"

Did he ever. "Key to my success as an attorney," he heard himself say, and then when she asked him to explain that, he did. She asked a question, which he answered, and before he knew what was happening they were in Tulsa.

He quickly became consumed with finding a parking spot in the crowded terminal lot. As a consequence, it didn't hit him until he was dragging his briefcase out of the backseat of his car that he'd just spent over an hour in conversation with a woman talking mostly about himself—and he had enjoyed it!

The thought literally froze him in place for a moment. Then Paige Ellis tossed her plaid scarf around her neck and tucked the ends into the front of her bright gold, three-quarter-length coat, looking more polished and lovely than a woman in cheap clothes ought to. Grady shook himself, recalling that she was in an emotional stew at the moment and probably wouldn't remember a word that had been said between them. Her distraction had no doubt led to his own.

Feeling somewhat deflated, he trudged toward the terminal. She fell into step beside him. It had apparently rained in Tulsa the evening before, and little glossy patches of damp remained along the pavement. Paige failed to see one, and the slick sole of her brown flat skidded, so naturally Grady reached out to prevent her from falling. Somehow, she wound up in his arms. She beamed a smile at him, stopping the breath in his lungs. After that he couldn't seem to find a way to let go of her, keeping one hand clamped firmly around her arm until they were safely inside the building.

Thirty minutes later as they moved from check-in to the passenger screening line he began to worry that arriving a mere hour ahead of their departure time had been foolishly shortsighted. Thanksgiving, after all, was the busiest travel day of the entire year.

Paige chattered about first one thing and then another. His fear that they might not make their flight was reason enough not to interrupt her ongoing one-sided conversation about… He lost track of what it was about. But it allowed him to worry for them both, then to be relieved when they walked onto the plane and into their seats with minutes to spare.

When she reached for the in-flight magazine, he knew a moment of mingled relief and disappointment. Apparently, she thought he would be interested in an article, for she began a running commentary on a piece about the latest in computer technology.

Grady remembered his brother saying that because he lived with four women he heard at least 100,000 words per day. At that moment, Grady didn't doubt Dan's assessment. But surprisingly Grady found himself interested. Afterward, they found themselves discussing her work.

Paige Ellis, it turned out, was a marvel of ingenuity and self-discipline. Not only was she a self-taught medical transcriptionist, she had her own cottage industry. By means of a small business loan, she had supplied state-of-the-art computer transcription equipment to four other women, all of whom worked out of their homes and were paid by the hour. By concentrating on doctors in the smaller communities around Fayetteville, Paige had garnered the lion's share of the transcription contracts in the area. Due to the lower costs of her business format, she was able to undercut her competition substantially.

"Thank the good Lord," she declared happily, "I will have the time I've been dreaming about to spend with my son before it's too late." She laughed, and then, to Grady's shock and dismay, she suddenly began to cry.

For Grady it was like being pulled out of a comfortable chair and thrust on to a torture rack. He didn't know what to do or say, so he just sat there like a deer frozen in the headlights and listened to her.

"He's eleven now. Eleven! I've missed *four* birthdays!"

Grady already knew from reading the case file that Nolan Ellis had ostensibly taken the boy for a two-week camping trip at the end of June, three-and-a-half years earlier. It was to have been Vaughn's birthday gift from his dad, and they were to have returned before the boy's actual birth date of July 1. The camping trip, of course, had been a ruse meant to give Nolan a two-week head start to disappear, and it had worked like a charm. Only as she'd sat alone hour after hour, she told him, waiting to light the candles on Vaughn's birthday cake, had Paige begun to realize that the two weeks of her son's absence might well turn into a lifetime.

The particulars of the divorce were likewise already known to Grady, though the Jones firm had not handled it. That, in his opinion, was most unfortunate, something she matter-of-factly confirmed as the story spilled out of her.

High school sweethearts, she and Nolan had married young. By the time their son had reached the age of four, Nolan had decided that he didn't want to be married, after all. Resentful over his "lost youth" and the burden of family responsibilities, he had simply walked out.

Even more shocking, the divorce papers had alleged that Nolan might not be Vaughn's father. Angry and hurt, Paige had signed without even consulting an attorney. Only later did she realize what Grady, or any other halfway competent attorney, could have told her: she had, in effect, signed away her and Vaughn's right to financial support.

She'd realized her mistake when she'd transcribed notes concerning a case in which one of her clients, a medical lab, had been called upon to verify paternity so that child support could be levied. After hearing Paige's story, a helpful lab technician had arranged for Vaughn to be tested and had also recommended an attorney who dealt with paternity cases. When Nolan predictably resurfaced several months before Vaughn's eighth birthday, Paige had been ready. She'd hit Nolan with a court order, proved that he was Vaughn's father and been awarded substantial monthly child support. Nolan had been livid, but he'd seemed to calm down fairly quickly.

"I did think he might disappear again after the court decision went against him," she said, sniffing, "but after he stuck around for a while, I started to believe that he really wanted to be a father to Vaughn. That's what my little boy wanted, and who could blame him? Every little boy wants a daddy. I never dreamed Nolan would take Vaughn and disappear."

"It's not your fault," Grady said, wondering when his arm had come to be draped about her shoulders.

"I can't help wondering if he's missed me," she whispered.

"Little boys want their moms, too," Grady assured her.

"Do you really think so?"

Grady realized suddenly that all this chatter was a product of her emotional state, so when she turned that hopeful, tearstained face up to him, what else could he do but tell her about his own experiences?

"I know so. I was six when my mom died, and nothing's been quite right in my world since."

How on earth they got from talking about losing his mom to talking about his divorce, he would never know. At some point he started telling her how his marriage had fallen apart.

"So, she left you to marry your boss," Paige clarified sharply, both surprising and puzzling him.

Embarrassment and pain roiled in his gut, but he'd come so far already that he didn't see any point in pulling back now. "Technically he was her boss, too, since we both worked for the same Little Rock law firm."

"And how did that come about?" Paige wanted to know.

Grady shrugged. "I asked them to hire her."

Paige folded her arms at this. "So let me get this straight. First she refused to stay in Fayetteville and join your family's practice."

"There aren't any opportunities for advancement in a small family partnership," he explained.

"Then, the firm in Little Rock hired *you*, and wanted you bad enough to take *her* in the bargain. Right?"

Eventually he nodded. "Right."

"So she used you to get into a firm she couldn't have gotten into on her own, then she left you for someone with more power and prestige." Paige threw up her hands, exclaiming, "Well, at least she stayed true to form!"

"T-true to form?"

"It's obvious, isn't it? She manipulated you, and when she found someone else who could offer her more, she traded up."

He was so taken aback by the idea that for a moment he couldn't even give it proper thought. Paige must have taken his silence for censure, for she suddenly wrinkled her pert little nose, sighed and muttered, "Okay, I shouldn't be judging, but such selfishness gets to me."

His family had hinted at the same thing, that Robin had left him for his boss not just because the man was elegant, affable and downright loquacious but because she was greedy. It hadn't made sense at the time. His bank account was hefty enough, after all. Since then he'd avoided thinking about it because it was too painful.

Now, after several years, he could see things from a different perspective. Robin had used him. That didn't make the hurtful and numerous accusations she'd thrown at him any less true. Did it?

He shook his head. Robin was correct about him

being inept with women. Had she not pursued him, he doubted that they'd have ever gotten together. One-on-one with a woman, his tongue stuck to the roof of his mouth and his mind went completely blank. The more attractive he found her, the worse it was.

Usually, he amended silently, glancing sideways at Paige.

It was nuts to think that he might be any different with Paige. If his poor communication skills and emotional ineptness were not enough, there was his clumsiness. Okay, maybe once he'd been fleet of foot and a force to be reckoned with on the athletic field, but those days were long gone. That he'd been able to discuss them, even briefly, with Paige Ellis had been terribly flattering, which had led to hours of conversation. The fact that he'd enjoyed those hours so much suddenly made him seem especially pathetic.

None of this meant anything to Paige, after all. She was an admitted sports freak; he'd allowed her interest in the fact that he'd once played college football to become more personal than it was surely intended to be.

Disturbed, Grady let his seat back, mumbling that they had a long day ahead of them, and closed his eyes. She agreed with him and curled up in her seat, but she did not sleep. He knew this because he didn't sleep, either.

They changed planes in Atlanta, and on that last, short leg of the trip, he avoided personal conversation by discussing business, beginning with a particular form that she needed to sign. He'd mentioned it before, but she'd been in too much shock to really understand at that time.

"In other words," she said, after he'd gone over the whole thing once again, "if I sign this, we'll be pressing charges against Nolan in South Carolina as well as Arkansas. Is that correct?"

Pleased that she'd grasped the concept this time, he reached for an ink pen. "Exactly."

"But I'm not sure that's what I ought to do."

His hand stopped with the slim, gold-plated barrel of the ink pen still lodged within the leather loop provided for it. "I beg your pardon?"

"I'm not sure I want to prosecute Nolan."

Grady's tongue seemed to run away with him. "Why on earth not?" he demanded. "The man kidnapped your son!"

The spike-haired lady across the aisle turned a curious gaze on them, and Grady realized he'd raised his voice.

"You think I don't know that?" Paige said with some asperity. "Believe you me, I know what it's like to miss your child with every fiber of your being, minute by minute, hour after hour, day after day after week after month…. And I realize that I'm about to do the same thing to Nolan that he did to me. The pain of that may be punishment enough."

"That's not the point," Grady told her urgently, doing his best to keep his voice down. "This is about protecting you and Vaughn."

"That *is* the point," she insisted, sliding into the far corner of her seat and folding her arms. "I can't let this be about retribution, and right now, for me, it is."

"I don't understand."

"I don't expect you to. Suffice it to say that I've been seeing a counselor for some time now, and she, along with my Christian ethics, warn me against seeking any sort of vengeance."

"What about what's best for your son?"

"I think this is what's best for my son," she stated firmly. "Nolan is his *father*. Do you think he wants his father punished? I don't think so."

"I would," Grady insisted. "Knowing he kept me away from my mother, I surely would."

Paige shook her head. "You only say that because you can't see the other side. You haven't been a parent. You don't know what it means to put the welfare of your child first. I'm sure Dan would understand what I'm trying to say."

That stung, far, far more than it should have. She was correct, but that didn't keep Grady from feeling great alarm on her behalf. As far as he was concerned, allowing Nolan Ellis to walk around free was a reckless and frightful thing for this woman and her son. His every instinct screamed for prosecution on every possible level, but all he could do was point out the legal loopholes that she would be leaving open if she failed to follow his advice.

She listened, but he could tell that he wasn't convincing her. Frustrated, he searched for a way to compel her to accept his reasoning.

"No one would blame you if you locked him up and threw away the key!"

"That's beside the point."

"Then what is the point?"

"Doing the right thing."

For a moment he could only stare at her, wondering if she was for real. "This *is* the right thing."

She stared back and finally said, "I'll pray about it." With that she turned away from him.

Confounded, Grady watched her bow her head and retreat into herself. He'd made his best case, giving her good, solid legal advice, but he might as well have saved his breath. Obviously they didn't communicate as well as he'd thought.

This wasn't the first time his legal advice had been rejected, after all, not by a long shot, but he'd never been more disturbed about it.

Popping his seat back again, he folded his arms and shut his eyes, determined to finally catch a few minutes of rest or at least some peace.

Both would prove to be in very short supply.

They touched down at the Greenville-Spartanburg International Airport at a quarter past eleven that morning. After renting a car, they drove to the Greenville County Sheriff's Department where Vaughn waited, having spent the previous night in a group foster care facility. Grady had not pressed Paige for a decision about prosecuting Nolan, which was good since she truly didn't know what she was going to do.

Now that the moment to see her son again—after

three years, six months and one day—had finally arrived, Paige was so nervous she felt ill. Pressing a hand to her abdomen and surreptitiously gulping down air in an effort to settle her stomach, she walked through the heavy glass door that Grady held open for her. They met briefly with a polite, efficient uniformed officer who checked their paperwork and led them through a narrow hallway to a private conference room.

Her heartbeat grew louder and the knots in her stomach pulled tighter and tighter with every step that she took, so that by the time Grady paused with his hand on the plain, brushed steel doorknob, she could barely breathe.

"Ready?" he asked softly.

Reminding herself that Vaughn might be ambivalent at first, she pulled her spine straight and nodded. As that heavy, metal door swung inward, she began to tremble. Grady pushed into the small, crowded room. She practically ran over him, suddenly so eager that she could not contain herself.

Everything registered at once: pale walls, pale floor, pale, rectangular table flanked by lightweight metal chairs with blue, molded vinyl seats. A green-and-white bag with some team logo printed in red sat in the center of the table, stuffed so full of clothing that it couldn't be zipped. Two women—one young, white and plump with a brown ponytail, the other African-American, slender and slightly older—occupied two of the chairs on the near side of the table.

Across from them sat a boy, a stranger, who shot abruptly to his feet.

Paige's first thought was that they'd made a mistake. This could not be her son. He stood at least as tall as her own five feet, with no trace of the bright copper-blond hair that had crowned her baby boy. Instead, the thick, fine locks falling haphazardly over his brows, tangling with the thick lashes rimming his warm brown eyes, was a rich auburn. Then he tossed his head defiantly, and she caught a glimpse of a jagged scar just above his right eyebrow, the scar he'd gotten tumbling headlong off the porch into the shrubbery.

"Vaughn!"

How she got around the table she didn't know, but when she threw out her arms, he flinched and backed away. She'd been told to expect this, and yet disappointment seared her trembling heart. Sucking in a deep breath, she forced her feet to slow.

It was like approaching a feral animal, once domesticated but now wild. He seemed uncertain, but she sensed that he definitely recognized her. Carefully, her lips quivering, she slipped her arms around him. Perhaps it wasn't wise, but she had to, *had to,* hold him, if only for a moment.

"Mom," he whispered in a voice she would never have recognized and yet somehow knew.

Only with great effort did she manage not to sob, but stopping the tears completely was impossible. She smiled through them, cupped his slender, oval face in her hands, pulled it gently forward and laid her forehead to his as she had so often in the past.

"Thank You, God. Thank You. Thank You."

Chapter Three

Vaughn let her hold him for a time, but then the two women at the table introduced themselves, and he pulled away. The young one was a caseworker with Child Protective Services, the other a Victims Services agent with the county sheriff's office. After making themselves known, they seemed content to sit back and observe, leaving Paige to focus once more on her son.

He had backed into the corner of the room, his arms tightly folded across his chest. It was not a good sign. Paige tried not to take offense. It was only to be expected. He'd spent the last three-and-a-half years with his father. He was bound to be confused. She couldn't help noting that he was a handsome boy whose shoulders were already broadening, and now that she got a good look at him, she realized something else.

"You look like my dad."

He frowned. "No, I don't. I look like *my* dad."

"You're built like Nolan," she agreed quickly, aware that she was tiptoeing through a minefield here, "and you have the same coloring, but that's my father's chin and nose you've got." He bowed his head, as if rejecting anything she might say. Paige gulped and searched for some way to meaningfully engage him. "Do you remember your grandfather?"

Vaughn snorted, glancing up at her sullenly. "'Course. I wasn't *that* little when he died."

He'd been five and inconsolable. The memory of how he'd cried for his grandpa wrenched her heart. Had he cried like that for her? She wouldn't ask, for both their sakes.

Chairs scraped back as first the Child Protective Services caseworker and then the Victims Services agent rose. "I think we've heard all we need to," the VS agent said, her dark face parting in a smile that was half congratulatory, half sympathetic. "You should have some paperwork for us."

"The desk officer has it," Grady replied.

"Yes, of course." She stepped forward and addressed the boy. "You take care, Vaughn. Happy Thanksgiving."

He did not so much as acknowledge her words. The CPS caseworker skirted the table and hugged him.

"Cheer up, honey. It's going to be okay." He nodded glumly, but didn't speak. She patted his shoulder and turned to Paige. "Happy Thanksgiving."

"A very happy Thanksgiving," Paige murmured,

clasping the woman's hand. "Thank you both from the bottom of my heart."

"Just doing our jobs," she said.

The two women quickly exited the room. The instant the door swung closed, Vaughn all but attacked. "What happens now?"

"We're going home, son," Paige said gently. "I thought you knew that."

"I know I gotta go with you," he declared, his voice breaking with the weight of his emotion, "but it's not my home, not anymore. What I mean is, what happens to my dad?" He started to cry. "They got him in jail! He always said you'd put him away if you found us. That's not right! He doesn't belong in jail!"

"Don't worry," she urged, pulling him into her arms again. She couldn't let herself be hurt by his concern for Nolan. What counted now was putting Vaughn's fears to rest. She knew what she had to do, had known how it would be. Taking a deep breath, she firmly stated, "I have no intention of pressing charges against your father."

"That may not be wise," Grady warned, but she shook her head at him, convinced that she was right in this.

As much as she believed Nolan had wronged her and their son, as much anger as she'd carried with her over their separation, no good would be served by punishing Nolan legally.

"Does that mean they'll let him go?" Vaughn asked hopefully. "I'll leave with you if they'll let him go."

"You'll go with her anyway," Grady pointed out to Vaughn, pitching his voice low. "You don't have a choice. Paige, you need to think about this."

"I have thought about it."

"We need to consider this carefully," Grady argued.

"My mind's made up, Grady."

"For pity's sake, Paige!" Grady Jones erupted, and that triggered Vaughn.

"It's none of your business!" he shouted at Grady, then rounded on his mother. "What's he got to say about it, anyway? Just 'cause he's your boyfriend or something, that doesn't—"

"He's *not* my boyfriend!" she exclaimed, grasping the boy by the tops of his arms. "He's my attorney."

"*One* of your attorneys," Grady corrected smartly.

"*One* of my attorneys," she snapped, glaring at him over her shoulder.

Vaughn shuffled his feet and bowed his head, muttering, "It's still none of his business."

"It's not his decision, but it *is* his job to advise me," Paige pointed out calmly.

"For all the good it does," Grady muttered.

Paige ignored him, looking to her son, who asked, "So Dad can go home?"

"I can't say what the South Carolina authorities will do," Paige told the boy, "but your dad won't stay in jail because of me, Vaughn, I swear it." Sliding one arm around his shoulders, she turned to face Grady. "Can the South Carolina authorities keep him if I don't press charges?"

Grady clenched his jaw and looked away, but then he answered. "No."

"What about the state of Arkansas?"

He fixed her with a level stare. "They may want him held for failure to pay child support."

She could feel Vaughn trembling beside her and lifted her chin. "What if I speak in his favor, petition for leniency on his behalf? Forgo the back payments?" Grady was so clearly appalled by the mere suggestion of her intervention that she felt her temper spark.

"That would not be wise," he rumbled.

"That is not an answer to my question."

"You haven't thought this through," he insisted.

She took that to mean that her intervention on Nolan's behalf would likely result in him doing no time. She turned back to her son. "I'll keep him out of jail," she promised.

Vaughn slumped with obvious relief. Paige put on as bright a face as she could manage and announced, "Our plane doesn't leave until almost three, so Mr. Jones made lunch reservations for us at a hotel downtown."

Vaughn put on a sullen face and grumbled, "I'm not hungry."

"No? But it's Thanksgiving, and you love turkey. I know you do. Especially the drumstick." He made a face at that, and she supposed that his delight with drumsticks at Thanksgiving dinners past seemed babyish to him now. She quickly went on, changing the subject. "We should be home before nine this evening."

He lifted his head, looked her in the eye. "My home's in South Carolina."

She felt her heart drop, but swallowed down the part that seemed to have lodged in her throat. "But Nobb's your home, too," she said softly. "You'll see that if you just give it a chance. I've missed you so much, Vaughn, more than you can possibly know, and we're going to work everything out, I promise."

He said nothing, just ducked his head, sighed and dragged his feet toward the door with all the enthusiasm of a condemned prisoner on his way to the gallows. Pushing aside her heartache, Paige reminded herself that this was to be expected. Only God knew what adjustments they had in store for them, but then only God could make them a family again.

Grady determined that he would not let his own dissatisfaction with Paige's decision not to prosecute her ex-husband color the meal. He was furious with her, worried about her and just generally disgruntled, but after an hour or so in the boy's icy, hostile company, he decided that *his* mood was definitely the brighter of the two.

Paige, for all her quiet joy and steely determination, could not lighten the atmosphere. Nevertheless, she tried, commenting gently on the quality of the food and the service, remarking what a treat it was not to have to cook Thanksgiving dinner for herself, asking quiet, neutral questions about Vaughn's life, most of which he answered with as few syllables as possible.

Did he like school? Sometimes.

What was his best friend's name? Toby.

Favorite junk food? Barbecue potato chips.

Last book he'd read? Didn't know.

She appeared to take no offense at his sullen, almost belligerent replies. When the meal arrived she prayed over it, simply bowed her head and began, as if it was perfectly normal.

"Father, we have so much to be thankful for today. I cannot thank You enough for bringing my son back to me. You have heard my prayers, and I know that You will continue to do so. Give each of us wisdom now, Lord, as we work to make of our lives what You would have them be, and bless the Jones brothers for all that they have done on our behalf. Amen."

As she spoke softly, Grady looked around the room self-consciously, while Vaughn sprawled in his chair, glaring at him. Grady noted with some surprise that several other diners had also bowed their heads.

The meal crept by with Paige pretending not to notice that Vaughn wasn't eating. She did try to deflect his glower from time to time, without much success. Grady fumed, uncertain just what the boy's problem was. The crazy kid seemed to blame him, Grady, for his father's problems!

Didn't he understand how lucky he was to be back with his mom? At his age Grady would have done anything, *anything*, just to share one more meal with his mother. In Grady's opinion, Vaughn Ellis should be on his knees, kissing his mother's feet instead of worrying about his self-centered father, and it was all Grady could do not to tell him so.

As soon as the meal was finished and Grady paid the check—determined that this was one part of the trip that wouldn't find it's way onto Paige's bill— Vaughn demanded to see his father. Paige turned troubled, pleading eyes to Grady, and he found himself almost sorry that he hadn't had the foresight to arrange any such thing. Almost.

He shook his head. "Can't be done, not on this short notice and a holiday."

"I'm sorry, Vaughn," she told the boy sincerely, an arm draped lightly about his shoulders. "You can call him later."

Grady shook his head at that, at a complete loss. Didn't she know what Nolan would do if she gave him just half a chance? He'd already absconded with her son once. Did she think he wouldn't do it again? Grady decided that he was going to have a long talk with his brother about this once he got home. Maybe Dan could make her see reason. What it would take to reach the boy, Grady couldn't even imagine, but he was glad that he wasn't in Paige's shoes. This, he thought morosely, should have been such a happy day, not tense and silent and barely civil.

The ride to the airport was gloomy at best. Sitting in the backseat with her son, who seemed determined to ignore her, Paige didn't even try to make conversation. They had to visit a shop in the airport in order to purchase a second bag and get the boy's clothes safely stowed for the trip, but when Paige began to repack his things, Vaughn elbowed her aside, grumbling that he would do it.

She backed away, her arms locked about her middle as if she was trying to hold herself together. Grady found himself at her side, his voice pitched low.

"He doesn't know what he's doing right now."

She flashed a wan smile at him. "I expected it to be difficult," she said softly, "but I thought my son would at least be glad to see me."

"Well, sure he is," Grady insisted, though they both knew better.

Her eyes gleamed with liquid brilliance, brimming with a kind of bittersweet pain that made Grady want to howl. "I don't know him anymore," she whispered brokenly. "I don't even know my own son."

"You'll get to know him," Grady rumbled, squeezing her fingers quickly. "It'll be okay," he told her, wishing for an eloquence he'd only ever found inside a courtroom.

Her smile grew a little wider. "You're a good man, Grady Jones."

His heart thumped inside his chest. Vaughn rose from his task then, sparing Grady from having to find a reply. He pointed toward the ticket counter, muttering that they had to get the boy checked in for the flight, and walked off in that direction. Only later, when the flight clerk was ready to receive the boy's luggage, did it dawn on Grady that he'd left Paige and the kid to manage the bags.

He was still mentally kicking himself for that a half hour later when they arrived at the departure gate, having passed through security. The place was surprisingly crowded, and Grady frowned. Weren't these people supposed to be home eating turkey? He concentrated on finding seats for them in the waiting area, then parked himself against the nearby wall.

Paige had bought Vaughn a couple of magazines in which he'd shown interest at the store, but the brat shook his head mutely when she offered them to him. Deflated, Paige shot a resigned look to Grady, and it was all he could do not to shake the kid. Grady tried not to watch the careful way in which she approached the boy, as if he were a wounded animal, but he couldn't seem to take his eyes off them, and every time her son rebuffed her, his temper spiked a little higher.

By the time they were finally able to board the flight, Grady was gnashing his teeth. What was wrong with the kid? Didn't he see how unfairly he was treating his mother? She hadn't created this situation; his father had.

Only after they changed planes in Atlanta did Paige again try to communicate with her son. She asked gentle question after gentle question and received in reply only shrugs and sharp glances from the corners of his eyes. When she began to talk about her plans for Christmas, explaining what she and Matthias had discussed, Vaughn finally deigned to speak.

"Who's Matthias?" he demanded, screwing up his face.

Paige smiled. "Didn't I say? Matthias Porter is our boarder."

"What's that?"

"Well, he rents a room in our house."

"So we're poor?" Vaughn surmised caustically.

"No, we're not poor. We're not rich but certainly not poor."

"Then how come you're renting out rooms?"

Paige looked down, and for a moment Grady thought she'd tell the kid how much money she'd spent finding him. Instead she said, "Matthias had nowhere else to go. He's elderly but too healthy for a nursing home and too poor to live on his own."

"What happened to his family?"

"I don't think he had much. His wife died, and he was left all alone," Paige told the boy softly. "Like me."

Vaughn looked away at that. "I'm sorry," he said, his voice like shards of glass, "but if you've got Matthias now, why don't you let me go back to Dad? Or else he'll be all alone!"

Grady saw the naked pain on her face, even after she squeezed her eyes shut, whispering, "Oh, Vaughn."

A moment later she reached up and pressed the boy's head down on her shoulder. He let it stay there, but he wasn't happy about it. In fact, looking at them, Grady didn't think he'd ever seen two more miserable people in his whole life. He'd have given his eyeteeth if he could have somehow made it better.

It had never occurred to him that Vaughn wouldn't be eager to return to his mother, that the boy might actually prefer his father. Didn't the kid realize that his father had literally stolen him from his mother?

Grady began to understand that finding her son had been a beginning for Paige rather than simply the end of her search. Her waiting and wondering was over, but now she had embarked on a long, new, difficult journey with her son, and that trip promised to make this one look like a romp in the park.

It was dark when the plane landed in Tulsa. Vaughn perked up a bit when he saw the Mercedes, asking his mom, "This yours?"

"No," she answered evenly. "It belongs to Mr. Jones."

Vaughn's manner was almost derisive as he climbed inside, as if she had somehow proven herself a failure in his eyes by not owning the car. Grady had to bite back the impulse to point out that Vaughn's precious dad had been picked up in a four-year-old truck with a crease in the tailgate.

As chatty as Paige had been on the drive from Arkansas, she was that silent on the long drive back from the airport in Oklahoma. In fact, if a single word was spoken during the first hour, Grady remained unaware of it. Vaughn leaned into a corner of the backseat, crossed his arms and feigned sleep, while Paige sat beside him and bowed her head. Every time Grady looked into the rearview mirror, there she sat with her head bowed, as still as a statue. He began to think that, unlike Vaughn, she really had fallen asleep. Then Grady saw her lips moving and realized that she was praying again.

She looked up at the sigh that gusted out of him, and their eyes seemed to meet in the mirror, though he doubted that she could actually see him. A small, tender smile curved the corners of her mouth before she looked away again. He couldn't imagine that her smile was for him, but it kept him looking at her in the mirror when he should have been concentrating on his driving.

Eventually Vaughn sat up and complained that he was hungry. Considering that he hadn't eaten his Thanksgiving dinner, Grady wasn't surprised. At Paige's request, Grady found an open drive-through at one of the little towns that they passed along the way to Nobb. Vaughn ordered a burger, tater tots and a drink that looked like it could fill a fifty-five-gallon drum. Grady didn't say anything about the kid eating in his car, though it was not something Grady normally would have allowed.

Vaughn had wolfed down the food and was sucking air through his straw by the time Grady turned on to Paige's drive. For the first time, the boy showed some interest in his surroundings. The house came into view, and for an instant Grady thought he saw something pleasant in the boy's reflection in his rearview mirror before Vaughn sat back and remarked derisively, "Hasn't changed a bit."

Grady held his tongue, recalling perfectly well that

the address given on Nolan's arrest record had been that of an apartment complex in Curly, South Carolina, a small town on the outer edge of Greenville County. He heard Paige murmur that she'd had the back porch remodeled into an office, but Vaughn didn't ask why as Grady parked the vehicle and got out.

The big black dog came down from the porch to greet them, and Grady assumed that his car was now familiar enough that the animal wouldn't bother barking. The thing hadn't let out a peep when Grady had arrived in the dark that morning, but no sooner did Vaughn step out of the Mercedes than the dog sat back on his haunches and lived up to his name, throwing back its head and slicing the air with yips and yowls and some sounds Grady had never before heard a living creature make.

Vaughn clapped his hands over his ears, while Paige attempted to scold the dog into silence. Light spilled out of the front door. Matthias appeared, and as before a command from him shut off the awful cacophony.

"Howler!"

Subdued now, the dog's pink tongue lolled out of its mouth as it waited eagerly for Vaughn to pet it. Instead, he stomped toward the house, leaving his mother to retrieve the bags that Grady pulled from the trunk of the car. Matthias came down the steps toward the boy, a smile—or at least what passed for a smile—on his craggy face.

"Don't mind old Howler," the old man said. "He's all alarm and no guard."

Ignoring Vaughn's scowl, he stuck out a hand, but the kid twisted past him and all but ran into the house, slamming the door behind him. Matthias stood for a moment, gazing toward Paige, who sighed. She seemed tired and sad. Finally, the old man turned and made his painful way up the steps and back inside.

Paige turned to Grady. "I tried to prepare myself," she said, and he heard the trembling uncertainty in her voice. "Knowing intellectually how difficult it might be and going through it are two different things, I guess."

He wanted to tell her that time would heal all wounds, that the worst was past her, anything to make it better. But what did he know? As she'd pointed out earlier, he had no experience as a parent and no hope of it. She likely would not appreciate words from him, anyway, so he just hoisted the bags and muttered, "I'll carry these in for you."

"No," she said, taking them from him, "you've done enough. Thank you. With all my heart, thank you."

He shook his head, shocked by the urge to hug her. Instead he asked, "You going to be okay?"

She smiled tremulously. "Oh, yes. My son is home. He isn't happy about it, but I knew he might not be, and I really have tried to prepare myself to deal with it."

"I don't know how anyone could prepare themselves for this."

"I've been seeing a Christian psychologist for the past two years."

"Didn't know there was such a thing."

"Oh, yes. Why wouldn't there be?"

He shrugged. "Just never thought about it."

"I wanted someone who shares my beliefs. My pastor recommended her."

"Ah. Makes sense, I guess."

"Dr. Evangeline's been very helpful," she said. "I'm really not surprised by Vaughn's behavior."

Just disappointed. Heartsick. Weary. She didn't have to say it. Grady saw it in the droop of her slender shoulders, the tilt of her head, the dullness of her beautiful eyes.

Grady looked to the house, escaping the weight of her emotions by wondering what might be going on in there. "I guess."

Her gaze followed his, and she whispered, "I can't help wondering what Nolan's told him about me, though. I mean, how did he explain taking him away from me?"

Grady hadn't thought of that. "Well," he said slowly, "any number of ways, I guess."

"And none of them good," she muttered, adding wistfully, "He was barely eight when they disappeared, just a little boy. He wouldn't know what to believe or what not to." She looked to the house again. "Now he's almost a teenager, and I have to accept that there's no making up for lost time. He has to learn how to have a mom again."

It occurred to Grady that he and Vaughn had something in common: they'd both been denied their moms at very young ages. Suddenly Grady thought of the last time he'd seen his own mother.

No one could have guessed that day as she'd dropped him off at school that she would never make it back home. To his shame, he'd shrugged away the kiss that she'd pressed to his cheek as he'd gotten out of the car, and he hadn't looked back or waved a farewell even though he'd known that she would watch him all the way through the door of the building.

He'd never seen her again. When his dad had shown up at the school later that morning with his brother sobbing at his side, Grady had known that something awful had happened, but he'd never expected to hear that his mom was gone forever. He hadn't believed it. Sometimes he still didn't believe it.

Grady didn't tell any of that to Paige. He had never told it to anyone. It was just something that he lived with. Suddenly Vaughn didn't seem like such a brat. No doubt the kid was terribly confused right now. Remembering what that was like, Grady hoped that the boy would soon come to see how lucky he was to get his mom back.

Clearing his throat, he said that Dan would probably be calling her in the next couple of days. She thanked him again, and then there was nothing left to do but get back into the car and head home alone.

He should have been relieved, and on one level he was. It had been a long, trying day. Still, he couldn't help feeling that he was abandoning Paige.

His last sight of her was in his car's left side mirror. Bathed in the rosy glow of his taillights, she stood there alone with a bag grasped in each hand, a small woman with a big job before her.

If he'd been a praying man, Grady would have said a prayer especially for her. As it was, he fixed his gaze forward and drove home, even more troubled than the last time he'd done so.

Chapter Four

Paige listened to the door slam and dropped down onto the sofa, sighing inwardly.

Nothing she'd done or said in the past month had made her son the least bit happy. He'd hated his room on sight. Too "babyish."

She'd rearranged everything and bought new linens and window treatments, keeping her regret buried as she'd put away the boy he'd been, all the things she'd treasured to remind herself that he was real and belonged in this place. He hadn't seemed particularly pleased once the changes had been made, but given how often he retreated to his room in a huff, he must have felt more comfortable with his personal surroundings than before.

Today's huff had to do with his impending return to school. Or perhaps it was the gifts he'd received yesterday for Christmas. Or the "do nothing" environment of Nobb. It was all tied up together somehow.

She'd kept Christmas low-key, realizing that it might not be the celebration for him that it was for her. Recalling the dreary Christmases she'd spent without him, she tried not to dwell on the fact that this one hadn't quite lived up to her expectations. He'd spent most of the day bemoaning the fact that he was missing out on a hunting trip his father had promised him.

Before noon on this first day after Christmas he'd declared the video games she'd bought him "boooring," the radio-controlled car "junk," the clothes "lame." Then he'd complained that he didn't have anyone to do anything with.

Realizing that she was not yet *someone* to him, she'd made the mistake of suggesting that they invite over a few of the kids from church. He'd rolled his eyes, already having made known his feelings about church, which according to his dad was for "weaklings and nut jobs."

She wondered if Nolan had always thought that, even during the years that he'd attended with her, starting when they were dating in high school. After Vaughn's birth Nolan's church attendance had grown increasingly sporadic, until it finally ceased. Once that had happened, the divorce had quickly followed, but Vaughn didn't need to know that.

Or did he? She wasn't sure, and since she wasn't certain, she kept her mouth shut. Everything she believed told her that it was wrong to point out Nolan's faults to his son. Yet, she wanted him to understand the importance and value of regular worship. Reminding herself that if she was confused, then he must be even more so, she held on to her patience. And her convictions.

Because Vaughn had nixed inviting over any of the youth from church, she had wondered aloud if he might want to call some particular friend from school. He'd laughed aloud at her idea of contacting one of the boys from his class, declaring that those who didn't attend the local church were even "dumber" and "hickier" than those who did. In fact, the whole school was "stupid," he'd declared, and he wasn't going back after the first of the year. Paige had quietly but firmly refuted that, which had sent him slamming into his room.

Their counselor, Dr. Evangeline, had strongly recommended public school for Vaughn. Paige's first impulse had been to hold him out until the start of the new semester, giving them a chance to get to know one another again, but Dr. Evangeline had insisted that Vaughn needed the socialization, needed to find replacements for the buddies he'd left behind in South Carolina. When the doctor had pointed out that because of state attendance standards, keeping him home those three weeks between Thanksgiving and Christmas vacations could cause him to be left behind a year, Paige had been convinced.

She constantly fought the impulse to hold him close and never let go again, so it had been difficult to take him down on the Wednesday after Thanksgiving and enroll him in the Nobb Middle School, which was part of the large, wealthy Bentonville district. He'd hated it from day one.

He hated Dr. Evangeline, too, a fact he'd made known during their first joint session with her. It hadn't been pretty. Since then he'd repeatedly said that a "guy" would do better, understand more, "actually listen, maybe."

Paige worried that Vaughn had a problem with women in general, starting with her. He not only disdained the psychologist to the point of rudeness, he disliked his female teachers—though the lone male in the group hardly fared any better—complained that the husband of the couple who taught his mixed Sunday school class deferred too often to his wife, and made sure that Paige knew how far short she fell of the Nolan ideal in parenting, running a household and everything else.

In short Vaughn hated everything and everyone in Arkansas, including her. Maybe most especially her. Those sentiments had grown darker and more vocal over time, especially since Dr. Evangeline had suggested that Vaughn should not be allowed contact with his father at least until he settled into his mother's household again. That, more than anything else, had enraged Vaughn.

Now Paige no longer knew what the right thing to do was. She only knew that her son resented not being allowed to call his father and that it was just one item on a very lengthy list.

Matthias limped into the living room, his cane

thumping pronouncedly on the hardwood floor with every step. The weather had turned sunny and mild, but his arthritis had not noticeably improved. That had nothing to do with the frown on his weathered face, though.

"It ain't my habit to give advice unasked," he announced, "but I'm makin' an exception here and now."

Resignation weighing heavily on her, Paige crossed her legs, denim whispering against denim. "Go ahead. Say it."

"It's time to tie a knot in that boy's tail."

"And how would you suggest I do that, Matthias? Take a belt to him?" They both knew that was out of the question.

"Stop letting him walk all over you. Ever since he's been here you've bent over backwards trying to please, but the world just ain't ordered to his liking. We know who he's got to thank for that, even if he don't. Maybe it's time he was told."

She shook her head. "I don't think it's wise to run down his father to him. That's Nolan's game, and it's bound to backfire. It's bad enough that Vaughn's life has been turned completely upside down without me trying to turn him against his dad."

"He can be glad it ain't up to me," Matthias mumbled, heading back into the kitchen where she had a pot of stew bubbling on the stove and corn bread baking in a cast-iron skillet. "I'd show him upside down."

Paige closed her eyes and fought the bleakness of

despair with the only tool she had. *Lord, help me do what's best for my boy,* she prayed silently. *Show me what needs to be done and give me the strength and patience to do it. Help him understand how much I love him, how much You love him, and thank You for bringing him home to me.*

She could only trust that one day Vaughn would be thankful, as well.

"Happy New Year."

"Hmm?" Grady turned away from the window, a cup of coffee in hand to find his brother standing in their father's kitchen, grinning.

"What'd you and the old man do last night, party until the wee hours?"

Grady snorted. "Hardly. I might have been the youngest one here, but I went to bed as soon as the ball dropped in New York."

"Party pooper," Howard groused, coming into his kitchen with one arm draped around his daughter-in-law's shoulders. "Look what Katie brought us."

She slipped free of Howard and carried the enameled pot with its glass lid in sight of Grady before placing it on the range.

"Spaghetti?" Grady noted, surprised.

Katie turned her dentist-perfect smile on him. "You're not superstitious, are you, Grady?" Katie asked.

"Black-eyed peas are just more traditional."

She scrunched up her nose. "Never could stand them."

Grady shrugged, wondering if Paige Ellis would

serve black-eyed peas on New Year's Day. He immediately regretted the thought. She should have been
out of his head long ago. But at odd moments like this,
she suddenly sprang to mind. He couldn't imagine
why.

After the long debriefing he'd had with his brother
on the Monday after Thanksgiving, Grady had re-
frained from asking Dan if he'd heard from her. Other
than being pestered more than once by Janet to submit
his billing report and expenses from the trip to South
Carolina, the case had not been mentioned again
except in passing. Grady couldn't help wondering
what the last six weeks had been like for Paige,
though.

Had the boy come around? Was he walking the
woods that surrounded her old house with that dog at
his heels, pretending at some childish fantasy? Did he
gaze at his mother with worshipful eyes now and
grimace halfheartedly at the way she babied him?
Had he made friends with Matthias?

"Where on earth are you?" his father's voice asked.

Grady realized with a jolt that the conversation had
carried on around him. He shook his head, gulped his
coffee and said that he needed a good rest in his own
bed tonight. He couldn't for the life of him remember
why he'd started sleeping over at his dad's on New
Year's Eve, anyway. Except, of course, that he never had
anywhere else to go, and Howard always claimed to
need help with the party he routinely gave. He'd started
doing that about the time Grady had gotten divorced.

They were a matched pair, Grady and his father, despite the thirty years between them, both big and square-built with deep, rumbling voices and hands and feet the size of platters. Both alone.

"Do you know what your problem is?" Howard asked, and Grady just barely managed not to roll his eyes.

"Here it comes," he groaned.

He didn't really resent his father's lectures. His father's concern for him was a good thing. They had never discussed those difficult early years after his mother's death when the distance between them had seemed to stretch into infinity. But it was after his divorce, that he'd discovered how firmly his father was in his corner.

"Your problem," Harold said, ignoring Grady's irreverence, "is that you spend too much time alone."

"And you don't?"

"That's different."

"I've been alone four years, Dad. How about you? More like thirty-four, isn't it?"

"Thirty-three. But I've had my family. When are you going to start one, Grady?"

"As soon as some woman throws a rope around him and drags him back to the altar," Katie said drolly.

"That's pretty much what the last one did," Dan noted.

"I blame her for this," Howard announced gruffly.

"You blame Robin for everything," Grady pointed out. "It's not her fault that I'm no good with women."

"She certainly didn't help things," Howard grumbled.

"Listen," Dan said in an obvious effort to change the subject, "we're throwing a football party in a few weeks. I want you both to put it on your calendars."

Howard shook his head. "Don't count on me, son. I've already got plans."

Dan raised his eyebrows at Grady. "Well, can I count on you, then?"

"I'll get back to you."

Dan sent a significant look at his wife, who smiled and said, "I have a couple friends coming who I'd like to introduce you to."

Single, female friends, no doubt. Grady turned back to the window that looked out over the deserted golf course, hiding his grimace.

His family loved him. They tried to be supportive, and he tried to be appreciative, but he was getting real tired of being everybody's favorite charity case.

It was time he got a life.

He wondered if Paige Ellis was as much of a sports fan as she'd claimed.

"He did not! You take that back!"

Paige heard the angst in her son's voice even before she recognized the anger and resentment. She'd run out to find a grocery store open on New Year's Day and grab cans of the black-eyed peas Vaughn had insisted they were supposed to eat for dinner. Vaughn and Matthias were arguing when she returned to the house. Dropping the bag with the cans on the end of the counter just inside the kitchen door, she glared at the pair of them, Matthias in particular.

"What's going on?"

Vaughn's face set in mutinous lines, while Matthias's eyes clouded. "I was just pointing out a few facts of life to this youngun," the old man grumbled.

"My dad did not kidnap me!" Vaughn declared heatedly.

Paige sent Matthias a quelling glance. "I don't see anything to be gained by discussing this subject." She turned to the counter and began removing the cans from the bag, saying brightly, "I got the peas. They may not be the brand you like, but I was lucky to find any at all. I didn't realize how many people abide by that old custom."

"I'll tell you what's to be gained," Matthias said doggedly. "The truth. Any other woman would've put that man away for what he'd done."

"Matthias, stop it," Paige ordered, whirling around, but it was already too late. Vaughn was already screaming at her.

"It's all your fault, anyway! He wouldn't have had to take me if you hadn't kept us apart!"

Paige fell back against the counter. "What are you saying?"

"He didn't have any choice but to take me! You kept him away 'cause he wouldn't give you money! That's why he wasn't around for so long! You wouldn't let him be a dad! And now you're doing it again!"

Paige gasped. After the divorce she'd gone out of

her way to include Nolan in Vaughn's life. She'd begged him to come around. He'd complained that her demands on his time were unreasonable, saying that Vaughn wasn't old enough to miss him. He'd even threatened to tell Vaughn that he wasn't his father if she didn't give him some space.

Only after she'd proved his paternity and won back the right to child support had he taken any real interest in his son, and only then to punish her. She hadn't cared, so long as Vaughn was happy. Now to hear her son say that she'd kept Nolan from being a dad to him was almost unbelievable to her.

She gulped and stammered, "W-we always have ch-choices."

"I don't!" he yelled. "'Cause if I had a choice, I wouldn't be here!" With that he tore from the room, rocking her sideways as he shoved past her.

"Now look what you've done!" she cried at Matthias, but the old man shook his head sorrowfully.

"Not me, girl. That Nolan's the one who done this, and you aren't helping that boy by not telling him the truth."

Paige closed her eyes and put a hand to her head. "Even if he could hear and believe the truth, Matthias, I couldn't tell him. You just don't understand the harm it does a child when his parents defame each other."

"His father don't have no problem defaming you."

"All the more reason for me to take the high road."

"Just be careful you ain't setting yourself up for a

bad fall," Matthias warned. "If you don't make that boy understand that his daddy's a lying, scheming—"

· "*Stop*," Paige interrupted firmly. "Just stop. Don't you see? No one can make a child 'understand' such a thing." She shook her head. "I don't even want him to know it, Matthias. I want him to believe that his father loves him as much as I do. I want my son to grow up believing that both of his parents treasure him beyond anything in this world."

"Wanting a thing don't make it so," Matthias insisted. "You're setting yourself up for disappointment, if you ask me."

It was on the tip of her tongue to say that she hadn't asked him, but she swallowed the impulse as he limped out of the room. Matthias only wanted what was best for her, but she had to think of what was best for Vaughn.

Grady leaned against the window ledge behind his brother's desk and tried not to stare at her. He'd been surprised when Dan had called and asked Grady to join him and Paige Ellis in his office. His dealings with Paige Ellis should have been at an end. Even if legal assistance was required, her case was Dan's responsibility, not his. Yet, he'd answered his brother's summons without complaint, interrupting an important telephone conversation in the process.

Her hair was a little longer, he noted, as if she hadn't found time to get to the stylist recently. Shadows rimmed her exotic sea-green eyes. For a moment he thought she'd taken to wearing smudged eyeliner; then he'd realized that she was tired, so tired that even the tiny smile she'd found for him had seemed to require great effort on her part.

"Anyway," she said, glancing at Grady and then at her hands. "I just thought I should run it by you before I made a firm decision."

Dan cast a veiled look at Grady, who knew instantly what he was thinking. The safety issue loomed large in both their minds.

"The contact would be limited to the telephone, I take it?" Dan asked.

She nodded. "Since you made it impossible for Nolan to return to Arkansas without risking prosecution, it has to be."

At least she'd acquiesced to that much, Grady told himself. Dan shot him a helpless look, and Grady cleared his throat, prepared to be the bad guy. "That was my doing, and I thought letting Vaughn call his dad was a lousy idea from the beginning."

"I know you did," she said softly. "My former counselor agrees with you."

"But the new counselor does not?" Dan surmised.

Paige sucked in a deep breath, her chest rising beneath the lapels of her brown velvet jacket and the plain front of the simple plaid sheath dress under it. "That's right. He feels Vaughn will benefit from regular, unhindered contact with his father."

"But the old counselor apparently thought it was harmful," Grady pointed out. Paige took it as a bid for clarification.

"She concluded that talking with his father would keep Vaughn from making peace with his new circumstances."

"Obviously my brother finds merit in her argument," Dan said. "I think I agree with them, though I have to tell you that this is not a legal issue. There is nothing at this point to legally prevent Nolan from maintaining contact with your son."

"We could fix that if you want us to, though," Grady added.

She shook her head. "I'm not here to find a legal impediment. I—I just want to do what's best for my son."

If you were sure what that was, we wouldn't be having this conversation, Grady thought. He truly wanted to help her.

"Can I ask you something?" At her nod, he went on. "Why did you switch counselors?"

The slowness of her reply told him that she was choosing her words with great care. "My son relates best to men."

Dan made a sound somewhere between recognition and conclusion, and Grady knew what he was going to say before he said it. Groaning inwardly, Grady could only listen.

"I'm wondering if a male in this role is the best choice. I mean, we've had experience with this issue ourselves. Our dad's failure to bring a solid female influence into my brother's life created some difficulties for him, as they both would tell you."

Grady briefly closed his eyes. "I don't think Vaughn could have a more solid female influence than his *mother*, Dan."

"Right!" Dan waved a hand, swiveling side to side in his chair with what Grady hoped was extreme embarrassment. "I didn't mean to imply... Actually the situations aren't that similar. Ours was a male household after our mother died. Grady was only six, so it's no wonder he never learned how to relate to women."

Grady groaned aloud this time. "Thanks loads, Dan," he rumbled.

"I—I probably wouldn't have, either," Dan went on lamely, "if not for my wife."

To Grady's surprise, Paige Ellis sat up very straight. "Who says Grady doesn't relate to women?"

Dan chuckled uneasily, as if he thought she was making a bad joke. When he realized that she was serious, both eyebrows shot straight up into his hairline. Paige glanced at Grady and caught him with his mouth hanging open. She flopped back in her chair, huffing with what sounded suspiciously like indignation.

"That's ridiculous," she scoffed. "I spent at least eighteen straight hours with your brother, and I assure you he's perfectly capable of relating as well to women as men." She nodded decisively here and added, "Better, in fact, than a great many men of my acquaintance."

Now Dan's mouth was hanging open. He managed to get it closed, babbling, "Ah. Um, I see. That's...good."

Grady grinned. He couldn't help it. In fact, a chuckle escaped as he came to his feet. But, it was time to bring this discussion to an end before his brother got the wrong idea.

"All right. I think we're through here."

"Yes, I really shouldn't take up any more of your time," Paige agreed briskly, rising from her chair, "especially since I came in without an appointment."

"Think nothing of it," Dan replied graciously, leaning over the desk to offer her his hand.

She shook hands, then allowed Grady to steer her toward the door. He did not dare to so much as glance in his brother's direction as he moved with her across the room and through the next, which was mercifully empty, Janet being away from her desk.

"It was good of you and your brother to see me on such short notice," she said as he walked her straight past the receptionist in the outer office and through the door at the glass front of the suite to the bank of elevators beyond.

"You happened to catch us both free," he lied, pushing the elevator button. The door slid open at once, and the moment for them to part ways had arrived, but he found himself oddly reluctant to do so. Impulsively, he stepped into the elevator with her, an action which required explanation. Belatedly he provided one, saying, "I'm ready for a cup of coffee. Can I buy you one?"

She paused a moment, then smiled and said, "Why not?"

"Good."

He punched a button, and the elevator gave a little lurch before dropping slowly toward the ground. He let silence eat up the seconds while he tried to think of what to say without letting on how pleased he was by her defending him.

She just stood there grasping the strap of her handbag while it dangled in front of her, watching the floor numbers light up one by one. Thankfully the building was only five stories tall. That was enough time for him to panic at a topic for discussion, which he used the moment they stepped off the elevator.

"I, um, know you don't want to hear it, but I have to point out that by not pressing charges against your ex-husband, you've left yourself open to legal action on his behalf." She stopped dead in her tracks, going pale, and he instantly regretted his words. Grasping her by the arm, he started her forward again. "I didn't say he *would* file an action, only that he *could*."

"What sort of action?"

He steered her toward the coffee trolley in the building lobby. "Petition for visitation." She caught her breath. "I didn't say he'd get it."

They reached the trolley, and she stood quietly while he purchased two small coffees. He could see her mind working over the problem of her ex as she added milk and sugar to her cardboard cup and turned with him toward a padded bench set back among a veritable jungle of potted plants.

"I thought you took it black," he commented sitting down.

"Oh. I'm, uh, experimenting."

He watched her sip, barely controlling her grimace, and he could've kicked himself. "You don't even drink coffee, do you?"

She wrinkled her nose. "I'm cultivating a taste. For black, I think."

Appalled at his own stupidity, he removed the cup from her hand and set it aside before swigging down a hefty slug from his own. "Obviously my addiction to this stuff just made me assume that you drank it, too."

"There are worse things," she pointed out, "than being polite enough to offer something you like to someone else."

"*You* were being polite when you accepted," he murmured. "Guess we're just polite folks, you and me."

She smiled and swayed sideways, giving his shoulder a little bump with hers. As if…as if they were friends. Or something. He gulped, then choked down more coffee to cover it.

"About Nolan," she said abruptly. "How could he get visitation if he can't even enter the state?"

Grady forced his mind back to the issue. "He can't unless he can convince a judge he won't interfere with your custody. You could still close that door by pressing charges."

She shook her head. "I know you're right, but I just can't risk alienating my son any further."

"Well," Grady said, "we still have time. We've made it clear to Nolan's attorney that if he does anything stupid we can still file charges."

She closed her eyes. "I pray it doesn't come to that."

He shifted, holding the cup of coffee between his knees with both hands. "Not going well, I take it."

Sighing, she shook her head. "It's as if Vaughn's forgotten all about our life together, as if the last three and a half years have completely canceled out the previous eight."

"Sounds like a defensive thing to me."

She sent him a sharp look. "What do you mean?"

He wasn't use to opening up to people, but he'd make an exception for her. "There was a time when I tried to forget how it had been before my mother left. Died. Before she died."

Paige's slender fingers curled around his hand. "Why?"

He saw how badly she needed to know, and he told her as best he could. "Because it hurt so much to remember. Forgetting was the only way I could…" He used her analogy. "Find any peace."

Her grip tightened. "Thank you for telling me this."

He let go of the cup with that hand and folded his fingers around hers, saying, "You know, my brother's right. The truth is I do have a difficult time relating to women. I—I never know what to say. I can't figure out how women think or what they want o-or expect."

"I don't believe that," she declared, shaking her

head. "You don't have a problem with women any more than you've forgotten your mother. You're just a little shy."

Shy? A big burly guy like him? He pushed the thought away, and shook his head.

"No, I'd rather cut out my tongue than make conversation with a woman. Usually."

She laughed, and her grip on his hand relaxed, but she didn't relinquish it entirely. "Nonsense. Now can I ask you a question? Do you think the male psychologist might be a mistake? I got several references, and they say he's the best."

Grady shrugged, flattered that she was actually sitting here asking his advice on what was a strictly personal matter. "Who knows? If you like him, use him."

"I don't like him. He acts like our problems are ridiculous, as if the solutions should be glaringly obvious to anyone with half a brain."

"Well, there you go," Grady declared, offended for her sake. "Dump him and go back to the first therapist, or else find another."

"I don't want someone else," she stated flatly, surprising herself as much as him apparently. "I know Dr. Evangeline. I trust her, even if I don't always agree with her, and she shares my religious convictions."

"Then why change?"

"Vaughn hates her."

"And likes the new guy," Grady surmised.

"I don't think so, actually. I think he hates all of us."

Grady looked at her, but she didn't appear as wounded as she did relieved. Nevertheless, he heard himself saying, "He doesn't hate you. He hates the situation. My dad thought I hated him, but I just missed my mom."

She smiled. "You don't know how glad I am to hear that."

He shrugged and hid his delight behind his coffee cup, muttering, "No charge."

She laughed again, and he privately marveled. What was it about her that made it so easy for him to talk to her? Maybe he wasn't as inept as he had always believed. He suddenly knew why he'd come down here with her. Sucking in a deep breath, he summed up his courage and plunged in before he could think too much about it.

"Listen, my, um, my brother's having this football-watching party at his house...." She was looking at him with those enormous green eyes, as if trying to figure out where he was going with this, and all at once he wasn't so sure himself. "Um, he's got a giant-screen TV," Grady finished lamely.

She looked down at her hands. "That's nice."

Nice. The death knell for romance.

He bit back a groan. What was he thinking? He couldn't ask her out, especially not to a party at his brother's house! Might as well shoot himself now. Yet, he couldn't just let her walk away.

Suddenly he thought of the cards he'd recently stuffed into his wallet. He normally carried only business cards, but Katie had had personal ones printed for him as a Christmas gift, and he'd made a show of tucking a few into his wallet. He'd never expected to have any use for them. Fishing his wallet from his hip pocket, he found the card and offered it to her.

"Maybe you'd like to have this. You know, in case… Well, just in case."

She took the card and stared at it so long that he had to restrain himself from snatching it back.

"I don't recognize this number," she finally said.

"Right. It's, um, my cell phone."

To his vast relief, she smiled. A moment later, she took her leave. Grady dropped his head into his hands and moaned.

She would never call, of course, but at least he'd made an effort. It was more than he had ever done with anyone else.

Chapter Five

Vaughn covered the mic in the telephone receiver with one hand and looked up at his mother. "You're not going to stand there and listen, are you?"

Paige tamped down her irritation at the question. She'd gone against the advice of everyone she knew and allowed Vaughn regular contact with his father, provided he agreed to return to Dr. Evangeline for counseling. He had seemed slightly less belligerent since then, but he obviously didn't want her overhearing his conversations with Nolan.

She turned to leave the kitchen, saying, "Call me when the water starts to boil so I can put the rice in." She reckoned that would give him twelve to fifteen minutes to talk, but she checked her watch as soon as she was out of sight, knowing perfectly well that if she left it to him he wouldn't call her until the pot had boiled dry.

After fourteen minutes she went back into the

kitchen to start dinner. Vaughn hung up and swung around, his sienna eyes challenging her in a manner with which she had become all too familiar. She waited for it, going about her business.

"You hate it that I want to go home."

"You are home, Vaughn."

"This'll never be my home! I want my dad, and he wants me!"

She looked him straight in the eye and softly said, "I know exactly how he feels. Believe me, I know too well what it's like to pray for the sound of your voice. Every day and every night for three and a half years, I prayed just to know that you were safe."

Vaughn's face went blank as she spoke. He stood staring at her for a moment as if he didn't quite know how to react. He didn't speak another word to her that whole evening, answering direct questions with nods, shrugs or shakes of the head. As the days passed, Vaughn grew more sullen and withdrawn.

Matthias was certain that Nolan was somehow directing the boy's behavior, and Paige didn't doubt that on some level it was true, but she couldn't find a way to change it. Every instinct she possessed told her that cutting off communication with Nolan would only backfire. She decided to try to speak to Nolan himself about it, calling him one evening after Vaughn had gone to bed.

Not at all contrite, he literally laughed at her. "Why would I want to help Vaughn be happy in Arkansas?"

"Because it's best for him."

"He wants to be here with me. Haven't you figured that out?"

"That's not the issue."

"Oh, you always think you know what's best for everyone, don't you?" he complained. "You still can't accept the fact that the divorce was best for me, and you never will."

"Actually," she said, pinching the bridge of her nose, "under the circumstances the divorce was best for both of us, but that doesn't matter. All I care about now is what's best for Vaughn."

"And that's why you'll eventually send him back to me," Nolan announced smugly.

She knew then that Nolan would not try to help Vaughn through this because he counted on Vaughn's misery convincing her to do the noble thing. He knew her well. He understood that if she truly became convinced that Vaughn could not reconcile himself to living with her, she would send him back to his father rather than see him continue to be miserable.

First, however, she'd have to find the strength to do it, and at present she was far from convinced that Vaughn would be better off with Nolan. What she'd learned about Vaughn's life with his dad told her that he had not been properly supervised. The written reports from Vaughn's teachers in South Carolina described a boy with a lengthy record of absenteeism who came to school often unkempt, unprepared and sometimes hungry.

If that wasn't enough, Vaughn's behavior was. This

Vaughn habitually rebelled at the notion of having to do what was expected of him, unlike the sweet and compliant boy he had previously been, and the only leverage Paige had was those telephone calls with his dad. Afterward, he was often glum and even more belligerent than before. It had become a vicious circle that threatened to wind tighter and tighter until it spiraled completely out of control.

They almost reached that point on the Monday that Paige received Vaughn's first report card, which she accessed online, having signed up for e-mail notification. Because she was pleased when he climbed into the truck that afternoon, she leaned over and smacked a great big kiss on his cheek.

He looked at her as if she'd gone crazy. "What was that for?"

"That was for one A, three Bs and three Cs. I saw your report card online today," she told him, checking traffic and pulling away from the curb.

"Oh, yeah," he mumbled, looking away, "I guess you're supposed to sign a copy of it."

"Did you bring your copy home with you?"

"Uh, guess I forgot." He didn't forget, and they both knew it, but she didn't scold him. He couldn't just accept her approval and let it be, though, grumbling, "I don't know what the big deal is. Three Cs isn't all that great, and the A was in PE."

"I don't care. It's an improvement over your last report card, that's what counts."

He scowled. "That's just 'cause school here is easier."

She cast a doubtful glance his way. "I'm sure it doesn't have anything to do with you actually doing your homework and showing up for class."

He erupted at that. "There you go again! Always hounding me about homework and stuff. Dad never stayed on my back like you!"

She snapped. Before she even realized what she was doing, she'd whipped the truck over to the shoulder of the road and turned on him. "Would you tell me, please, what it is that *will* make you happier here?" She raised a hand before he could even open his mouth. "I didn't say *happy*. You've made it clear you're not going to let yourself actually be *happy* no matter what! And leave your father out of this, will you please? I just want to know what it's going to take to make you a little bit happier with this situation!" She held up her thumb and forefinger, about a quarter of an inch apart, to demonstrate how small a thing she was really asking of him.

He clamped his jaw mulishly and folded his arms, staring straight through the windshield. She opened her mouth to blast him again, and that's when he answered her. "I don't have anything to do here, nothing fun, nothing I used to do!"

"Name one thing," she demanded.

"Hockey."

She blinked, not only because it was unexpected but because it was such a simple, pointed answer. "I take it you don't mean watching hockey, because I know you watch the games on TV."

"Duh." He curled his lip, just in case she hadn't fully realized yet how stupid he found her statement.

Exasperated she demanded, "Well, how am I supposed to know these things if you don't tell me? Do you want to *play* hockey?"

"Of course, I want to *play* hockey," he all but sneered, turning his hands palm up for emphasis. "I'm good at hockey, believe it or not."

"Of course, I believe it. Why wouldn't I?" He glanced at her, some of the wind seemingly taken out of his sails. She was feeling calmer but hadn't decided yet if losing her temper had been a good or bad thing. Gripping the steering wheel, she checked the traffic and pulled out, muttering somewhat sheepishly, "Now all we have to do is find you a hockey team."

She knew just where to begin her search, too, with the only hockey fan she knew.

That card with Grady's personal cell phone number had found its way into her hand repeatedly since he'd given it to her. She'd stared at it often, knowing full well that she had no excuse to call. Grady was her attorney, not her friend, and if he somehow made her feel wise and capable and able to unravel the enigma that her life had become, it was only because he was a particularly able legal counselor.

Yet, the last time she'd seen him, for one tiny moment, she'd thought Grady might be asking her out. He'd only been making conversation, of course, but just for an instant, her heart had raced and her spirits had soared.

It hadn't mattered how ill-advised dating one of her attorneys might be—or dating anyone for that matter. Of all the times in her life to consider taking that step, this was undoubtedly the worst. Still, she couldn't deny that Grady was a very attractive man, and nice, to boot. At least he could point her in the right direction.

She waited until after Vaughn went to bed that night. He didn't like her hovering, as he put it, while he was getting ready to turn in, so she kept her distance after reminding him that it was time to call it a day. What she really wanted to do, of course, was stand and watch him perform the myriad little rituals she had so missed in his absence, but he grumbled that he wasn't a baby. Instead, she sat patiently, one eye on the clock in the living room, until the yellow line of light that showed beneath his door went black, before she retreated to her own room.

Opening a drawer in her bedside table, she took out the card that Grady had given her and read the numbers printed upon it. In truth she knew them by heart, so many times had she looked at them. Another glance at the clock told her that the hour was fairly late, but it wasn't going to get any earlier if she sat there dithering. She picked up the telephone receiver and dialed.

Grady couldn't believe his eyes when he saw the tiny screen of his cell phone light up with her name. He'd given up wondering if she'd call. After the way he'd botched a simple invitation the last time they were together, he figured she'd finally accepted what everyone else took for granted about him: he was hopeless at getting to know women, and there was really no reason for a woman to try to get to know him, especially this one.

A woman like Paige Ellis could have her pick of men. Still, she'd called, and it would be rude not to talk to her.

Deciding to go for a light, breezy tone, he punched the correct button, lifted the tiny phone to his ear and said, somewhat cheekily, "Well, hello, stranger."

"Umm…hi! This is Paige Ellis."

He smiled at the warm, welcome tone of her voice. "I know. Your name came up on the caller ID."

"Oh, of course." She cleared her throat, and for one awful moment he feared he'd blown it already. Then she responded in a teasing tone. "I suspected you were not a morning person on our drive to Tulsa. I hope that means you're a night owl and it's not too late to call."

"So you figured out I'm not a morning person, huh? Guess my growl was worse than I thought. I didn't bite you, did I?"

She laughed. "Not even a nip. Actually you were very gracious. I hope you're not just being gracious now. Should I call back tomorrow?"

"Nah, I never hit the sack before eleven."

"Not even when you're getting up at two in the morning?"

It was his turn to chuckle. "In that case I make it ten. So what's up? You didn't call to check my bedtime, did you?"

She laughed again. "I'm looking for a youth hockey league in the area, and I'm desperate."

"Desperate but lucky," he quipped. "I happen to have a buddy who's a hockey freak. He turned me on to the sport, actually. And it just so happens that he's coach, commissioner and sponsor of the local youth league all rolled into one."

"You call it lucky. I call it blessed, and you, Grady Jones, are a blessing."

For several moments, he literally floundered. Finally, he sputtered, "Uh, n-no one, th-that is, what I mean..." He cleared his throat and pulled his thoughts together. "I take it this is for Vaughn."

"Who else? Seems he played hockey back in South Carolina. I'm hoping that getting him on a team here will make him more satisfied with his situation."

"I see. Well, the season began in September, but it runs practically year-round. This being January, we're less than four months in, so it ought to be possible to still get on the team. Should I call my guy and see what he has to say about it?"

"Of course, I want you to call your guy. I know it's an imposition, but my son wants to play hockey. It won't make him happy, mind you, but if I thought it would improve his attitude by one iota, I'd impose on a total stranger."

After that, she said that she had to go, he imagined that she seemed as reluctant to end the conversation as he was. He promised to talk to his hockey buddy about the possibility of Vaughn getting into the local league and get back to her soon. A moment of silence followed, and somehow he felt the gentle, gathering import of it even before she softly spoke.

"I meant what I said, Grady. You've been an answer to prayer for me more than once, and I thank God for that."

He spoke before he could think. "Makes me wish I believed in prayer."

She didn't laugh this time. Instead she was silent, then said, "Oh, Grady, that breaks my heart."

Breaking her heart was the very last thing he wanted to do, but he didn't know how to tell her so or even if he ought to. He swallowed, his own heart beating entirely too rapidly, and finally managed to say, "Aw, don't pay no mind to me."

"I will pay you mind," she said, though what that might mean he couldn't begin to guess. "Better, I'm going to hold you in my prayers, Grady Jones, and you'll see. I'll prove it to you. Prayer works. Because God's real, and He loves us."

"I wouldn't know about that," he told her softly, surprised by the sound of yearning in his own voice.

"You'll see," she vowed again. "You'll see."

Oddly enough, he hoped she was right, but he had to wonder if that wasn't pushing hope too far.

* * *

Grady nodded as Matthias retreated and Paige rose from behind her desk. He looked around the narrow room. It was colder than the rest of the house, which explained why she was wrapped up in a bulky cardigan sweater. Her face had lit up when she'd first seen him, and she was smiling so broadly now that he couldn't mistake his welcome. Then he spotted the fax machine atop a high table in a corner, and he suddenly knew how ridiculous it had been for him to come here.

He'd expected to spend the whole afternoon of Valentine's Day in court, but when the other party had failed to show, the case had been summarily dismissed. No shortage of work awaited him at the office, but when he'd found on his desk the papers that Jason Lowery had sent him concerning the youth hockey team, he'd made the impulsive decision to personally deliver them to Paige.

It had never occurred to him that he could fax them to her. Instead he'd driven all the way out to Nobb to hand-deliver them, which had absolutely nothing, surely, to do with the fact that it was Valentine's Day. Did it?

He felt like a schoolboy who'd just discovered girls didn't necessarily have cooties, horrified and elated at the same time. It couldn't have been more embarrassing if he'd shown up with chocolates and roses.

She removed the headset and came around the desk toward him. "I didn't expect to see you today. What are you doing out our way?"

He had no choice but to brazen it out. Thrusting the papers at her, he said, "I thought you should have these right away."

She scanned the papers, her tilted eyes rounding. "Oh! I knew there'd be gear to buy, but this list is endless!"

"Most of it's small stuff," Grady pointed out, "but before you worry about that, we first have to convince Jason to give Vaughn a tryout. Right now he's just willing to meet and talk."

"Okay," she said, sounding determined. "That's a beginning." She laid the papers on the corner of her desk and bent to remove a stack of files from the only chair in the room except for the larger one behind her desk. "Can I take your coat?"

"No, thanks. I can't stay long."

"Well, have a seat anyway. Matthias usually has a pot of coffee on, if you're interested. I warn you, though, it probably won't be what you're used to."

He shook his head, stepping forward and gingerly lowering himself into the rather spindly wooden chair. "No, thanks. I just want to explain Jason's situation to you."

She leaned against the front of her desk, crossing her slender, corduroy-clad legs at the ankles. "Jason is your friend, Jason—" she craned her neck to consult the papers on her desk "—Lowery, I think it is."

"Right. Jason's a couple years younger than me."

"That would make him how old?" she asked, smiling.

He blinked, taken off guard. Then he realized that she could only have one reason for asking—and it didn't have a thing to do with Jason Lowery. "Uh, thirty-seven, I think. I'll, um, be forty in August, so he's thirty-seven or eight."

She nodded, her smile not faltering in the least. "I think you mentioned that he's married."

"Yeah, uh, with a couple kids, boys. The oldest one's about Vaughn's age."

"That's good."

"Yeah. The thing is, there's just the one team in that age bracket around here, and it's sort of an elite group. They don't have the level of interest or parental involvement they need to field more than one team, so naturally they take the best, most dedicated players, and it's mostly tournament play, which involves travel, making it a fairly expensive endeavor."

She deflated a little. "I see."

"But, hey, one thing at a time, right? Meet and speak, that's the first step. If Jason thinks Vaughn's really got the drive, he'll try him out. After that, we'll see."

She nodded, murmuring, "At least Vaughn can't say I didn't try for him. When is this meeting?"

"Up to you. Jason's at the rink three evenings a week, Tuesday, Wednesday and Thursday. And usually Saturday, if the team's not traveling. But, uh, not tonight, since it's Valentine's Day."

"I'm sure his wife appreciates that," Paige said. "I'd normally have choir practice tonight, but it's been suspended so couples can go out."

Grady toyed with the idea of a dinner invitation and discarded it. Valentine's Day was not the time for a first date. When was the time for a first date? he wondered. Pushing that thought away, he asked instead, "Sing, do you?"

She wrinkled her nose. "That's a matter of opinion. I can carry a tune, at least, and Dr. Evangeline felt I needed something in my life that isn't focused on my son."

Grady wondered if she might have room for another kind of personal involvement besides choir. The idea alone scared the fool out of him; yet he heard himself saying, "I could go with you guys, if you like, to the meeting with Jason, I mean."

She smiled. "A personal introduction by a friend couldn't hurt. If you're sure you can spare the time."

"Wouldn't have offered otherwise. Tomorrow night too soon?"

"Not soon enough for my son, if I had to guess. So, yes, tomorrow would be great."

"Okay. Jason says practice starts at seven so we ought to get there about eight. I can be here by, say, seven-fifteen."

She shook her head. "This time, we'll come to you. I insist. It just doesn't make sense for you to come out of your way. How about we meet you in your office parking lot about seven-thirty?"

He said heartily, "Excellent! I've got a deposition tomorrow, and that covers me in case it runs over."

"Okay. It's a date then."

He wished it were. "I'd better let us both get back to work."

"I'll walk you out," she said, straightening away from the desk. "It's about time for me to pick up Vaughn, anyway."

She signaled that he should go first, and they moved through the narrow hallway to the living room. Even before they fully entered that room, the front door opened and Vaughn stepped inside. Grady felt the brush of her shoulder as Paige rushed past him to reach her son.

"What are you doing here? How did you get home?"

Vaughn shrugged. "Justin Gordy's mom brought me. I forgot to tell you we got out early today."

"You should've called me!"

"It's not like I have a cell phone," he retorted, which sounded to Grady like the continuation of a previous argument.

"There are phones at the school," she pointed out.

"The lines were, like, a mile long," he complained. "Guess I wasn't the only one who forgot to mention it was an early-release day." Paige lifted a hand to press her fingertips to her temples. "It's not like you don't know the Gordys," Vaughn argued smartly, and she nodded.

"You're right. You're right. Samantha Gordy's in my Sunday school class. It just shook me. I-I was about to go get you when you came in."

Vaughn had stopped listening to her, having

realized Grady was there. "Why's *he* here?" he demanded suspiciously.

Paige smiled at Grady. "Mr. Jones has arranged an interview for you with a local hockey coach."

For a moment, uncluttered joy transformed the boy's expression, so much so that Grady found himself suddenly worried. What if it didn't work out? If Vaughn didn't make the team, not only would he suffer, his mom would, as well.

"Oh, man!" Vaughn exclaimed, putting a hand to his head. "I don't have any of my gear! I can't even practice!"

"Hang on," Grady said, "this is just an interview. I can't guarantee a tryout."

"I get it," Vaughn assured him, somewhat disdainfully. "It's not my first interview."

Grady relaxed a little. Obviously the kid had some real experience with hockey—and a huge attitude problem that Grady tried hard to ignore.

Vaughn looked to his mom again. "I gotta get my hands on some gear. I don't stand a chance without it. I'm too rusty."

Paige glanced at Grady, then smoothed a hand over her son's head. "I understand. We'll just have to cross these bridges as we come to them, though. Something will work out, I promise."

"Not unless I get some practice," he insisted.

"The coach will loan you gear and give you time to practice if you think you need it," Grady informed him.

Vaughn closed his eyes. "Oh, man, I gotta ace that tryout."

Taking his hands, Paige sat down on the edge of the couch. "I think we should pray about this, right now. It'll help put your mind at ease."

For a moment, Vaughn seemed reluctant, but then he bowed his head. Paige began to speak quietly while Grady stood there like a log.

Here, he thought bleakly, was the reason why it would never work between them. Paige wasn't just a believer; she was a practitioner. She didn't just talk about it, she *lived* her faith. A woman like that would never give a doubter like him a serious chance, and even if she did, he was bound to disappoint her.

Grady swallowed a lump in his throat. He could no longer pretend that he'd beat a path to her door on Valentine's Day just because he'd had an unexpected couple of hours on his hands. Now he had to face the truth. Though he had romantic thoughts about Paige Ellis, they could never be more than simple friends.

Friendship was something, though, he consoled himself. It was certainly more than a mere attorney-and-client relationship, and much more than he'd had with any other woman since his divorce.

He'd taken a real step forward. Finally.

Just because it felt like a step in the wrong direction, didn't mean that it was.

Did it?

Paige ended her prayer and looked up, smiling

beatifically. Vaughn took a deep breath and let go of her hands.

"Can I call Dad and tell him the news?"

Her smile grew strained. "Finish your homework first."

Vaughn made a face, but he trudged off toward the kitchen, shrugging out of his backpack and muttering, "Dumb report."

"Haven't you forgotten something, Vaughn?" Paige asked, halting the boy in his tracks. He turned, and she jerked her head at Grady, who instantly wished she hadn't.

Vaughn frowned, but he faced Grady and addressed him. "Thanks for getting me the interview."

"No problem. I'm glad your mom asked for my help."

Vaughn started to turn away again, but Grady cleared his throat. Reluctantly Vaughn faced his mother and said, "Thanks."

Paige accepted that with calm grace. "You're welcome."

Vaughn made his escape.

There's another reason not to get romantically involved with Paige Ellis, Grady told himself, watching the kid hurry from the room. He didn't know how much of Vaughn's insolence toward his mother he could put up with. One day he'd collar the kid, and Paige would be mad at him. That, Grady feared, was something he could not endure. Bottom line, it was best that he not do something where he might have to.

Shaken, Grady took his leave. It would have been

better, he believed, if he hadn't come, and if he had any sense he'd find a reason not to accompany them on Thursday. But he knew he wouldn't.

Apparently, he didn't have a lick of sense. Not when it came to Paige Ellis, anyway.

Chapter Six

Vaughn literally could not sit still. Repeatedly ignoring his mother's admonitions to keep his seat belt buckled, he bounced around in the backseat of Grady's car, babbling about his favorite hockey players and the brand of new skates he wanted. Paige prayed that he would make the team and that she could afford the gear required to play.

Vaughn asked Grady about the coach and the facilities; Grady told him about Jason but didn't know anything about the rink. Riding in the front with him, Paige occasionally flashed him a wry smile, grateful for his patience.

When they reached the rink, Vaughn was out of the car before the engine died, but then he literally sauntered toward the entrance, flipping a nonchalant wave at a sweaty player walking toward a top-end luxury SUV with his parents. Grady made it around the car about the same time that Paige got to her feet, and it belatedly occurred to her that she might have waited for him to open the door for her. He closed it instead, and they stood side by side watching the strutting sway of Vaughn's shoulders, then traded looks before breaking out in grins.

"I'd say he's got the attitude that Jason's always talking about," Grady said beneath his breath.

"Who knew cocky could be an improvement?" Paige whispered.

Grady chuckled softly. "I'm sorry it's been so rough for you."

"It hasn't been a picnic," she admitted, "but it's better than not knowing whether he's dead or alive."

"It takes a strong woman to go through something like that and come out on the other side without bitterness," he told her.

"Oh no, I'm bitter," she said flatly. "God knows I resent what Nolan did to us. I have to work every day at not acting on that bitterness. How about you? You must have some resentment over your divorce."

He shrugged. "I guess. I don't think about it much anymore. I realize now that we were never really suited. I couldn't talk to her."

"How did you wind up married then?"

He spread his hands helplessly. "Like my brother said, ours was an all-male household after my mom died, so I didn't grow up around women. I liked girls, but I always felt dumb around them, so I just kept my distance. When Robin showed an interest in me, I let myself be swept along. Eventually she started talking about us getting married like it was a given, and I figured it was the thing to do. I wasn't *un*happy about it."

"You might not have been unhappy," Paige said, "but it sounds like you didn't love her."

Grady didn't deny it. He stroked a hand through his thick, wavy hair. It was sandy brown, much warmer than his brother's premature silver, she mused, the perfect foil for those electric-blue eyes.

"I tried," he said, "I wanted to be married, and I wanted to make her happy, but I never said the right thing. No matter what the problem was, I never could say the right thing to her. It's always been that way."

"I don't get that," Paige protested, drawing her brows together. "You're not like that with me."

One corner of his mouth curled into a lopsided smile. "Maybe I finally grew up. Robin always said I needed to."

"Looks like," she teased, sweeping her gaze over him. She didn't realize that she was staring until he spoke.

"We better get inside before Vaughn body checks some unsuspecting pedestrian."

She smiled, nodded, and walked with him into the building, where they found a surprising number of people milling about in the foyer. She spotted Vaughn talking animatedly with a pair of boys about his age, pads and helmets tucked under their arms, skates slung over their shoulders by the laces. One of them dropped his equipment to shuck his jersey, and Paige was surprised to find that he was much slimmer beneath the bulky pads than she'd assumed. Next to him, Vaughn looked substantially more solid.

A woman called from across the room, and the boys hurried off in her direction. Vaughn turned, looked around and jogged over to Paige and Grady.

"Guys say Coach is tough but cool. He likes aggressive play and emphasizes defense."

"Sounds about right," Grady confirmed.

"They say they're weak on offense."

Grady looked at Vaughn. "What position did you play before?"

"Forward."

"That should work."

"I take it forward is an offensive position?" Paige asked.

"That's right," Grady said, but Vaughn rolled his eyes.

"Don't you know anything, Mom?"

"Not about hockey," she admitted blithely, noting Grady's glower. She pushed through swinging doors into the arena, Vaughn and then Grady following.

Grady was instantly hailed and went off to speak to his friend. Suddenly Vaughn clutched Paige's forearm with both hands. She recognized the combination of hope, eagerness and fear in his expression and knew that he wanted this badly.

She patted his fingers where they gripped her arm and whispered, "You can do this. I know you can. And don't forget, I'll be praying for you."

He visibly relaxed, nodding decisively and pressing

back his shoulders. When Grady called to them, waving them over, Vaughn moved out in front and greeted Jason Lowery with a firm handshake and obvious eagerness. After introducing everyone, Grady came to stand next to Paige, letting Vaughn speak for himself.

Lowery was a good-looking man, tall, dark and unabashedly male. All that saved him from being devastatingly handsome was a white scar bisecting one eyebrow and a nose that had obviously been broken a number of times. He struck Paige as intelligent and affable but rather intense.

They chatted for several minutes before Lowery clapped a hand onto Vaughn's shoulder and escorted the boy to a seat in the bleachers some distance away. Paige got the unmistakable message that her input was no longer required.

Grady stepped in front of her, distracting her attention from Vaughn. "We've done everything we can," he told her, and she nodded, folding her arms against her fluttering middle. "Now it's up to him. Don't worry. He can handle it."

"I'm sure you're right," she said, meeting his gaze.

He smiled, his whole face softening. She saw something in his eyes that momentarily confused her.

"What?" she asked.

Grady quickly looked away. Then he winked at her. "A man always likes to hear he's right."

She laughed, and suddenly she knew what she'd seen. Her pulse sped up. Oh, yes, she knew that look. It had been a long time since she'd seen the interest to kiss her in a man's eyes, but she recognized that look when she saw it.

Thrilled, she smiled in a way that she hadn't since she was a mere girl. Then she glanced past Grady to her son and sighed inwardly. This was the wrong time for that look. Unfortunately, the right time might be a long while coming. If ever. Vaughn seemed none too friendly toward Grady, and Grady wasn't exactly delighted with Vaughn's attitude.

Grady took her by the arm and turned her away from the pair talking intently. "Let's walk. This could take a while."

Nodding, she let him lead her back the way they'd come. They reached the area near the doors where a bulletin board was mounted on one wall, and they wandered over to check the notices posted there. Paige saw a lengthy list of used gear for sale.

"This helps," she said, studying the list. "I priced some of the gear new on the Internet, and I don't mind telling you it took my breath away."

Grady was perusing another long sheet of paper. "Looks like you might also have to rent rink time so he can practice."

"Rats." She moved over to take a look for herself, then caught her breath. "That's not all! I have to pay for lessons! He can't be on the ice alone!"

"It's only for a short while," Grady said, his hands landing atop her shoulders as he stepped up behind her.

Paige knew that she would pay whatever she had

to, if it would help Vaughn make the adjustment to being with her again. "Can't be more expensive than private investigators and attorneys," she added. "Not that they aren't worth every penny."

Grady chuckled and lightly massaged her shoulders, drawling, "Honey, there are times *I* can't afford me."

She didn't really hear anything after the endearment, which washed over her in a hot rush. She turned, wondering if he'd meant that the way it had sounded, but before she could even make eye contact with him, Vaughn's anxious voice distracted her.

"Mom. Mom! Coach needs to see you."

Focusing on her son, Paige hurried to follow him around the bleachers to an area in the back, where the coach was digging gear out of several large cloth bags. He told Vaughn to find a helmet, jersey and pads that would work for him before turning to Paige. The jersey, pads and helmet were on loan. She could rent skates, but Vaughn would need at least one stick, gloves, shorts large enough to fit over the pads and, of course, skates.

Jason wanted to try Vaughn out in exactly one week, provided they could find at least four hours of practice time in the interim. Fortunately, the rink rental was included in the instructor's fees. After recommending two different instructors, the coach warned her that if the boy lived up to his expectations, she would need to have him in Little Rock the following weekend for competition.

"We take the ice at 8:00 a.m. Saturday," he told her, "which means he'll need to be there Friday and stay overnight."

Gulping, Paige said, "I understand."

She and Grady helped Vaughn haul his borrowed gear to the car. The boy chattered in delight every step of the way but fell silent as they were driving back toward the law office where they'd left their vehicle. When they came to a stop at a traffic light, Paige twisted around in her seat to see what had distracted him. Her breath caught, and tears filled her eyes. Vaughn sat with his head back against the seat, eyes closed, his hands clasped and lips moving silently in prayer.

Paige quickly faced forward, not wishing to intrude on her son's conversation with God. Her gaze collided with Grady's along the way. Glancing at his rearview mirror, he let her know that he realized what was going on in the backseat. She wiped away her tears with her fingertips, smiling tremulously. Grady produced a paper napkin, and she laughed softly when she saw the logo of a coffee shop on it. He smiled and then his hand gripped hers for a second before the light changed.

Bowing her head, Paige followed her son's example. Anything that could send him to God was something to be thankful for.

The instructor blew his whistle, and Vaughn slid to an abrupt halt, his skates spewing tiny slivers of ice.

Paige had been watching him skate laps for some time, and before that he'd been facing off against another boy and the instructor, a man named Juli, short for Julian, Jefferson.

If the coach minded the feminine-sounding sobriquet, he didn't show it, and considering his height—which must have been six-five, at least—he could have made his displeasure vividly known. In contrast, the other instructor wasn't much taller than Vaughn himself but built like the proverbial brick wall.

Juli skated over to Paige, seated in the home team box, and leaned against the partition wall. "Kid's sharp. If this is rusty, I can't wait to see him a month from now."

"So you think he'll make the team?"

"He will unless he smart-mouths Jason. Lowery doesn't take any lip. He likes attitude, but he wants to see it, not hear it, and he expects his skaters to play smart, which means legal. I don't know what Vaughn's last coach's philosophy was, but some coaches think bad manners are the price you pay for aggressive players. That doesn't cut it with Jason Lowery, though."

Paige sighed. "I heard Vaughn sassing you earlier, and I'll speak to him."

Juli nodded. "It's frustrating to go up against somebody twice your size, but losing your temper doesn't make you a better player, and Vaughn has to learn that." He smiled and added, "I think he's got the message."

"I'll make sure he does," Paige said, hoping that Vaughn would take this lesson to heart. He'd been relatively happy lately—except after talking to his dad.

Jefferson skated off to set up the four boys present in a man-on-man scrimmage, with himself as goaltender. Paige turned her head just as Grady stepped over the bench to settle down next to her. She smiled in surprise.

"What are you doing here?"

He shrugged inside his overcoat. "Case was continued. I didn't see any point in going back to the office at this hour of the day. Besides, I'm curious. How's it going?"

"Vaughn has to learn to control his temper."

"Ah. Well, sports are good for that, believe it or not. With the right coach."

"Jason appears to be the right coach."

"He is." Grady patted her hand where it rested on her knee. "Besides, Vaughn wants this bad enough to deliver what's expected of him."

"It's just that hockey is so violent," Paige worried aloud.

"Any sport can be," Grady said, "if hotheads prevail. You're a sports fan, you know what I mean."

She nodded. "He would pick the one sport I know the least about."

Grady laughed. "I'm betting that the more you learn about hockey, the more you'll find to appreciate. Hockey is similar to soccer in some ways, as physical as football, fast or faster than basketball.

Requires as much hand-to-eye coordination as tennis, as much judgment as golf. Roll all that into one and put it on ice, and that's hockey."

Nodding, she let go of her worries. "It's made such a difference in his attitude. Why, he's almost pleasant."

She wouldn't think about what might happen if he didn't make the team. Why borrow trouble? It was enough that Vaughn no longer brooded at the dinner table; he chattered. He continued to seem troubled and pensive after talking with his father, but he'd actually forgone the daily telephone conversation on a couple occasions lately, either because he was eager to get to the rink or had too much homework.

Matthias seemed thrilled with the changes in Vaughn. She'd even heard the two of them laughing together, and Vaughn had thanked her effusively for the skates she'd bought him. He should have. They'd cost a fortune.

After a half hour or so, the instructor called a halt. No sooner did Vaughn reach her than he blurted, "I'm starved!"

Recent experience had taught Paige to be prepared, and she handed over a protein bar at once. He downed it in two bites, even before he got his skates off. After guzzling at least a quart of sports drink, he asked for something else to eat, catching her off guard.

"Uh, we'll stop for something on the way home, I guess."

"I have a better idea," Grady announced. "I'm

ready for dinner myself. Let me buy you two a couple of steaks."

Before she could even reply, Vaughn exclaimed, "Great!"

"But you're all sweaty," she pointed out.

"Aw, come on, Mom, I'm hungry!"

Grady lifted his eyebrows at Paige, who gave in. "Oh, all right." She opened her shoulder bag to get at her cell phone. "I'll just call Matthias while you get out of your pads."

They piled into the car a few minutes later, Vaughn proclaiming that he was going to eat a whole cow. They discussed where they should go and decided on a popular chain restaurant.

It turned out to be a good selection. Grady ordered the most expensive steak in the house and pronounced it acceptable. Vaughn got his favorite, battered, fried onions, and Paige was able to have a good salad. She and Grady sat across from Vaughn in the roomy booth, while Vaughn gave Grady a running commentary on today's practice, admitting, "I blew my cool."

"Just so you know," Grady said casually, "Jason won't put up with that kind of thing."

Vaughn nodded. "That's what Juli said."

"Juli?"

"Julian Jefferson," Paige explained, "the instructor."

"One of those guys out there today?"

"The tall one."

Grady looked at Vaughn. "He lets you call him Juli?"

"No way!" Vaughn answered. "I call him Coach to his face."

"But Juli is what he goes by," Paige said.

Grady shook his head. "Now there's a guy confident in his manhood."

"Actually," Vaughn weighed in, "he said the players on the other teams used to call him Juli to get his goat, so he just decided to go with it, and now it's not an insult anymore."

Grady nodded. "Smart. I'm liking this Juli."

Vaughn considered and agreed. "Yeah. Me, too. At first I thought, well, he's not my real coach so, like, what difference does it make, you know? But, he's the coach right now, and he can still teach me stuff."

"That's a good way to look at it," Paige said, pleased. "I'm impressed that you realize that he deserves a certain respect, Vaughn, and also that you see he has something to teach you, even if it's just that you should control your temper when you play."

"Losing your temper gives the competition an edge," Grady commented. "Once they see you can be pushed into losing your cool, they'll use it against you."

"I know," Vaughn said, an edge to his voice. "My old coach, he used to say the same thing, but sometimes it's hard, especially when someone razzes you. One guy, his dad was in jail, and all the guys on the other team knew about it, and they kept saying stuff." Vaughn glanced accusingly at Paige, and she knew that he was thinking about his own father's short jail stay.

"I hope you see how inappropriate and unfair that sort of tactic is," she told him gently, but he just shrugged.

"When I win at something," Grady rumbled, "I like to know it's because I have superior skills and play a better game."

"I don't think having superior skills is a problem for Vaughn," Paige commented, trying to lighten the mood.

"What would you know about it?" Vaughn asked. "Just 'cause I'm your kid doesn't automatically mean I'm a good player."

"Hey, she may be prejudiced," Grady snapped, "but she's enough of a sports fan to recognize a real athlete when she sees one."

Vaughn looked skeptical. "Yeah?"

"Yeah," Grady grumbled, sounding irritated.

"H-Haven't you noticed that I watch basketball on TV every chance I get?" Paige asked hastily, disturbed by the air of confrontation.

Vaughn put on a sulky, defensive face. "I thought Matthias was the one turning on the games."

Paige waved a hand and reached for a piece of bread, purposefully keeping her tone light. "As far as Matthias is concerned, golf is the only sport that ought to be televised."

"You probably even watch golf," Grady surmised, cutting into his steak.

"What's wrong with golf?" she asked, feigning indignation.

"Not a thing," Grady replied calmly. "I've watched

tons of golf with my dad, and it's every bit as exciting as watching paint dry." Vaughn laughed, and the moment of tension faded. "Playing golf, now that's something else," Grady went on.

Paige relaxed. They bantered about the merits of various sports until the meal was finished and Paige admitted, "Okay, okay, so I don't know anything about hockey."

Both Grady and Vaughn said, "I'll teach you."

They scowled at each other, and Paige jumped in with, "It'll probably take both of you!"

"I'm sure you'll catch on quick," Grady encouraged.

Vaughn shrugged as if he couldn't have cared less whether she ever developed an understanding of hockey or not. Would he ever get tired of punishing her for turning his world upside down? She wondered if he'd done the same thing to his father once he'd realized he wouldn't be going home to her again after that camping trip.

She put the thought away. The past didn't matter. What counted was right now, this moment, and the future that she was building with her son.

That future likely did not include Grady Jones in any substantive way. The renewed tension at the table told her that.

Unaccountably saddened, she reached for her handbag, saying, "It's getting late. We'd better go."

Vaughn sucked up the last quarter inch of soda in the bottom of his glass and slid toward the edge of the booth while Grady signaled the waitress for the check.

"Can I split the bill with you?" Paige asked Grady, dipping into her bag for her wallet.

"Nope."

"At least let me get the tip."

"Uh-uh. I invited you out, remember?"

"But—"

"Vaughn," Grady interrupted, tossing the boy his car keys, "explain the meaning of the word *no* to your mom, will you?"

Vaughn looked at the keys, then he took his mother by the hand and tugged her toward the exit, saying, "Come on, Mom. Let's wait in the car."

She let him lead her out of the restaurant. He unlocked the car and climbed into the back, cracking, "We ought to take this thing for a spin while Money Bags is settling the bill."

"Don't call him that," she ordered, catching the door before Vaughn could pull it closed, "and if you're ever stupid enough to go joyriding, try not to pick an attorney's car."

"What difference does it make so long as you don't get caught?" he retorted.

"It makes a lot of difference, Vaughn," she said more sharply than she'd intended. "Joyriding is a crime."

"Like I'd ever do it!" he protested. "I was just kidding."

Paige grimaced, knowing she'd overreacted. "I know you wouldn't, but mothers are supposed to give advice."

"Well, if you're gonna give me advice, I'm gonna give you some. When a guy invites you out, don't try to buy your own dinner, especially when he's got lots more money than you."

She crouched to bring herself eye level with him. "Grady didn't invite *me* out. He invited *us* out."

"Yeah, right, and he's *just* your lawyer."

"I—I guess we're friends," she stammered. "Does that bother you?"

He shrugged, saying coldly, "What do I care? At least, there'll be somebody here for you when I go back to Dad."

Paige felt every bit of her hope vanish. "Oh, Vaughn."

"I'm sorry, Mom!" he blurted. "But Dad needs me. Your life's together. You've got friends and a business, church and stuff like that. He's got nobody but me!"

"If your dad can't get his life together, Vaughn, you can't do it for him," she pointed out.

"You don't understand!" Vaughn exclaimed. "He depends on me to keep him on track!"

"You're not the parent!" she argued desperately. "You're the child, Vaughn. He's not your responsibility."

"But he's my *dad!*"

"And I'm your mother! And I love you!"

He stared at her, helpless. "I know, but so does he. It's not fair. I should get to choose who I want to live with, and when I'm twelve, I can."

"Is that what you think, that you can just wait me out until you're twelve, then convince a judge to send you back to South Carolina?"

He didn't answer that because Grady appeared just

then. Splitting a look between them, he asked, "What's going on?"

"Nothing," she replied tersely, rising and closing the door.

Grady opened up the front for her, and she slipped onto the seat and buckled her safety belt. He walked around to drop down behind the steering wheel before reaching back for his keys, which Vaughn slapped into his palm without comment.

"What'd I miss?" he asked, eyeing Vaughn.

Paige sent him a despairing glance and shook her head. Vaughn said nothing. After a moment, Grady started the car.

When they reached the parking lot of the ice rink, Vaughn bailed out of the car and strode toward his mother's SUV without a single word to anyone. Paige stayed where she was to speak to Grady.

"He thinks that when he's twelve he can tell a judge he wants to go back to Nolan and that will be the end of it."

Grady made a face. "It wouldn't be quite that easy."

"But could it happen?"

"Maybe. Not likely, but...I warned you that you were leaving yourself open by not filing charges."

"What difference does it make?" she asked bitterly. "If, after everything, he wants to go back to Nolan then—"

"Let's cross that bridge when we get to it," Grady interrupted. "He won't be twelve until July, and I can't imagine that he'll want to go back by then."

She shook her head, fighting tears. "You didn't hear him earlier. He thinks he has to go back. He says his dad needs him. It's like he's the parent and Nolan's the child."

"Don't worry," Grady urged, squeezing her hand. "If it comes to a court fight, we've got plenty of ammunition."

She gulped, knowing that her fight with Nolan must never come to a courtroom. "I thought things were getting better, but he's just biding his time here."

"Maybe he thinks that now," Grady said, "but you're a great mom. He'll change his mind. You'll see."

Paige gave him as much of a smile as she could manage. "Thank you for dinner."

He tapped the tip of her nose with his forefinger. "My pleasure."

"You're a good friend, Grady, and a good attorney, even if I don't always take your advice. It's just that I have to think of my son first and foremost."

"Yeah, I got that," he rumbled, and for a moment she thought he'd say more. When he didn't, she did.

"I'm sorry if Vaughn got on your nerves tonight."

He made a face. "It's not that. I just don't have much experience with kids. I didn't mean to come across as surly."

"You didn't," she told him, "but I don't think it matters. He seems to be hoping you'll take me off his hands, frankly."

She'd meant it as a joke, but Grady didn't seem to

see it that way. In fact, he looked stunned by the idea, which disappointed her more than it should have. She figured she'd better cut her losses and run.

"Well, good night."

"See you."

She got out of the car, wondering if she really would be seeing him again. Not anytime soon, if she had to guess, and who could blame him? Vaughn could be difficult if not downright hostile.

Maybe, all things considered, it would be better if she didn't see Grady again. Apparently she'd misread him. For so long she'd been too consumed with finding her son to even think of forming a romantic relationship, and now was obviously not the time to begin.

She couldn't deny that she was disappointed, but then she'd never been tempted to lean on someone else the way she was tempted to lean on Grady Jones. Something about him made her feel safe and validated, which was nonsense because they seemed to disagree as often as not. He didn't even share her faith!

From now on, she decided, she would keep her relationship with Grady strictly business.

On the other hand, someone had to show Grady how much God loved him, and if not her, then who?

Confused, she knew that she'd just given herself something else to pray about.

Chapter Seven

"So how come you don't have any family?" Paige heard Vaughn ask as she walked into the kitchen.

Matthias shrugged over his oatmeal bowl. "Me and my wife didn't have no kids, so when she died I was alone."

Paige poured a bowl of corn flakes for herself and stirred yogurt into it. She hated milk, always had. Vaughn, fortunately, loved it, which was why he picked up his bowl just then and slurped down what was left. Afterward, he started to wipe his mouth on his sleeve, glanced at her and opted for a paper napkin instead.

Paige leaned against the counter and hid a smile behind her spoon. These small, everyday things thrilled her. They were what she had missed most during his long absence.

"Didn't you have any brothers or sisters?" Vaughn asked Matthias, returning to his theme.

Matthias reached for his coffee cup. "Had some sisters once, but we lost touch a long time ago."

This was news to Paige. Pushing away from the counter she said, "I didn't know that."

Matthias stared into his cup. "Like I said, we lost touch a long time ago."

"Were they older or younger than you?" Paige asked.

"Older. I don't know if either one of 'em is even still alive." He put down the cup and pushed up to his feet, using the table for leverage.

"Even so," she said thoughtfully, "you could have nieces or nephews."

He shook his head. "So far as I know, neither of 'em ever married. Ain't it time to leave for school?"

"In a minute," Paige said, scraping up another bite of cereal and yogurt. "Get your stuff together, son."

"Okay."

She poked the bite into her mouth, and while she chewed Matthias followed Vaughn out of the room.

Paige pondered what she'd just learned, wondering why Matthias had seemed uncomfortable talking about it. Likely he found the subject sad, but it could be something else, something he didn't want to say in front of Vaughn. She determined to speak to him about it in private, away from Vaughn's sharp ears.

A few moments later, Vaughn yelled that he was ready. Paige rinsed her bowl and left it in the sink before hurrying out to grab her coat and take her son to school.

Her cell phone rang before she got back to the house. Apparently some mix-up had occurred at the office of one of the doctors who used her transcription service, resulting in two of her employees receiving incomplete recordings. She had to drive into Bentonville to resolve the matter, which put her way behind in her own work and left no time for conversation.

She worked through lunch, making do with crackers and cheese, one eye on the clock as she raced to make up for lost time. Vaughn came in from school starving as usual, and she took an hour to spend with him before hurrying back to her desk until dinnertime. She forgot all about talking to Matthias.

It was exactly twenty-two minutes past two the next afternoon when he limped into the office, Grady Jones at his heels. The look on Grady's face told Paige that something was very wrong. She came to her feet, ripping off the headphones without first turning off the recording.

"I came myself," Grady announced unceremoniously, "but if you want Dan, I'll take you to him."

"What's happened?"

He extracted a sheaf of papers from his inside coat pocket and tossed them on to her desk.

"I was wrong," he apologized. "Nolan didn't file for visitation. He's filed for full custody."

Grady sat next to Paige on the sofa in her living room, holding her hand. Worry rumpled her forehead.

"I don't understand," she said. "After what he did, how could he possibly hope to win legal custody?"

Grady tamped down his anger and reached for the professional detachment that he'd abandoned back at his office the moment he'd realized what Nolan had done. The anger was multifaceted.

He was angry with Nolan, of course, but also with Vaughn, who might well have shared potentially devastating details of Paige's life with his father. On another level, he was angry with himself for not having pushed harder for filing charges. He was also angry to a degree with Paige, who had left herself unprotected in her zeal to please an ungrateful little brat who might never be reconciled to his situation.

Grady was even angry at God, if He existed, for allowing this to happen.

"Nolan's claiming that you are an unfit mother."

"That's ridiculous!" Matthias erupted, addressing them from the center of the floor, where he stood with his weight braced against the head of his cane. "He can't prove that. Paige is a fine mother. No kid ever had better."

"He's claiming that you belong to a cult," Grady went on.

"A cult!" Paige exclaimed in disbelief. "That's insane!"

Grady consulted the papers on his lap. "The Community of the Redeemed."

"That's my church. It's not a cult!"

"He says you give them considerable sums of money."

"I don't *have* considerable sums of money, but I give above my tithe, if that's what he means."

"He contends that you don't make a move without the approval of the group," Grady went on. She had to fully understand the charges that Nolan was making.

"I consult my pastor and others from time to time," she said, "but they don't dictate what I do!"

Grady shuffled the papers, cogently presenting the argument as outlined in the emergency petition. "They quote an expert who contends that the church has no affiliation with any recognized body and describes its tenets as secretive."

"That's nonsense! We're independent and nonde-nominational, but many churches are. There's nothing *secretive* about it."

Grady scanned the attached report. "Says that two investigators from the Foundation for Research on Cults tried to clarify the group's beliefs and were pressed for personal encounters by the leader—let's see, that would be Richard Haynes. They interpreted this as secretive and manipulative."

"Talk about blowing things out of proportion!" Paige declared, rolling her eyes. "I know what happened. These two 'investigators' called the pastor to ask him questions of a spiritual nature, and he did what he always does. He offered to meet, pray and discuss it with them. He likes to counsel people in person. He says it gives him better insight. There's nothing wrong with that, and it's not secretive or ma-nipulative. It certainly doesn't make the church a cult."

"A cult!" Matthias crowed. "Ha! That's rich. Their so-called expert don't even know what a real cult is! Maybe they think all churches are cults. I could tell 'em about cults, the ignorant, no-account weasels."

Something in the way Matthias spoke alerted Grady. He fixed his gaze on the grizzled old man ranting in the middle of the room, his mind racing.

"What do you know about cults, Matthias?" he interrupted.

Matthias shut down in midrant, a hunted look coming over him. "What's that?"

"You heard me. I want to know what you know about cults. More importantly, I want to know *how* you know. Because you do, don't you?"

Paige scooted closer to the edge of the sofa. "Don't be absurd. What would Matthias know about cults?"

"They named him as your handler," Grady revealed, clutching the papers in one hand, his gaze trained on Matthias. "I thought it was pure convenience, him being here in the house with you and possibly attending the same church. But it's more than that, isn't it, Matthias?"

The old man closed his eyes. "Father in Heaven, forgive me," he said. Stumbling backward he came up against the recliner and fell down into it, dropping his cane and bringing both hands to his face. Paige flew off the couch and to his side.

"Matthias! Are you all right?"

"Paige, honey," he said, gripping her hands with his, "I did this! I been a fool near all my life, and I paid the price, but I never expected it to fall on you, never in a million years."

"Perhaps you'd better answer my questions," Grady instructed firmly, ignoring Paige's glare.

Matthias slowly nodded, and Grady listened with growing concern as the old man told the story of a young couple, prosperous farmers, married several years and desperate to conceive a child.

"No one could tell us why there was no babies," he said sadly. "Back in the fifties, they didn't know much 'bout such things. Then a preacher came to town, a traveling evangelist with a band of followers. They called themselves the Seed of Israel."

Charismatic and persuasive, the preacher had convinced Matthias and his wife that their barrenness was due to the sin of greed, and he'd declared that once they'd "surrendered all to God," they would be exceedingly blessed. Before it was over, the Porters had sold off everything they owned and given all their money to the fellow and his followers. Eventually the band of believers had dwindled to a hardy few who'd become increasingly insular, estranged from extended family and friends and controlled by the man they called Brother Israel.

"I actually told my sisters I didn't want nothin' to do with 'em," a shamefaced Matthias confessed to Paige. "I thought, at the time, that Satan was using 'em to pull me away from the true religion."

"Oh, Matthias," she said, "how awful that must have been for all of you."

"I looked for 'em later," he told her miserably, "after Brother Israel died and ever'thing fell apart, but they'd moved away, and I couldn't find out where."

Brother Israel, it seemed, had dropped dead from a stroke during one of his raging, hours-long sermons. The remaining believers had disbanded, leaving the Porters with nothing.

"Truth is," Matthias confessed, "my wife and me never recovered. We moved up this way and farmed on shares or leased land 'cause no one was gonna loan real money to a fool like me."

"You're not a fool," Paige said, on her knees beside his chair. "We all make mistakes."

He patted the hand she placed on his forearm, saying, "It don't matter no more, girl. We made a decent life for ourselves here, put all that behind us. It was years before I even heard the word cult, but that's what the Seed of Israel was. Seemed like they was springing up all over in the seventies. Believe me, wasn't nothing new."

Grady cleared his throat. A headache threatened by the time Matthias had finished his tale. "Obviously Nolan has somehow dug up this story and twisted it to suit his purposes."

"But how could he have found this out?" Paige asked.

"He, or his attorney, has probably done just what we did and hired a private investigator." Grady shook his head, putting up a hand to massage one temple. "I've got to tell you, Paige, it wouldn't take much for a good trial lawyer to spin this into a real nightmare, especially if Vaughn testifies for them."

"But he wouldn't do that!"

"Nolan got this idea somewhere," Grady pointed out. "If not from Vaughn, then from who? I'm not saying Vaughn deliberately told his father things that he could use against you, but I imagine they can make whatever he's said sound pretty indicting. Our defense is going to have to be equally compelling, and the first thing you have to do is distance yourself from the church."

"Don't be ridiculous! We'll just have Pastor Haynes explain what the church believes."

"That might work with a judge, Paige, but with a jury?" Grady shook his head, sick at heart. "I sure wouldn't bet on it. In fact, if I was on the other end of this, I would *insist* on a jury trial."

She put her hands to her head, sinking back on her heels. "I can't believe this."

"I'm so sorry," Matthias said mournfully.

"It's not your fault," Paige insisted. "Nolan did this."

"But I gave him the ammunition, girl. Even if he don't already know 'bout my past, he's bound to find out, and you don't know how sorry I am about that."

"We don't know what he knows," Grady said, "and that's part of the problem, but you're no more to blame than the rest of us, Matthias. I should have insisted that we put Nolan Ellis away when we had the chance. We'll have to file charges on him now. It's our only leverage."

"You know I can't do that," Paige said simply.

Grady couldn't believe he was hearing this. "You *have* to! This isn't just about upsetting Vaughn anymore. There's too much at risk."

She lifted her chin. "I'd risk anything for my son, if you don't know that by now."

"Oh, I know it!" he snapped. "And obviously so does Nolan!"

Matthias lifted a hand, forestalling further argument. "We can't fight them if we're fighting each other."

Sighing, Grady pressed a hand to the back of his head, which had begun to throb. "On that we can agree," he said.

Matthias nodded, his jaw working. "It must be me that put this idea in their heads, so I guess the best thing I can do now is to take myself as far away from here as I can get."

Even as Grady reluctantly agreed, Paige shot up to her knees. "Don't be silly! Where would you go?"

"That doesn't matter right now," Grady said. "We'll find a place for him."

"He has a place," she insisted, "and I won't hear of him leaving home because of Nolan's nonsense."

Grady closed his eyes and counted to ten, trying to retain his grip in the face of growing dismay. "Paige," he reasoned, "just for once, would you please listen?"

"Fine. I'm listening." She subsided, folding her arms and sinking back down on to her heels, a mulish expression on her face. He'd seen that very look on Vaughn's face. Apparently mother and son were more alike than he'd realized.

Grady marshaled his thoughts. "Okay. Now, in order to mount an effective defense against these potentially devastating charges, we have to do certain things. Number one." He held up an index finger. "As I've already said, we have to distance ourselves from anything that can be made to resemble a cult. Two." He held up a second finger, rushing on before she could react to his first assertion. "Vaughn has to be made to understand how serious this situation is." She started shaking her head, but he plowed on. "We have to know what he's said to fuel this claim!"

"No." She got up, leveraging her weight against the arm of Matthias's chair, and faced Grady squarely. He groaned, recognizing that calm, stubborn expression. "Under no circumstances will I put my son in the middle of this."

"Paige, you've got to listen to reason. When this thing comes to trial—"

"It won't come to trial!" she exclaimed, suddenly moved to tears. "I'll send him back to his father before I put him through that. And I won't disavow every-thing important to me just because someone else is willing to twist the truth!" She whirled away from him. "Matthias, you're not going anywhere. Do you hear me? This is your home. I need you here, espe-cially if worst comes to worst and Vaughn—" She broke off, trembling from head to toe.

Both Grady and Matthias rose to their feet. Matthias was closer, and he'd wrapped his ropy arms around Paige before Grady could even begin to get to her. He shook his head, confident that she must change her mind, certain that she wouldn't. Her back to him, she laid her head on Matthias's bony shoulder, and the old man sent Grady a worried, tearful look.

Grady bowed his head. He understood why she didn't want her son caught up in something this ugly. He understood that her church was important to her because of her faith. He understood that Matthias was precious to her, second only to Vaughn.

What *she* didn't seem to understand was that she was going to lose her child, and perhaps much more, if she didn't let him help her.

"Paige, please think about this. You've got to fight back. If you don't and this gets out… Think what something like this can to do your business."

She laughed, a mirthless, watery sound that broke Grady's heart. Lifting her head, she turned.

"Do you honestly think I care about that?"

"So that's it?" He threw up his hands. "You let Nolan haul you into court and lose everything?"

"No! It won't come to that. I never said I wouldn't fight, but I won't put my son in the middle of it, let Matthias leave *or* give up my church."

"Then what's the point? How else can we fight this?"

Paige swallowed. "This town is full of people who will testify on my behalf. They know the church is not a cult. And there's Dr. Evangeline. I've been seeing her for nearly two years. She's a clinical psychologist. Who better to tell the court that I'm not in a cult?"

"These townspeople, are they members of the church, too?" Grady asked.

"Some. But there are others who aren't."

"And didn't you tell me that Dr. Evangeline has some connection to the church?"

"She's a Christian and a member of a Christian practice. Many churches recommend her organization."

Grady shook his head. "You're taking a big chance going at it this way."

"And Paige, honey," Matthias put in, "just 'cause you won't bring Vaughn into this don't mean his daddy won't."

She bit her lip, but after a moment she shook her head. "I have to do this my way."

"Then you better think of this," Grady ground out. "Doing it your way is going to be expensive. Doing it *any* way is going to be expensive. You can't afford to lose your livelihood, and if it gets out that you're connected to some cult, that could happen."

She shrugged, folding her arms tight. "So we'll just have to keep it quiet."

"Interview, prepare, depose and call a whole town full of people to the witness stand," he drawled sarcastically, "on the q.t.? Right. Baby, you're going to need more than a lawyer to pull that off. You're going to need a magician!"

She lifted a hand to the small gold crucifix hanging from a delicate chain at the base of her throat. "But I have better than that, and He will take care of everything."

Grady lifted a hand to the back of his neck, dropping his head in defeat. What had made him think that he could talk to her? He couldn't even make her understand what a risk she was taking. He should've let Dan handle this. In fact, he never should have gotten involved with Paige Ellis at all.

For her sake, he wished he could believe in a loving, omnipotent God who protected the faithful from heartache, pain and loss, but he'd never been more doubtful or afraid.

Paige shook her head. She'd been doing so for the past hour and more, but she couldn't seem to stop. Unfortunately, she didn't know what the answers were, only what they were not.

"Even if Dan agreed," she said to Grady, sitting across the kitchen table from him, "I couldn't let you work for nothing."

He wrapped a big hand around the mug of coffee that Matthias had poured for him and heaved a deep sigh. The poor man had been holding on to the very edge of his temper all this time. Such steely resolve was to be admired, but Paige couldn't let that sway her.

"And why not?" he asked, his tone verging on a growl. "All attorneys work pro bono cases. It's expected."

"I'm not indigent, Grady," she pointed out. "I managed before. I'll manage again."

"That was *before* hockey," he said glumly.

So it was. The traitorous thought that it might be a blessing if Vaughn did not make the team flitted through her mind, but she dismissed it instantly.

"Of course," Grady said, not quite meeting her gaze

over the rim of his mug, "Vaughn might not make the team. For any number of reasons."

She half smiled, understanding clearly that he was offering to speak to the coach, and shook her head again. "I couldn't take that from him."

Grady set the mug down and folded his arms against the scarred tabletop. "Won't make any difference if Nolan gets him back, now will it?"

Paige rubbed her eyes. "No," she conceded, "but I won't punish my son for a situation created by his father. I want him to be happy, whatever that takes."

"Well, you won't have to worry about legal fees for a while anyway. We've, ah, got this new billing service, and they're, like, way behind. It could be, I don't know, months before they get current."

Grady was a terrible liar, but she wouldn't tell him so. He was trying so hard to help. And a delay in billing *would* be perfect.

"There, you see?" she said, trying desperately to inject a note of levity. "By the time billing catches up to me, I may have won the lottery."

"Now that'd be something," Matthias chimed in from the living room, "winning the lottery without ever buying a ticket."

She wanted to laugh, but it really wasn't a laughing matter. Not only could she lose legal custody of her son, but her good name was at stake. Worse, Matthias would be hurt if his past came out. In addition, her church and all its members could be labeled cultists, its mission to spread the good news of salvation severely handicapped.

While the expense of defending herself was worrisome, it fell far behind those considerations. Nevertheless, she couldn't ignore the facts. Even with the extra time that Grady was essentially promising her, certain expenses connected with something like this would not wait: special fees, court costs, investigators and experts… The list was endless.

And it could all be for nothing, Paige thought morosely.

Perhaps she should send Vaughn back to his father before this went any further, for everyone's sake. Yet, she couldn't quite give up the fight yet.

Neither, unfortunately, could she fight this in the manner that Grady wished.

"You never know how or when God will work something out," she said, as much to herself as the man sitting across the table from her.

"And what if it goes against you?" he asked.

"All I have to know is that God will take care of us, one way or another."

Grady frowned. "Doesn't seem to me like God's doing a very good job at the moment."

"It wasn't God Who filed that custody suit," she said. "That was all Nolan, exercising his free will."

He nodded, whispering, "I wish I could have your faith."

"You can," she told him. "It's yours for the asking."

He looked up in surprise, then he shook his head. "Oh, no, not for me. I've been a doubter too long."

"Yes, for you, and maybe that's the point of this,

Grady. Maybe God's teaching us all to rely more completely on Him. So far as I'm concerned, if that's all that comes from this mess, then it will be worth it."

Grady ran a blunt fingertip around the rim of his cup, pensive and solemn, and she knew that he was thinking over what she'd said. After a moment he looked up and asked, "How can you say that? I know how much you love your son, how hard you fought to get him back."

"Yes," she said, "but Grady, don't you see that my prayers have already been answered? For all the time that Vaughn was missing, I prayed to find him, to know that he was well, to have him home again. Yes, I found him. I know that he is well, as well as can be expected, anyway. I've had him home. I believe he's better off here with me, but God sees what I can't see, and whether Vaughn stays with me or returns to his father, my prayers have been answered. For that I praise God."

"It's not fair," he said. "You're a good mother, a good person. You don't deserve this."

"Thank you." She gripped his hands with hers, her heart turning over. "But it's not about fairness. We can't expect a painless life, Grady, not in this world. With pain comes solace, though."

She couldn't help wondering if that wasn't part of why Grady was here, to provide her solace. No one had ever made her feel safer, stronger, more certain than this man, and she had no doubt that God had brought him into her life for a reason.

He ran his thumbs across her knuckles. "I just don't want to see you get hurt again because of something Nolan's done."

"Nolan may have chosen this path, but I choose to walk it with God. That means I have to do what's best for everyone involved, not just myself. Doing it any other way would hurt me more than anyone else."

Grady sighed. "Okay," he grumbled. "We do it your way."

She closed her eyes, thanking God for the man who sat across the table from her. She prayed for wisdom and that, whatever happened, God would be glorified in this situation. She prayed as well that Matthias would find the peace he needed, and that Vaughn, Grady, even Nolan, would come closer to God.

For herself she requested strength, because whatever happened now she knew she was going to need it.

Chapter Eight

On the evening of the hockey tryout, Vaughn was subdued but surly. Grady understood that the kid was nervous, but he didn't see why he had to growl at his mother, who had done everything in her power—to her own detriment—to make her son happy. The second or third time it happened, Grady wanted to reach through the rearview mirror and shake the kid until his teeth rattled. He might have tried it if Paige hadn't been so serenely pleasant. Her, he wanted to hug.

That was getting to be a problem, frankly, an impulse he was having more and more trouble curbing. He really had no business working on her case, but he couldn't bring himself to step aside and leave it to Dan, who seemed all too willing to do whatever she wished with a minimum of argument.

Grady didn't *want* to argue with her, but he couldn't seem to help himself. He often found himself railing at her, and that just wasn't like him. She must not have minded too much because she'd allowed him to come along to the tryout, although he'd practically insisted. That wasn't his usual style, either.

Looking back, Grady realized that he'd seldom insisted, let alone argued, with Robin. He'd just gone along with whatever she'd wanted, including getting married. He regretted that his marriage had failed, of course, but he finally understood why. Obviously Paige had been correct in her assessment that he hadn't really loved Robin.

They hadn't loved each other. He'd been a means to an end for Robin, and she had been an easy, passive answer for him. He hadn't had to strain himself to win her, hadn't had to think of the right words to say, hadn't had to guess her needs or wishes or emotions. By keeping his opinions and thoughts to himself and going along with whatever she'd wanted, he'd thought he was making her happy, but he hadn't troubled himself to find out if that was true.

It was different with Paige. More than anything else in the world, he wanted her to be happy—even if he had to fight with her to make it happen. He wasn't arrogant enough to assume that he alone knew what was best for Paige, but he did know a thing or two about the law and what remedies it offered. It hurt him that she was so reluctant to accept those remedies when that was basically all he had to offer her. Yet, he admired her determination to do what she felt was right.

She was so quick to put everyone else first, though,

that he felt someone ought to look out for her. Consequently, he'd defend her as vigorously as she would allow against Nolan's absurd accusations, while doing everything he could to alleviate the other burdens that she bore. That was exactly why he'd decided to secretly give her a helping hand with her finances.

If Vaughn made the hockey team, which seemed likely, then he was going to need gear. Grady had seen to it that Paige was going to get a very good deal on that gear, such a good deal that neither she nor Vaughn could possibly pass it up. He'd also offset the other expenses as much as he'd dared. Knowing how stubborn she could be about these things, though, he'd talked his way into accompanying her and Vaughn to the tryout.

As he pulled into the rink parking lot, he could hear Vaughn breathing in as if he was steeling himself. His eagerness apparently trumped his apprehension, however, as he was out of the car almost before Grady got the transmission in park. He popped the trunk to allow Vaughn to dig out his mostly borrowed gear and took a moment to encourage Paige with a smile.

"Here we go," she murmured, at least as anxious as Vaughn. "It may not make any difference in the long run, but I pray he makes it."

Glancing around to be sure that Vaughn was out of earshot—she insisted that the kid be kept in the dark about the custody suit—Grady succumbed to the need to reassure her.

"I've been thinking about it, and I really believe we

can win in court. You're the best parent, and I'm pretty good in a courtroom, if I do say so myself."

Paige lifted a hand, cupping his jaw as tenderly as if he were a fragile, priceless sculpture. "Grady," she said, a touch of exasperation in her tone, "I keep trying to tell you that this can't go to trial. I won't put anyone I care about through that, not Vaughn, not Matthias, not my church, not even myself. And not you. I know you'd do the best for us that you possibly could, but I also know in my heart of hearts that in the long run a trial would do more harm than good." She shook her head. "Don't you see? Either Nolan backs down before it gets to that point, or I've already lost because my son will never forgive me if I do those things that will win an argument in court."

Grady fought every urge that rushed through him. He wanted to hold her, to protect her, to demand that she let him pulverize her ex in court, to tell her how much he cared for her, but he didn't dare. Oh, he didn't doubt that on some level she cared about him, too. She cared about everyone who came into her orbit with a selfless goodwill that amazed and even shamed him. It wasn't the same thing, though. He very much feared that he had fallen in love with her and that she could never feel the same way about him.

Vaughn tapped on the passenger window just then, juggling an armload of hockey gear. "A little help?" he complained.

Paige got out of the car to help Vaughn, and Grady followed them into the building. A half hour later, he sat next to Paige in the stands, gripping her hand as Vaughn made a mad dash toward the goal with the puck, his stick expertly shepherding that little black disc toward the net.

The boy had come out of the box on attack, catching everyone else on the ice off guard, including Jason, who'd lost his whistle in a gasp of surprise when Vaughn had punched through the face-off, darted out to snatch the puck from his own partner and whisked it in to make his first shot on goal. The assistant coach who was functioning as goalie caught just enough of the puck to send it careening off the goalpost. Otherwise, Vaughn would have scored while his erstwhile teammate for the two-on-two scrimmage was left standing midzone with his mouth open.

The pair of thirteen-year-olds deputized to give Vaughn a workout couldn't do anything but try to catch up as Vaughn fielded his own rebound, banked it off the wall and intercepted it again with a lofting swing that sailed it over the goalie's shoulder. Jason hobbled the whistle, finally getting it back between his teeth in time to call play to a halt just as the puck dropped into the corner of the net.

Grady was on his feet next to Paige yelling loud enough to drown out the whistle while Vaughn beamed a smile up into the stands that rivaled the lights overhead. A laughing Paige applauded, while Jason put his hands on his hips and shook his head, clearly impressed. A moment later he put the four skaters to another face-off, with strict instructions for Vaughn to pass the puck to his teammate this time.

Vaughn dutifully followed instructions. Then in the next two minutes he managed three shots on goal, all of which the assistant coach was lucky to stop. For the remainder of the exercise, Vaughn thwarted every attempt of the opposition to so much as get near the goal, let alone shoot on it, proving that his defensive play was as good as his offense. By the end of the exercise, the two older boys were clearly in awe of Vaughn, his own teammate seemed half-afraid of him, and both coaches were over the moon.

It came as no surprise, then, when Jason asked the boy to stay for practice with the whole team and quickly provided Paige with a schedule for the remainder of the season. Quite a crowd had gathered by the time the regular practice was ready to commence, and it quickly became clear to the other parents that the team had a new star. Off the ice, Vaughn seemed a little smug, but on it he was all business, and Grady had no doubt that Jason Lowery would soon take care of that immature arrogance.

One especially awkward moment came when one of the team fathers sidled up to Grady and asked, "Where did your son play before?"

Paige looked past Grady to the man and answered simply, "South Carolina," letting Grady explain that he was only a family friend.

"And a hockey nut," Paige added, flashing a smile up at him.

A hockey-mad friend of the family, he thought. Yeah, that was him, all right. No doubt that explained why he'd secretly paid for a boatload of top-of-the-line gear, the very latest of everything a player could want, the sum of which Jason offered to Paige at a fraction of its actual cost immediately following practice.

"It's used but it's the best available," Jason said.

Vaughn tore into it, thrilled to find price tags still attached. Jason flashed a guilty, apologetic look at Grady, who felt his face heat as the whole ruse threatened to come undone.

"Wh-what do you know," Jason stammered. "Some of it does still have the tags attached." He cleared his throat, obviously trying to think up a plausible reason why "used" gear would still have the store price on it. "Did I, uh, say 'used'? I should've said secondhand."

"Some folks buy out the sporting goods store before they even know whether or not their kid'll make the team," Grady supplied helpfully. "Right, Jason?"

"Uh, right."

Paige widened her already large, green eyes. "Why didn't they just return it?"

"Yeah," Grady muttered. "Why didn't they just return it?"

"Uh. It was on sale?" Jason ventured uncertainly.

Paige laughed. "Of course!"

Seeing her delight, Grady relaxed, and when he relaxed, Jason relaxed, so much so that he was entirely believable when he informed her that he was waiving the usual enrollment fee due to the fact that the season was almost half over. She accepted that with only a mild exclamation of surprise and didn't even question the ridiculously low room rate that Jason quoted her for that weekend's tournament stay in Little Rock.

Vaughn was too busy exclaiming over the new gear to give any thought to how it had just happened to come together in one place. Smart enough to take advantage of that, Grady grabbed up an armload of pads and gloves, heading to the car with them. Leaving Paige behind to complete the purchase, Vaughn followed Grady with his new team uniform, chattering happily.

It was too chilly to stand outside in the dark waiting for Paige, so after loading the new stuff into the trunk Grady and Vaughn got into the car. Several minutes later, Grady began to wonder what was taking so long. Vaughn, who was tired because of all that physical activity, had curled up on the backseat and was half-asleep, so Grady decided to look for her without him.

"I'll lock the car doors and hurry right back. Okay?"

"Whatever."

"Don't open up for anyone else."

Vaughn lifted his head off the seat "I'm eleven, not a baby." He dropped his head again and closed his eyes.

For a moment Grady was torn between going to look for Paige and giving the little smart aleck a piece of his mind. Then suddenly he realized that he was being more idiotic than Vaughn, who was, despite his skill on the ice, merely a child. Children were allowed to be cheeky and foolish; adults should know better.

Vaughn was just a boy in a tough spot, torn between two parents who couldn't live together. For the first time Grady wondered what he would have done in Vaughn's position. He could not be thankful for his mother's death, but he was suddenly glad that he hadn't had to choose between his parents.

From that perspective, the whole situation looked very different from Vaughn's end. Of course, no decent father would steal a child and run away, leaving his mom to suffer, though Vaughn obviously didn't see it that way.

All he knew was that he loved his dad, who had been there during the years when his mom had not. It didn't matter to Vaughn whose fault that was. He loved his dad. Period.

Grady marveled that Paige, who had been most hurt by Nolan's actions, had been able to see from the first that Vaughn's feelings and his ideal of his father mattered. The normal response to the kind of loss and pain that Paige had suffered at the hands of her ex-husband was anger and the tendency to make a monster of the perceived enemy, exaggerating every fault and failing.

Instead, Paige saw the common humanity that she and Nolan shared as parents. Paige Ellis, Grady realized, wasn't completely "normal." Indeed, the woman was almost superhuman, and he could see only one reason for it.

A *feeling* swept over Grady, as if someone or something unseen had tapped him on the shoulder and whispered, "That's right. It's Me." It was a voice he'd never heard and yet somehow recognized. He turned away from the sight of the boy curled up languidly on the backseat of his car and closed his eyes.

Okay, he thought, shaken. *I take it back. She's right. God is real. So why haven't You fixed this for her?*

If he'd actually expected some sort of response, he was disappointed, but *he* suddenly found himself wondering if maybe that was what he was here for, to fix things for her. Hadn't she said, more than once, that he was the answer to a prayer for her? If God could use him for her benefit without him even knowing it, how much more might he be capable of if he willingly surrendered to be used?

Here's the deal, he thought, *I'll do anything You want for her. Anything.*

When he realized what he'd just done, he had to shake his head. He couldn't remember the last time he'd said a prayer.

Reaching blindly for the door handle, he got out of the car and trudged back toward the building. He pulled open the heavy glass door and immediately saw Paige standing against the wall just inside the front entry, her arms loosely folded. Intuition told him that it wasn't some facile misunderstanding that put her there. Frowning, he waited until some guy and a pair of giggling little girls walked past him and disappeared into the arena before he went over to Paige and asked the obvious.

"What are you doing?"

She dropped her arms and rocked away from the wall. "Waiting for you."

"Forget where the car was parked?" he asked drily.

Shaking her head slowly from side to side, she leaned forward and said, "No."

Obviously his cover was blown. "Did Jason—"

"He didn't say a word," she interrupted. "He didn't have to. What's that old joke? I was born in the morning but not *this* morning?" Pursing his lips, Grady hung his head and prepared his arguments. She knocked them all to flinders by softly asking, "I wonder, is it ethical to kiss one's attorney?"

His gaze zipped to hers, finding it warmly glowing, and his heart just melted. "Absolutely not," he reassured her, "but if you don't kiss me, I'm going to kiss you."

"Well, in that case," she said, lifting her arms around his neck and leaning into him.

His heart stopped as she pulled his head down until they stood nose to nose. The top of her head barely reached his shoulder, and he was painfully aware of how dainty and fragile she was, but when she touched her lips to his, none of that mattered. How his hands came to span her waist and lift her or even when he closed his eyes, he didn't know, but when she broke the kiss her feet were dangling off the floor.

He carefully set her down again, hugging her close, even though it hurt to breathe just then, as if his heart had suddenly overfilled his chest. She hugged him back, and he reveled in that embrace until she muttered in his ear, "If you ever do anything like that again, I'll have to fire you."

"Now wait just a minute." He fastened his hands at her trim waist and held her back, the argument falling out of his mouth. "When it comes to the law stuff, you call the shots," he told her. "I don't always agree with you, but you're the boss. I can live with that. But you *don't* get to tell me what to do in my personal life."

She lifted her eyebrows and brought her hands to her hips. "Not even when it impacts *my* personal life?"

He folded his arms. "You turn that around, then you tell me the answer."

"Hmm." She looked down at her toes, then up at him. "Okay, so you get to spend your money however you want, and I get to decide whether or not I'll let it benefit me and my son."

"Fine." They stared at each other for several seconds. He thought his heartbeat was going to strangle him. "So will you? Let it benefit the two of you."

"Yeah," she said, grinning, "and thank you."

He shook his head. "No, I wanted to. It's important to me."

She slipped her arm through his as she stepped to his side, "I'll make sure Vaughn knows who he has to thank for this."

"I—I'd rather you didn't. I'd rather you didn't even know, to tell you the truth."

She tilted her head, gazing up at him. "Why, Grady

Jones, that's the dearest thing I've ever heard you say."

He smiled, ridiculously pleased, and walked her through the door out into the cool night. "I know you probably gave Jason a check for the gear, but you really don't have to pay for it."

"Why go to the bother of writing a check when you would just tear it up?" she asked wryly.

He laughed, hurrying her across the parking lot to the car. "Could it be that you know me too well?"

She came to a halt before the passenger side door of his car and turned to face him as he reached for the handle. "What I know is that God keeps using you to bless me and mine."

He froze, that prickle of *something* blowing through him again. "If God's using me to somehow benefit you, that's fine by me," he said.

She blinked at him. "Do you mean that the way I hope you do?"

"You said you'd prove it to me. So, okay, I'm convinced."

She beamed, and he tapped her affectionately on the end of her nose. After putting her inside the car, he walked around the front end to the driver's side. Lifting his eyes heavenward, he whispered, "Anything. Anything at all."

As he slid behind the wheel, Paige urged Vaughn to sit up and buckle his safety belt for the ride home. It hit Grady then that winning over Vaughn would be the greatest service he could do Paige.

Vaughn might even change his mind about going back to his father if he and Grady were more than tolerant acquaintances. Meanwhile, of course, he'd keep working to knock down Nolan's case against Paige. Now all he had to do was figure out how to make a friend of a resentful eleven-year-old whom he didn't even particularly like.

For the first time since he'd realized that his mom would never come home again, Grady considered going to God for guidance.

Grady showed up in Little Rock that next Saturday for the tournament there. Paige knew he must've risen before dawn in order to make it in time for the game. She was pleased but couldn't help worrying about Vaughn's reaction. He seemed happy enough to see another friendly face and played well, but the team came in second, losing by one goal. Vaughn apparently thought it was because of him.

"I blew it. Our whole line played like second graders because of me."

Paige instinctively sought to reassure him. "It wasn't your fault. You obviously knew what you were doing."

"The team will adjust," Grady stated flatly. "If Jason didn't think you were worth shaking things up, he wouldn't have put you on the roster."

Vaughn seemed to accept that, giving his head a businesslike nod, and Paige breathed a silent sigh of relief. Later, while Vaughn was meeting with the rest of the team, she worried aloud to Grady that Jason might be putting a little too much pressure on Vaughn.

"He can handle it," Grady said. "In fact, if you really want to know, I was pretty impressed. There was one point when Vaughn set up a perfect shot and his wingman missed the pass entirely. I thought Vaughn might lose his temper then. He was looking awful frustrated, but he kept his cool, and the next time the kid was where he was supposed to be. If he hadn't missed the shot, they'd have tied the score."

Grady predicted that the team would win the next game, and they did, coming in second in the tournament standings.

The next tournament was some three weeks away, which suited Paige since she'd landed a much-needed new contract. When Jason scheduled scrimmage games in the interim, though, she found herself stretched thin by practices and scrimmages and longer hours of work. Still, she was reluctant to take Grady up on his offer to ferry Vaughn to and from practices.

"Look," he said, "I come to the practices anyway because I love the game. Why not let me drive Vaughn and save you some time a couple times a week?"

"But you'd be putting a hundred miles or more on your car every time you do it," she argued.

"So? Do you know how many times I've driven almost seven hours each way just to attend pro hockey games in Dallas?"

"In other words, this is a cheap way to get your hockey fix," she surmised, laughing. He just shrugged and smiled. She knew it was more than that, of course, and that both pleased and worried her, but she gave in anyway.

The first time Grady took Vaughn to practice, she made dinner for him, nothing fancy, just meatloaf with macaroni and cheese right out of a box. The second time she was still at the computer when they got back to the house, with hours of work still left to do, but Matthias had stirred up a skillet of beans and franks that couldn't have been blacker if he'd set fire to them. She wasn't entirely sure that he hadn't. On the third occasion, Grady called from the rink to say he was picking up something on his way back, and nothing she could say would dissuade him.

She hung up the phone and turned back to the computer, as grateful as she was disturbed. She was taking shameful advantage of a good man. Not only had he gotten Vaughn an interview that ultimately led to him getting on the team, he'd made it financially possible for him to play. Now he was making it possible for Vaughn to go on playing by allowing her to earn the extra money that made the tournament travel possible.

Grady wasn't doing it for Vaughn; she very much feared that he was doing it for another reason entirely. She just didn't know what to do about that, and the truth was that she wouldn't have changed it if she could have. It had been a long time since a man had cared about her, and no one had ever cared as selflessly as Grady Jones seemed to.

She was surprised by what Grady and Vaughn brought home. Grady had swung by a place in Bentonville that offered full, home-style dinners for carryout to the harried professionals who worked in the area. Vaughn grumbled about it not being typical fast food, then announced that he had chosen the roast pork option himself, complete with potatoes au gratin, mixed vegetables, yeast rolls and carrot cake.

"This is wonderful!" Paige exclaimed once they were all sitting around the table in her old-fashioned kitchen.

She heard Grady's stomach rumble, but he didn't pick up his fork, knowing the routine by now. Instead, he reached for her hand. Paige gripped his fingers and reached for those of Matthias, who linked up with Vaughn, who gingerly took Grady's other hand. They all bowed their heads. Matthias did the honors.

"Lord, we thank You for the food You've provided, and we ask You to bless it to the nourishment of our bodies, that we might be better servants of You and Your kingdom. Amen."

"Amen," Grady rumbled, and Paige squeezed his fingers before she slipped her hand from his. He didn't even seem to realize how often he did that sort of thing. The man who hadn't believed in prayer was becoming surprisingly comfortable with it. She couldn't have been happier about that.

They talked hockey while the food disappeared, mostly about the team's prospects for winning the next tournament, which were looking pretty good according to Grady. Then Paige walked him out while Matthias and Vaughn cleaned up after their meal.

"You know it's not right for you to carry in our dinner after putting yourself out to get Vaughn back and forth to practice," she said. "Feeding you is the least I should do."

"You're working long hours," he protested, stopping on the bottom step leading down from her porch and twisting to face her. Since she stood on the porch itself, their heads were about even. "I can't let you cook for me, and I like eating too much to let Matthias play chef."

She chuckled at that. "He cooks a few things well, but only a few, and we've gotten pretty tired of those, I'll admit."

There was no porch light, but the moon hung big and full overhead. Its delicate light bathed his face in silver, his blue eyes gleaming like jewels. It was a strong face, square and heavy-featured but unabashedly, unmistakably male. She loved the way his thick, earthy brown hair waved away from its side part and fell boyishly over his broad forehead.

"Carrying in for you beats eating alone any day," he said.

Her hand came up, seemingly of its own volition, and skimmed his cheek. "I feel like I'm taking advantage."

He scoffed at that. "You're humoring me, and we both know it."

She dropped her hand and bowed her head, realizing that she had to say this even if she didn't want to.

"Grady, I'm afraid I can't give you what you want from me, not with everything so unsettled with my son."

"It won't always be unsettled," he said carefully.

"Won't it? I just don't know. That's what divorce does to lives, it turns them upside down. When there's a child involved I'm not sure they ever get right side up again."

She was trying to tell him not to get his hopes up, but somehow she couldn't come right out and say it. Even if Nolan finally went away and left them alone, she wasn't sure that Vaughn would ever be comfortable with her dating. Sometimes Vaughn still spoke of Grady in a scornful tone, even though he had to see that they couldn't have managed to this point without him.

She'd prayed about the situation a good deal and still wasn't sure what God's intentions were. Was Grady for her? Or was she for Grady? Or was it more than that? She was almost afraid to hope, afraid she'd wind up hurting a good man.

"We'll see," Grady said lightly. "Meanwhile, I get my hockey fix and meals I don't have to eat alone. Works for me."

"If that's true," she whispered, "then I'm glad, but Grady, please, don't let me hurt you."

"Don't worry about that."

"I have to worry about it."

He shook his head, smiling. "And here I thought you had enough to worry about."

She laughed. "True."

"Look, if I can't manage this or I get tired of it, I'll

let you know. Okay? It's not like I've got anything better to do. Or don't you realize that you're dealing with a social misfit?"

"Puh-leze. Don't try to sell that snake oil around here, mister."

He laughed and stepped down onto the ground. "Tell Vaughn I'll see him Thursday." Flipping her a wave, he moved off toward his car. "Good night."

"Good night."

She stepped back into the shadows, watching until his taillights disappeared into the darkness before she went inside. Matthias and Vaughn were watching television. She had work to do, but she sat down with them until Vaughn went to bed, knowing that it was only because of Grady that she dared do so.

Chapter Nine

Over the course of the next month, Grady took so many meals at Paige's house that he felt like one of the family, and while he didn't seem any closer to really getting to know Vaughn, at least the kid wasn't rude. All in all, he considered that he was making progress, especially as Paige seemed to count on him more and more. They attended every scrimmage and hockey game together, but Grady continued to transport Vaughn to and from practices on his own, bringing in dinner as often as not.

Over the past few weeks Grady had interviewed Paige's pastor, Richard Haynes, as well as several of the members of his church, and they were honest, perfectly harmless, everyday folk whose faith, so far as Grady could tell, was genuine. Pastor Haynes was a slight, soft-spoken, middle-aged man with thinning hair and pale, friendly gray eyes. From the outset he had expressed the determination to protect his church and help Paige in any way possible, so Grady wasn't particularly surprised to walk into Paige's house one Thursday evening in the middle of March to find the man waiting for him.

After surrendering a family pack of fried chicken to Matthias and Vaughn, who carried the containers into the kitchen, Grady shook hands with the pastor and got right down to business. "Have you been in touch with FFROC?"

The Foundation For Research On Cults was the entity Nolan's attorney had sicced on the church. Once a fully credible organization, it had largely devolved into what trial attorneys often referred to as a "hired gun." In other words, its experts tended to tailor their reports to the needs of those who paid them, but Grady hoped that they were still serious enough about their research to want to actually do some when the opportunity presented itself. Haynes had promised to contact those investigators and answer their questions over the phone as they had originally requested.

The pastor nodded. "I've spoken to them all right, but they no longer want to interview me over the phone. Now they want to come to the church."

"And bring cameras," Paige added significantly.

Pleased, Grady shrugged. "Let 'em. We've got nothing to hide."

Haynes smiled and relaxed. "My thoughts exactly. We're set up for the end of April."

Paige glanced toward the kitchen door, reminding them to keep their voices down so Vaughn wouldn't overhear. "Does this mean we can knock down their claims about the church at least?" she asked Grady.

"I hope so. They'll try to twist everything to their advantage, though, so we have to get them on record."

"How do we do that?" Pastor Haynes wanted to know.

"Number of ways, but the most obvious is to tape the interviews yourself."

Haynes seemed vaguely troubled by that, but he didn't protest. "I don't suppose there's any privacy or confidentiality issue in something like this."

"None," Grady confirmed, "but I have to tell you here and now, that I'm going to want the tapes."

Haynes nodded thoughtfully and suggested that they pray about the matter, starting that very moment. Grady allowed Paige to pull him into a tight circle with her and the pastor, who quietly voiced an eloquent prayer for guidance. He petitioned God on Paige's behalf, as well, asking for God's leadership in her life. He even asked that God soften Nolan's heart and make him aware of the harm he was doing with his custody petition and baseless accusations.

They looked up to find Vaughn standing in the doorway to the kitchen. So much for secrecy. Haynes quickly took his leave, and Grady found himself lifting a protective arm about Paige's waist.

She put on a brittle smile, which faded the instant Vaughn asked, "Can I call Dad now?"

Paige audibly gulped, pointedly stepped away from Grady and answered, "After dinner."

Vaughn turned away without another word, and

Grady traded glances with Paige. She was clearly worried. "Do you think he knows what's going on?"

"He's not stupid, Paige. If his father hasn't told him already, he's bound to know something's up."

She sighed. "It's important to me that I not be the one to put him in the middle."

"You haven't."

"Thank you for not saying anything to him."

"I promised I wouldn't."

"I know, and I appreciate it."

He smiled. If she didn't know by now that he'd do anything for her, he wasn't nearly as obvious as he figured he was. "Let's get some dinner while it's still warm, hmm?"

She let him steer her into the kitchen, saying. "You can't keep bringing in dinner for us like this, Grady."

"As long as you insist on working these long days, I can," he stated flatly, "and haven't we already had this discussion?"

She sighed at that and let him seat her. Matthias showed no qualms about eating food carried in by Grady, and neither did Vaughn, although he was quiet during the meal. Then again, at the rate that he was shoveling it in, conversation was clearly impossible. He asked to be excused before dessert, saying that he'd save his cherry cobbler for later.

"Can I call Dad now?" he asked. "In your office? Since everybody's still eating in here."

Paige labored over a smile. "That's fine."

He was gone in the blink of an eye. Looking as if

he'd bitten into something sour, Matthias pushed back from the table, muttered that he wanted to catch some TV and limped out of the room. Only then did Paige drop her head into her hands. Grady shoved his plate away and reached a hand around to massage the nape of her neck.

"Every time I think he's starting to make the adjustment, he reaches out to his father and we're suddenly going in reverse," she complained softly. Looking up, she said firmly, "Hockey does seem to have a positive effect on his behavior, though."

"Does it?"

"It's either that or you," she noted drily.

Grady chuckled, secretly delighted to think that he could contribute anything positive. "Me?" he teased. "A positive effect? There are legions of mothers who undoubtedly would argue that with you."

She snorted and picked up her fork again. "Obviously you haven't carried in dinner for them."

"Nah, I'm particular about who I carry in dinner for. Even as a boy I wouldn't pick up dinner for just anyone."

He winked, and she sputtered in laughter. He wondered if there was any limit to how much of a fool he'd make of himself just to hear that sound.

He was still thinking about that some twenty or so minutes later when Vaughn finally wandered into the living room to stand staring at Paige and Grady, who sat side by side while Matthias flipped through the television stations. With Vaughn on the phone in the office, Paige couldn't go back to work, so Grady had dropped down onto the sofa beside her to wait. Vaughn looked sad, dispirited, sullen, even confused.

"Would you like your dessert now?" Paige asked, but the boy shook his head. "Everything okay?"

He shrugged, sent Grady a dark look and said, "I'm going to bed."

"So early?"

"Tired," he mumbled, dragging himself off to the bedroom.

Her expression troubled, Paige glanced at Grady before slipping off the sofa to follow Vaughn into his room. She came back a few minutes later.

"What'd he say?" Matthias asked baldly.

She shot Grady an unreadable look before muttering, "Same old same old. He wants to go back to South Carolina. He doesn't have any friends here."

"He has friends," Grady refuted. "I see him with the other guys on the hockey team. Some of them are jealous because of the way he plays, but most of them seem to like him. They joke around together off the ice."

"I know," she said. "I've seen it, too, but whenever I suggest inviting his teammates over, he makes some excuse."

Matthias cleared his throat. "I think I can help you there. He told me the other day that they're all rich kids. He says they got pools and media rooms and stuff like that. Said the guys would 'freak' if they could see where he comes from."

"He's ashamed of this place," Paige concluded, dropping down on to the couch dispiritedly.

"He could just as well mean South Carolina," Grady pointed out, patting her shoulder. "The point is that most of his teammates are from Bentonville, and their families are affluent."

"Guess that's why he don't want them to see him riding around in your old truck," Matthias said to Paige.

"No wonder he always wants you to take him to hockey," Paige admitted sadly. "I thought he was being thoughtful of my work schedule, but he wants the other kids to see him get out of your Mercedes instead of my old rattletrap."

Grady winced. Here he'd thought the kid was warming up to him. That's what he got for not realizing that Vaughn would feel out of place on an elite Bentonville team. Those kids must seem rich to him, and obviously Vaughn had a problem with that, so instead of hockey making him happier here, it was just making him more discontent.

Grady couldn't help feeling responsible since he'd steered Vaughn to the team. How could he fix things for Vaughn? He made a good living. He could afford a house in Bentonville, a new car for Paige, just about anything she or Vaughn could want. Vaughn could live as well as anyone on his team, and Paige would never have to spend another hour transcribing medical notes if she didn't want to.

How ridiculous a notion was this? They weren't even dating, for pity's sake. He hauled her kid back and forth to hockey practice and invited himself to the dinner table, but they were basically still client and attorney. He had about as much chance of convincing Paige to marry him as sprouting a second head, especially if she lost her son because he couldn't find a way to stop it.

Surely, he told himself, God wouldn't let that happen. But what did he know about it? All he really knew about God, he'd learned from Paige, and that was just enough to confuse him. How was he supposed to know what God had in mind?

Maybe it was time he figured that out. He'd been thinking about it for a while now, and it seemed like confirmation that it was time to take the next step. Thankfully, he knew just who could tell him what that next step should be.

Paige accepted the coming Sunday's sheet music from the church secretary, confessing apologetically, "These days I'd lose my head if it wasn't attached to the end of my neck."

Thin and thirtyish with short, mousy, tightly curled hair, Betty was meticulous to a fault. The pastor claimed that she would alphabetize the months of the year if the order hadn't been firmly established for centuries. It was downright embarrassing for Paige to admit to someone with Betty's organizational penchant that she couldn't keep track of her own choir music.

"Surely my folder will turn up before long," she offered lamely, adding, "If not, of course, I'll pay for it."

"Oh, don't worry about it," Betty said. "We'll just make copies of everything."

"In that case, I hope your user's license is current," commented a familiar voice.

Paige whirled around, absurdly pleased but also surprised to find Grady Jones standing in the doorway of the pastor's office on a Tuesday afternoon. "Grady!"

Pastor Haynes squeezed past Grady. "I'm sure we renewed the license when we were supposed to. Right, Betty?"

Betty tapped the twelve-month calendar mounted on the wall behind her desk. "April," she said. "We renew our license every year in April."

Pastor Haynes folded his hands with satisfaction. "There you are. All in order."

Grady tilted his head as if trying to decide whether or not to smile. He didn't. Instead, he made a statement. "Copyright issues have been getting a lot of play in the courts lately."

"I never thought about copyright," Paige admitted, looking again at the music in her hands. "But that can't be why you're here. What is it? Have we heard from FFROC again?" That acronym always made her want to roll her eyes, but as ridiculous as it sounded, the Foundation For Research On Cults was too awkward a title for easy conversational use.

Grady just stared at her, while Pastor Haynes dithered uncomfortably for a moment before starting as if struck by a sudden idea. "You'll be glad to know," he announced grandly, "that Betty will be taping our visit with the researchers."

"I make the sermon videos," she informed Grady. "It's a simple matter."

"Date and time stamp on the tape?" Grady queried.

She seemed offended that he'd even ask. "Well, of course."

"What happens if they want to look around the place?"

"I'll take the camera and follow."

"No offense, Betty, but wouldn't it be better to hire a professional?" Paige ventured uncertainly. "I would pay for it, of course." She cringed at the thought, but surely this was her responsibility. To her mingled relief and concern, Grady shook his head.

"I think it's better for the pastor's office to take care of it. At this point we're just keeping the process honest. If theirs isn't the only tape, they can't cherry-pick comments to support damaging conclusions. We, on the other hand, just want the truth to come out, and that's always an unassailable position. If it comes to court, however, we'll hire our own expert to refute everything their expert says."

"Not that it will come to court," Paige hastened to add.

Grady made no reply to that, just clamped his jaw before thanking the pastor. The two shook hands, and Grady headed for the exit. Paige glanced around and hurried after him, puzzled by his behavior. Something was up, but she hadn't the foggiest notion what.

She called out to him the instant she hit the sidewalk. He stopped but didn't turn around. Instead he stood waiting for her to catch up with him, one hand jingling the change in his pocket.

Clouds swirled overhead, hinting at rain one instant, jolting them with sunshine the next. They provided a perfect illustration of this situation, illuminating one moment, obscuring the next.

"You never answered me back there."

He glanced down. "Guess I forgot the question."

That was an obvious ploy, and it alarmed her. This was her church. He was her lawyer, not to mention her friend. Why would he come here like this and not tell her about it?

"What's going on?" she asked pointedly. "You didn't drive over on a Tuesday afternoon to ask if the church is licensed to use copyrighted music or hear that Betty is filming the FFROC investigation. If it has to do with my case, I think I have a right to know."

He shifted his feet. "It doesn't." With that he strode away again.

Despite the fact that her vehicle waited in the opposite direction, she went after him, a little angry now. "Grady, I want to know what's going on!"

He rounded on her. "Did it never occur to you, Paige, that it might be *personal?*"

She blinked at him. Personal? This was her church, after all, not his. She stepped back, catching her breath. What if this was about the two of them?

She'd known that Grady wanted more than a professional relationship with her for some time. And she wanted one with him. One day. But not now, especially not after the things Vaughn had said the other evening in his bedroom.

She hadn't told Grady what her son had said because she hadn't wanted to hurt his feelings. Grady had been so generous to them, especially with Vaughn, but even Vaughn knew why. He'd asked what Grady was still doing there, and she'd said something meaningless about just having finished dinner, and Vaughn had snapped at her.

"Don't lie to me. You keep pretending there's nothing going on, but I know better. He ain't coming around because he likes hockey!"

"But he does like hockey," she'd argued.

"Not as much as he likes you," Vaughn had sneered. Then he'd blurted, "Don't think I care, 'cause I don't! At least he's got money, and that's what you care about most."

She'd tried to tell him that wasn't true, but he'd thrown in her face how much she worked. It would have done no good to tell him that it was for him.

"From now on I'll take you to hockey practice myself," she'd promised, and he'd confounded her by exclaiming that he wanted Grady to do it. She hadn't known what to make of that until Matthias had explained later. Now she didn't know what to do about anything. She looked at Grady and realized what a wretched mess she'd made of everything.

"I—I'm sorry. I didn't mean to pry. I was just surprised to…see you," she finished lamely, watching him leave, driving off in his Mercedes.

Maybe it was better this way. She just didn't know anymore. All she knew was that nothing she did seemed to make anyone happy, not Matthias who thought she was too soft on Vaughn, not Vaughn who was doing everything in his power to distance himself from her, and not Grady who seemed to want—and definitely deserved—more than she was able to give.

She was simply too exhausted mentally, emotionally and physically to figure out what to do about any of it. Worse, she wasn't sure it even mattered.

Just yesterday Vaughn had announced that he would be riding the school bus from then on, something he had vehemently protested before. She'd realized that, far from winning him over, she was losing him. That time at the beginning and end of every day had been sacrosanct to her. No matter how pressing her work, how badly she needed the money or how busy their schedule, she'd always driven him to and from school. It hurt to think that Vaughn hadn't understood what those few minutes meant to her. Or that he had, which was why he'd put a stop to them.

The whole thing was deeply demoralizing, but he was due home in less than an hour, and she meant to be at the door waiting for him. She trudged back to her own vehicle.

Matthias was in his room with the door closed when she let herself into the house a few minutes later. Assuming that he was taking a nap, which he often did, she tiptoed into the kitchen to fix herself a cup of herbal tea. Even though the house felt overly warm to her, she hoped that the tea would prove restorative.

Intending to get in a few more minutes of work before Vaughn came home, she carried her steeping tea toward the back of the house. A knock at her front door halted her in midstride; she knew instantly who it was. Only three people in the world could walk up onto her porch without Howler trying to shatter all the windows in the house, and neither Vaughn nor Matthias would bother knocking. Hesitating only a moment, she turned back and set the teacup on the coffee table before opening up.

Grady shuffled his feet and asked grimly, "Can I come in?"

The irony of the situation didn't escape her. First she'd pressed him for answers, and now that he apparently wanted to talk, she was reluctant to get into it.

"You don't owe me any explanations, Grady," she said, folding her arms. "I—I just stopped by the church b-because…" He looked up, smiling slightly, and she saw instantly that something had changed, something important.

"You lost your choir music," he finished for her, crowding so close that she automatically backed up. He stepped into the room, closing the door behind him. "I was there because I needed to talk to someone," he told her. "I still do."

She licked her lips, blew out her breath and

stopped; stopped worrying, stopped being embarrassed, stopped backing away. This was Grady, who had become dear to her, who had so often been the answer to her prayers, whose generosity had, for fleeting moments, made her pigheaded son happy. She sat down on the sofa and waited for him to carefully fold up his big body.

"I had some questions," he began, "I wanted to talk to someone about them. Pastor Haynes seemed the right person."

She knew then what it was about. Gladness filled her. "Was Richard able to help you?"

"Yes and no. Some of it makes sense." Grady gripped his knees with his big, square hands and went on. "For instance, a conversation is more productive if there's a personal relationship involved. Otherwise it's like talking to air."

"Do you know what this is?" she asked softly. "This is proof that God answers prayers."

"Is it?"

"It is if you're thinking about your personal relationship with God."

He sat back and crossed his legs. "The thing is, I haven't really had a personal relationship with God. God and me, we've sort of kept our distance, if you know what I mean."

"I do," she replied. "Now God's calling you to Him, I think."

He rubbed his eyebrow. "It *has* been on my mind a lot lately, so I made an appointment with the pastor."

She smiled. "I'm absolutely sure he told you where that personal relationship with God starts."

Grady pinched the pleat of his slacks. "It's surprisingly difficult to think about, you know."

"In what way?"

When he looked up, sadness stood starkly in his gaze. "The cross."

She nodded, understanding fully. "The cross isn't easy to think about, until you realize why He did it, why He let us spill His blood. No, it was more than that. He *poured it out* for us."

"But that's the part that doesn't make any sense."

"Just stop and think about what you'd do for those you love."

Grady looked at her squarely then, and the understanding that she saw in his eyes stopped her heart. As alone as he sometimes seemed, as often as he argued with her about what she felt was right for her son, this was a man who understood love. She thought of his mother, his brother, his father, everyone he might love; she tried very hard not to put herself among them, but she couldn't deny that she wanted to.

"I see what you mean," Grady murmured. "I guess it just always sounded like a bad plan to me. Why would you plan to sacrifice your own son?"

"For the good of all the rest of Your children," she answered. "Besides, would Christ, Who is part and parcel with God, have had it any other way? After all, since He has the mind of God, He knew what the plan was all along."

"Oh, my," Grady said, sitting forward. He mulled it over for some time. Then he pushed a hand over his face. "Wow."

She couldn't have said it better. When his hand dropped again, it sought out her own, she gripped his fingers tightly.

"Would you pray with me?" he whispered.

"Gladly."

She closed her eyes and bowed her head. Tears leaked out from beneath her lowered lids, but she didn't even try to sniff them back. This moment deserved tears, tears of joy, and she was suddenly so very glad that she'd lost her music! She'd have missed this otherwise.

After several minutes she realized that he was not going to pray aloud. A calming serenity stole over her, but only after he increased the pressure on her fingers did she clear her throat and whisper a closing.

"Thank You for loving us enough to pay the price for our sins, and thank You for all Grady has meant in my life and Vaughn's. Bless him as he's blessed us, accept him as he's accepted You. In the name of Your Son. Amen."

She didn't really know who hugged who first, but it hardly mattered. Reveling in the strength of his arms, she laid her head on his shoulder and held on tight. It was as if her problems just lifted away at that point, faded into insignificance. For the first time since she'd found out about the custody suit, she felt safe. There in his arms, she rested from her travails. Worry, even thought, was momentarily suspended as she just let herself be glad.

The next thing she knew, Vaughn was standing there, the knob of the open door in one hand, his backpack in the other. He stared at them, his face like chiseled stone. Yet, she saw the terrible conflict behind his expression, felt the tug-of-war rending his heart. Weariness slid over her once more, a weight so heavy she could barely lift her head.

"Hello, Vaughn," she said dully, pulling back from Grady and letting her hands fall into her lap. She searched desperately for the right words and came up with only, "How was your day?"

Without a word, he bolted into his room, slamming the door. Paige sighed and lifted a hand to her head.

"I didn't mean to upset him," Grady said awkwardly.

She shook her head. "Everything upsets him."

"I thought he was coming to like me at least a little."

"Grady, my son doesn't even like *me*."

"That can't be. How could he not love you?"

"He won't let himself," she said, really feeling the truth of that for the first time. "He's afraid he'll have to stop loving his father if he does. That's what he's been taught, that it must be only one of us. I can't seem to make him see that it can be both." Grady slid his hand to the center of her back. The weight and the heat of it were a comfort and a pain at the same time. "You'd better go," she said gently.

His hand moved up to her hair, kneading the back

of her head. "I don't want to," he told her. "I never want to leave you these days."

She closed her eyes, thinking how easy it would be to lean on him, to let him solve all her problems for her, but she couldn't do that. Vaughn was not merely a problem to be solved; he was her son, and she couldn't allow her own affections to be divided right now.

"I'm so very glad you came," she said, "but it's better that you go now. I have to talk to him, and it'll be easier that way."

Grady looked at first as if he might argue, but then he nodded and got up. She walked him to the door, and they just stood there for a moment, facing one another, until she reached up and cupped his jaw with her hand. She smiled, and then she hugged him again.

"I'm so glad for you."

He clasped her to him. "You said you'd prove it to me, and you did." With that he left her.

She closed the door and put her back to it, thanking God and gathering strength for the confrontation to come.

Chapter Ten

Every step felt as if lead weights had been fixed to her feet, but Paige moved across the floor to Vaughn's room and went inside. Flat on his back on the bed, he stared up at the ceiling.

She looked around, taking in tan walls, a hockey poster, dark blue linens. The radio-controlled car she'd bought him for Christmas occupied one shelf; a few books stood on another. His backpack had been dumped on the desk in the corner. Clothes scattered the floor. A mound of hockey gear stood just inside his open closet door.

Everything was familiar. Yet this felt like a stranger's room, as if it belonged in someone else's house.

Vaughn pushed up onto his elbows and glared at her.

"That wasn't what you think," she said calmly.

He shrugged and plopped down on his back again. "I don't care."

"I think you do care, Vaughn. I think you care a lot."

He swung his feet off the bed and sat up. "I just don't know how you could like him better than Dad is all."

For a moment, Paige was too shocked to speak. She couldn't believe that Vaughn might imagine she still harbored feelings for his father, but apparently he did. She put a hand to her head, trying to think through this.

"Vaughn," she finally began, "I didn't want to be divorced, that's true, but after what your father did—"

"He didn't *do* anything!"

Again, she was speechless. "You can't still believe that. He took you away from me! It was your birthday. Don't you remember? He was supposed to take you camping, but instead he ran away with you."

Vaughn got up to go to his desk, where he began pulling books from his backpack with short, jerky movements. "I have to do my homework so I can call Dad."

She'd worked so hard not to criticize Nolan, bitten her tongue countless times, refused to descend to his level of indoctrination, but Vaughn was too smart not to know the truth.

"You'll never understand what it was like," she blurted. "I was terrified. I didn't know where you were or if I'd ever see you again. I looked for you for three-and-a-half years!"

"You made him do it!" Vaughn insisted hotly.

She tried not to be hurt. She tried so hard not to be hurt, but he was utterly determined to cast her in the villain's role. Suddenly she was too tired to fight him anymore, too drained to take the principled stand, the high road. Why even try?

Her voice trembled when she said, "No one ever makes your father do anything, Vaughn. He does exactly what he pleases. You know that."

Vaughn flipped open a book and pulled out the desk chair, completely ignoring her. She didn't bother reminding him that he was supposed to do his homework at the kitchen table; he knew, but he'd only do it if she forced him, and all she would get for her trouble would be his compliance. Never acceptance. Never that.

Defeated, she started to back out of the room, but he whirled around, demanding, "Do you still love him?"

The question took her off guard. "Who? Grady?"

"No! Dad! Do you still love my dad? He thinks you do. He says that's why you didn't send him to prison, why you won't."

Stunned, she opened her mouth, but no sound came out. Suddenly she understood that Nolan, in his self-centered arrogance, probably actually believed that she was still in love with him. No doubt he thought that was why she hadn't prosecuted him for kidnapping their son! The idiotic man couldn't even imagine that she might have done it for Vaughn, that she could put her son ahead of any need to punish him.

She slapped her hands to her cheeks. It was so appalling it was almost funny.

"I kept your father out of prison for *you*, Vaughn, not him. I didn't want the divorce, because I believe that marriage is supposed to be forever, but no, I do *not* still love your father. If he thinks I do, then he is sadly, badly mistaken."

"Do you love Grady then?" Vaughn demanded, his voice breaking.

She closed her eyes. He couldn't know how hard she'd tried *not* to think about loving Grady, and she still wasn't ready to think about it. "I don't know," she whispered.

"Liar!" he screamed. "Liar! I hate you! I hate living here. I wanna go home! I want to go home! I'm glad Dad filed the custody suit! I'm glad!"

The words hit her like hammer blows. He knew about the custody suit, had known about it probably from the beginning. That hurt worse than anything else.

She whirled away, bumping up against Matthias as she stumbled into the living room. He brushed her off, rigid with purpose, and stomped toward Vaughn's room. She made a futile attempt to waylay him before simply collapsing against the end of the sofa.

Vaughn had known. While she'd been doing her best to protect him, he may well have been plotting with his father to ruin those closest to her. It was almost more than she could bear.

"Your mother's nearly killed herself trying to make you happy!" Matthias shouted.

"I didn't want to come here!" Vaughn shouted back.

"When're you going to get it through your head that

your dad ran off from you and your mom both? Then he took you just to hurt her when she called him on it!"

"That's not true!"

"He even tried to claim you weren't his."

"Matthias, don't!" she pleaded, but Vaughn shouted over her.

"He did not! *She's* the one who said it! She even signed a paper! He showed it to me. He showed me!"

Paige closed her eyes, shaking her head.

"She didn't know what she was doing when she signed them papers," Matthias exclaimed, "but *he* did! He drew 'em up just so he could get out of paying child support, and then he ran off with you to get back at her for trying to make him pay."

"It was all about money for her!" Vaughn yelled. "He never could've given her enough!"

"Don't be an imbecile!" Matthias roared. "Look around you! Does this look like the home of a grasping, greedy woman to you?"

"Let Grady give her *his* money!" Vaughn sneered. "He's got lots!"

"He oughta! She paid him plenty of hers when she was looking for you!" Matthias declared.

"Shut up!" Vaughn sobbed. "I want my dad! I want my dad!"

Paige pushed up to her feet then and flung herself at Matthias.

"Stop! Stop," she begged. "You're hurting him. Can't you see that you're hurting him?"

She tried to put a hand over Matthias's mouth and

felt the hot, liquid path of his tears. It broke her heart, the old man and the boy both crying. Matthias tried to wrench away and stumbled. She clasped an arm around his shoulders and steered him toward his room, turning back to Vaughn when Matthias put out a hand to steady himself against the wall.

He stood just inside his room, tears running down his face. She took a step toward him, shaking her head in apology. He stepped back and closed the door. She knew then that it was useless, that she had lost.

The weeks and months and years of hoping against hope, the struggle, the counseling, the patience, all the noble intentions, they meant nothing to a boy who just wanted his father. She went to her knees, and this time all she asked for was the strength to do what she must.

Paige finally pulled herself together enough to throw together a late dinner for them, not that anyone actually ate. Matthias was too miserably contrite, and Vaughn too sullen. Paige, operating by rote, concentrated on simply surviving from one breath to the next.

Sometime during the course of that long night, though, she finally made peace with what had to be. She'd turned Vaughn's life upside down when it should have been the other way around, and now the only way to fix it was to let him go.

It was taking a chance, she knew, a huge chance, and ultimately it would mean uprooting her whole world because if Vaughn went back to South Carolina to live, then so, too, must she. At least that was what she hoped to do, not that she *wanted* to move. She'd lived her whole life right here in this little town in Arkansas, most of it in this very house, but what other choice did she have?

Vaughn hated it here. Right now he even hated her. So she was going to let him go. But how could she lose him again? Somehow she had to build a bridge between them, and when that was done, maybe she could make a place for herself in his life. To do that, though, to have any real influence with him, she had to let him go.

On the other hand, to know that he was well and cared for, she had to be where he was. It was that simple. If she suggested such a thing now, though, Vaughn would doubtlessly tell her that he didn't want her there, and she couldn't bear that. Not now.

So she would keep that part of the master plan to herself and pray for the best.

Heavy of heart, she went to tell him of her decision early that next morning, only to find his room unoccupied. The bed didn't appear to have been slept in. Horrified, she mentally kicked herself for not realizing that he might run. Wearing nothing more than her ratty old chenille bathrobe over flannel pajamas and fuzzy slippers, she grabbed her purse and tore out of the house to look for him, praying that he hadn't gotten far.

He had gotten no farther, in fact, than the front porch.

She almost collapsed with relief to see him sitting there on the top step, Howler wedged in next to him, the dog's big black head taking up the whole of Vaughn's lap. That he'd intended to run couldn't have been more obvious. He was wearing his backpack; another bag stood at his feet.

Paige shivered and closed her eyes, thanking God that he'd had sense enough to stay put. Swallowing, she set aside her purse and searched her mind for the right words, coming up with only, "It's all right, Vaughn."

He bowed his head and scrubbed at his face with his jacket sleeve. She leaned against the porch rail, her back to him, and folded her arms, huddling inside her robe.

"It's not just that I miss Dad," he said quietly. "It was *easier* before."

"I understand," she whispered. Before she'd found him again, he'd distilled his life to a certain pinpoint of reality. He hadn't had to think about any of the broader truths until she'd forced them on him. It was what kids did, what they were, what it meant to be a child, and she'd never wanted anything else for him.

"It was really simple there," he went on wistfully. "Here, everything's so complicated."

For a moment the tragedy of it all overwhelmed her, but then she pulled herself together, cleared her throat, and said what she'd been planning to say. "Do you think your father would give me visitation rights, Vaughn?"

He twisted around. Howler scrambled up and

wandered away while Vaughn stared up at her, his face tear-streaked. "I can go back? Are you saying I can go back?"

The hope that trembled on the air momentarily robbed her of speech, but she swallowed and managed to say, "He has to sign papers, though, Vaughn. I won't lose you completely again. I can't bear that. I can't."

He rose stiffly. "You mean it?" She saw the hope in his eyes, and it nearly killed her. Finally, she managed a nod. He jerked into action, bolting for the house.

"I have to call Dad before he leaves for work!"

Feeling weak, she turned to lean against the porch post, terrified and already grieving in her heart. She stayed there, staring at the horizon of the dawn sky until she found the strength to stand on her own again.

Now all she had to do was find the strength to let him go—and give up dreams she hadn't even had the courage to dream yet.

Matthias would be shocked, probably even angry at first, but eventually he'd see that this was the best way. If he wanted to go with her to South Carolina, fine, if not, he could stay on here in the house if he wanted. He could bring in someone else if he didn't want to live alone, and they'd remain in close touch.

Grady, on the other hand, worried her. Grady, who didn't understand that he was just shy, just a big, sweet teddy bear of a man who never quite got over missing his mother, had already been abandoned once. She hated, *hated,* to be the next woman to abandon him, but what else could she do? She must take care of her son, and she couldn't ask Grady to uproot his whole life and follow her, not when he had so many reasons to stay here and Vaughn barely tolerated him. Not when she couldn't promise him it would ever be different.

"Oh, Father God," she prayed, "make him see that I have to put my son first. Make him understand that I'm not the woman You meant for him."

She doubled over, gasping for breath, and wondered how it was possible to feel so keenly the loss of something that had never even been hers.

"You can't," Grady insisted, bending over her. "Sweetheart, listen to me. I can back him down. I know I can. I'm not saying that you should take it to court. You can't do that. I get it now. Really. But you don't have to give up custody of your son."

"Yes, I do," she said sadly, lifting a hand to his face.

It melted him, just turned him into mush, when she touched his face like that, as if it was precious to her, treasured. Grady went down on his haunches and covered her hand with his, pressing it to his cheek. He didn't care that his brother stood behind his desk, watching and listening.

"Will you see to it, Dan?" she asked softly.

Dan cleared his throat. "We'll craft you an airtight agreement."

She nodded, and Grady wanted to throw things, scream, rave. For all the good that would do.

"You can't trust Nolan, Paige," he pointed out helplessly.

"I know." She smiled to show that she appreciated his concern. "But I don't have any other choice, Grady. Besides, my faith's not in Nolan."

Grady closed his eyes. How could she do it? He knew how much she loved Vaughn, what lengths she would go to for that boy. And that was his answer. She could do it precisely because she loved her son.

"You really think this is best, don't you?"

"I wish I didn't," she whispered.

"Jason's going to be crushed," he said, half hoping to make her smile.

She merely nodded and dropped her gaze. "I hoped it would be enough, you know, the hockey. Enough to keep him satisfied here. With me."

"Boys can be so self-involved, Paige. They don't mean to be, but they can't help it. Take it from me. I was so angry when my mother died, and I punished my dad for it, like it was somehow his fault, like he wasn't as destroyed as I was."

"You may have punished him, but you really thought it was your fault, didn't you?" she said, smoothing his hair with the same tenderness he'd seen her smooth Vaughn's.

Grady gulped and nodded. "I thought that if she hadn't taken me to school that morning, she wouldn't have been hit by that truck."

Paige nodded knowingly. "But your father finally convinced you, didn't he? No matter what you said or did, no matter how angry you got, he just kept loving you until you understood."

That's what she was trying to do for Vaughn, Grady knew, love him to the truth.

"Yes," he whispered, "that's just what my dad did."

"Then surely you understand that Vaughn needs his father."

"Nolan isn't fit to be that boy's father," Grady bit out.

"Nevertheless, he *is* Vaughn's father," she said calmly, "and Vaughn has to believe that Nolan's worthy of his love. He can't bear to believe anything else. I hope, by doing this, he'll see that I'm worthy of his love, too."

"He will," Grady promised, trying hard to believe it.

"From your lips to God's ears," she said sadly.

His smile was bittersweet because not too long ago, he'd have scoffed at that and now he spent a significant portion of every day chewing God's ear, but he didn't kid himself that he had any special "in" with the Almighty. In fact, much of the time he felt like a toddler demanding his own way.

Even when he started out making his case like the very capable barrister that he believed he was, he'd find himself quickly reduced to sheer begging. Fortunately, he sensed that God was willing to be patient with him. He prayed for a portion of that patience for himself now.

He certainly hadn't exhibited patience when he'd pushed his way into this meeting. He'd been hurt, at first, that she'd come to Dan instead of him. Now he frankly didn't want any part of this. It went against everything in him, everything he felt for her, to send the boy back to his father.

It was apparently going to happen, however, and that meant she was going to need all the support she could get. *That* he could give her. He wanted to, he *needed* to. With Vaughn out of the picture somewhat, maybe she'd even start to think of him as more than her lawyer. Yet, he'd keep Vaughn here if he could because that was what she wanted.

"I should go," she said, sliding forward.

He pushed up onto his feet and helped her out of the chair, allowing his gaze to sweep over her.

She'd chosen a rather formal outfit for this visit, an asymmetrical suit with a slim skirt and fitted, collarless jacket of a pale violet trimmed in wide, yellow-gold bands. Her backless shoes were the same shade as the trim and the most trendy things he'd ever seen her wear, with long, pointed toes topped with tiny, feminine bows. She'd brushed her golden hair back behind her ears, and little gold buttons decorated her dainty earlobes.

She took his breath away, but then she did that in denim and flannel. Seizing her hand, he announced that he'd walk her out. After a few more words with Dan, she allowed him to escort her from the office.

"Let me drive you home," he urged when they reached the elevator. She shook her head, but he pressed. "I'm worried about you. You're upset. Let me do this. We'll come back for your truck later, or I'll find some other way to get it home to you."

"Grady, I'm sorry. I can't."

"For my peace of mind, if nothing else?"

She looked down at her hands and then up again, apology in her eyes. "I have an appointment, Grady."

"Oh? Prospective client?"

She shook her head. "I'm going to be traveling back and forth to South Carolina, frequently, and it's going to be expensive."

"Don't worry about the cost," he said, seeking to put her concerns to rest. "I'll help you. I have some frequent flyer miles built up and—"

"No." She shook her head emphatically. "I can't take your money or anything else anymore." She looked up, her big, soft, green eyes beseeching him, and added, "Because I can't give you what you need, Grady."

He felt a flare of alarm. "Yes, you can," he insisted, "not right now, maybe, but one day."

"No," she said again.

Panic setting in, he pulled her against him, folding her close. "You're the only one who can give me what I need, Paige. The only one."

"I'm not. I wish I were, but…" She closed her fists in the fabric of his coat as if she would hold him close, but then she pushed away. "I have to concentrate on my son. And I won't take advantage of you anymore, Grady. It's not right."

"Hush," he said, sliding his hands down her arms. "This isn't the time for this discussion. You have other things to concentrate on right now."

She made a sound somewhere between exasperation and laughter. "I think that was my argument."

"Okay, then, we're in agreement. Right?" He smiled down at her encouragingly. "Right?"

He could see that she wanted to continue arguing but didn't have the heart for it. He took hope in that.

"I have to go," she said, slipping free.

Grady swallowed a protest. "I'll, um, I'll call you. Okay? Or you can call me if you want to talk."

She just looked at him, then she suddenly went up on her tiptoes to kiss his cheek. "Thank you."

She was always saying that, and he really couldn't let her anymore. "I'm the one who should be thanking you. I wish you'd remember that from now on."

Worry and regret put a crease between her eyebrows. She sighed and shook her head, but then she turned away to punch the elevator button.

They stood side by side in silence until the elevator arrived. She stepped into it. He let her go with a smile, tucking his hands into his pockets, and then when the doors slid closed, he turned on his heel, striding straight back to his brother's office.

Dan looked up from his computer and leaned back in his chair, waiting for it.

"Ironclad," Grady dictated, pecking the edge of the desk with an emphatic forefinger. "You hear me? I want Nolan Ellis tied up so many ways he can't cough without her knowing it."

"You want to specify the cough medicine he can take?" Dan asked drily.

"This isn't a joke. I wish to God it were, but it isn't!"

He wished, too, that words set down on paper could truly control behavior, but he'd been practicing law too long to believe that.

Dan dropped his ink pen to link his hands together over his belt buckle. "You know what I think, Grady?"

Reaching deep down for patience, Grady pinched the bridge of his nose, growling, "What?"

"I think you're in love with that woman."

Grady snorted and parked his hands at his waist. "For all the good that does either one of us."

Dan cocked his head sympathetically. "Does it help," Dan asked, "to know that I'm praying for both of you?"

"Yes," Grady answered, his irritation dissolving. "Yes, it helps a great deal."

Dan smiled, slowly. "How did she do it?" he asked. "What?"

"Convince you that you couldn't go on ignoring God."

Grady clapped a hand to the back of his neck. "I don't know. By example, I guess."

"You mean she doesn't preach like I do."

"I didn't say that."

"You never say anything. That was part of the problem. I never knew what you thought, what you believed."

"You haven't preached at me in a long time, though."

"Not because I haven't wanted to," Dan confessed.

Grady looked down at his feet. "I thought you'd given up on me."

"Hardly. I just realized it wasn't doing any good."

"It did more good than you know. I just..." He looked up. "I had to come to it on my own, I guess."

"We all have to come to it on our own," Dan said.

Grady had never felt closer to his brother than he did in that moment, and he knew that it was because they were brothers in more ways than one now.

Oh, Lord, he thought, *hear my brother's prayers. I'm an idiot, but he's a good man, and he's known You a lot longer than I have. Please hear him, because she's been through so much, and she's so good. I don't know how she can bear to lose her son because I don't know what I'd do if I lost her.*

As if she'd ever been his!

Yet he had to believe that she would be; he couldn't imagine how he'd go on if he didn't believe it. Abruptly he understood that it was the same for her where Vaughn was concerned. She had to believe that Nolan wouldn't disappear with him again. She couldn't do what she had to if she didn't.

He was suddenly more frightened than he'd ever been before in his life.

Compared to his tryout just a few weeks earlier, Vaughn's leave-taking from the team was anticlimactic. Grady had asked to accompany them to the game, and Paige felt that it was only fair since he'd been such a big part of the hockey thing from the beginning. Surprisingly, Vaughn had agreed without much prodding from her.

He played his final game with fierce energy and, after a final victory, calmly delivered the news that he was leaving. Paige had told him that the unpleasant chore was his personal responsibility, and he performed it ably, shaking the coach's hand and thanking him. Vaughn balked, however, at saying goodbye to his teammates, and Paige didn't see any reason to force him to do it.

Jason seemed shocked and confused but resigned by Vaughn's brief announcement that he was moving back to South Carolina. Both Paige and Grady thanked him for his trouble and followed Vaughn out of the building. He practically dived into the backseat of the car the instant that Grady unlocked the doors, obviously hoping to avoid the other boys now exiting the building.

Paige knew just how he felt. Goodbyes were awful, and every day felt like goodbye to her now.

Just how little time was left became obvious on the following Tuesday as Paige looked down at the signed custody agreement that Grady had delivered in person. Just as she'd expected, Nolan had conceded to all their demands.

"Do you really think you can trust him to abide by this?" Grady asked again.

She almost told him then what she was planning, but somehow she couldn't. Not yet. Not until she knew for sure that it was going to happen. She still had so much to work out, and until she did, not even Vaughn would know that she intended to move to South Carolina to be near him. Why hurt Grady until she had to?

She shook her head. "No, but maybe he will for a little while."

All she needed was enough time for Vaughn to start to miss her. By then she hoped to have sold her business and made provisions for Matthias.

"What if he runs again?" Grady demanded.

"There's no reason for Nolan to run again," she said. "He's won. Why would he take Vaughn and disappear now?" Except to hurt her, but surely depriving her of her son a second time would be enough even for Nolan.

She carefully placed the papers on her desk. "Well, I guess it's time to make the flight reservations."

"Let me do it," Grady offered, rising from his chair. "How is Saturday? I can go Friday, if you want, but—"

"Grady, I can't let you go with us," she stated as kindly as she could.

"But you can't go alone," he argued.

Matthias had said the same thing, but while she could definitely use the support of a good friend in this, she couldn't see letting Grady accompany her. Vaughn's attitude toward him guaranteed that his presence would make a difficult journey even more so.

"It's best," she said simply, dismissing Grady's concerns.

He literally gnashed his teeth. "Why won't you let me help you through this?"

"You have. You are, but…" She gave him the truth. "I won't spend those last hours in my son's company with him sulking because I brought you along. He would, too. It's not fair, I know, but that's just how it is."

Grady sighed and muttered, "At least let me drive you to the airport."

"Better not plan on it," she said. "You could do one favor for me, though."

"Anything."

She looked down at the agreement on her desk. "I'd like you to explain this to Vaughn. I don't want his father to be able to lie to him about our agreement, and frankly I'm not sure he'll believe me."

"I'll take care of it," Grady said solemnly. "Bring him by the office. It'll feel more official that way."

They settled on Thursday, two days hence. After thanking Grady and walking him to the front door, she went back to her office and began calling airlines. She almost cried when she found a special fare leaving out of Northwest Regional, the local airport, the following week. She bought tickets for Wednesday.

That left her exactly eight days with her son, and she silently vowed to make their remaining time as fun and carefree as possible. It was too little too late, perhaps, and God knew she needed to work every minute, but she would have plenty of empty hours to catch up after her son went back to his father.

She could only pray that all her hours wouldn't be empty ones after that.

Surely, surely, Nolan wouldn't disappear with their son again, although he might if he knew what she was planning, which was a very good reason to keep it to herself until it was too late for anyone to do anything about it.

Vaughn plopped down in front of Grady's desk with an aloof air, which he immediately ruined with a sarcastic remark to his mother. "Your boyfriend's office is pretty cool."

Seeing Paige wince, Grady mentally grabbed hold of his temper and flattened his hands on the gleaming surface of his desk. "I am one of your mother's attorneys," he told the kid sternly, "but, believe me, any man would be blessed to be your mother's *boyfriend*. Now, I suggest you button that smart lip and listen to what I have to tell you."

Sullenly, Vaughn folded his arms, but other than narrowing his eyes, he offered no other reaction. Paige averted her gaze, flags of color flying in her cheeks. Grady cleared his throat and once more addressed the boy.

"You need to understand the agreement that your parents have signed."

Vaughn shrugged, but his insouciance was belied by a certain wariness in his eyes.

"First of all," Grady began, "your parents have agreed to shared custody, with physical custody to reside in South Carolina. This means that you'll live with your father, but he cannot change your address without informing your mom and working it out with her."

"I just can't lose track of you again," Paige explained shakily. "That's all this means."

Vaughn looked at her but didn't say a word.

"Your mother has the right to see you every other weekend," Grady went on, "beginning the second weekend in April."

"That's, like, just over two weeks," Vaughn said, sounding troubled.

"That's right," Paige said, swallowing. "Is that a problem?"

Vaughn inclined his head, eyelids lowering, and Grady thought he saw a bit of guilt in the boy's expression. Finally, though, he shrugged and muttered, "Dad says my old team will let me come back, and the games are always on Saturdays."

"That's fine," Paige told him softly, her voice thick with unshed tears. "You know I love to watch you play."

Vaughn blinked. "You mean *you're* gonna come *there?*"

"I thought you'd prefer that."

Vaughn smiled. "Yeah! That's great!"

Grady traded looks with Paige. Clearly, Vaughn wasn't displeased by the idea of spending time with his mother. He just hadn't expected her to actually put his needs and desires first, despite all evidence to the contrary. Grady went on.

"Your mother is also entitled to spend holidays with you."

"That's negotiable, though," she put in hastily. "I'm willing to alternate with your dad." Offering him a lame smile, she added, "We'll work something out."

Vaughn frowned, his gaze seeming to turn inward, but he said nothing.

Grady licked his lips and said, "You'll spend summers with your mother."

"We'll work that out, too," Paige added quickly. "I don't want you to miss out on any important camping or fishing trips."

Vaughn bowed his head, leaning forward slightly to grip the arms of his chair. Grady couldn't tell what the boy was thinking, especially as he seemed to have taken a sudden vow of silence. After a moment Grady continued his explanation of the agreement. When he got to the part about the child support, Vaughn suddenly looked at his mother.

"You mean, Dad doesn't have to pay you a bunch of money?"

She spread her hands. "Vaughn, I never cared about that, except when you were small and we couldn't pay our bills."

He frowned, muttering, "It's just, he doesn't make much."

"Child support is always predicated upon income," Grady informed him. "The court sets the payments based on the income of the parent who has to pay, and if the income level changes, the child support amount can be adjusted. All your father had to do was approach it legally, unless, of course, he could afford to pay and just didn't want to."

Paige gave her head a little shake, looking worried, and Vaughn opened his mouth, but then he seemed to think better of whatever he was going to say and subsided. Grady lifted an eyebrow and moved on.

"Your mother is under no legal compulsion to pay child support to your father," he began. "Nevertheless, she has arranged to make monthly payments into a special account in your name, one hundred dollars of which will be made available to you every month for your personal use."

Vaughn's jaw dropped. "A hundred bucks a month!"

"We can make it twenty-five dollars a week, like a real allowance, if you want," Paige suggested carefully.

Vaughn's excitement was palpable. "Honest?"

"I think he likes that idea," Paige said to Grady, smiling.

Grady bit his tongue, any number of snide remarks threatening to slide off it. Why hadn't they just offered the kid money to stay?

"And," Paige was going on, "when you're ready for college, the rest of the money will be there." Vaughn's eyes went wide. "Of course," she added, "you'll have to keep your grades up."

"I will!" he promised. "Honest!"

Paige nodded, smiling, though her eyes were suspiciously bright. "That and a hockey scholarship could very well pay for your entire education," she observed brightly.

Vaughn looked at Grady. "Can you get hockey scholarships?"

"I would imagine so."

He sat back as if dumbfounded, mumbling to himself, "Dad had to pay for his college himself."

"Actually," Grady snapped, knowing he shouldn't, "your father defaulted on his college loans."

Vaughn blinked, but a mulish expression overcame him as he turned to his mother to grudgingly demand, "What's that mean?"

Paige flashed Grady a censorious glare, but she answered her son. "It means he borrowed money that he didn't pay back."

Mouth tightening, Vaughn cast his gaze downward. "Maybe he couldn't afford to pay it back."

"Maybe so," Paige whispered.

Vaughn scratched the arm of the chair with one fingertip, silent once more.

Grady mentioned that the contract between his parents could be amended only by mutual agreement, then asked if Vaughn had any questions. He shook his head. Grady flipped the folder closed and sat back.

"I guess that's it, then. Unless you have something you'd like to say?"

Vaughn sat in stony silence, scratching, scratching, scratching. Grady glanced at Paige, who lifted a shoulder. Leaning forward, Grady softened his words.

"You know, Vaughn, it's not too late."

Vaughn looked up at that. "What do you mean?"

Grady spread his hands. "You don't *have* to go back to South Carolina." Vaughn abruptly dropped his gaze. "Or," Grady went on, "you could wait until the end of the school semester. That's only a couple more months."

After a moment during which Paige sat forward hopefully, Vaughn shook his head. "I oughta go now." He looked up then. "I mean, I want to go now." He turned to his mom. "O-on Wednesday, like we planned."

Paige nodded, slumping. "Okay. Sure. On Wednesday."

They sat in painful silence for a few more seconds. Then Paige got to her feet, shifting the strap of her handbag onto her shoulder.

She'd worn jeans and a navy blouse beneath a neatly tailored camel corduroy jacket. Grady drank in the sight of her.

"We'd better go," she said with forced brightness. "We'll miss the movie."

Grady followed them out into the hallway, wishing he was going with them. She smiled at him.

"Thank you, Grady."

He nodded, and she started off down the hall at a brisk pace. Vaughn glanced in his direction before turning to follow her. Grady would never know what impulse made him step forward and call out to the boy, but he did.

"Vaughn?"

The boy stopped, turned around and walked back to him. "Yeah?"

Grady glanced at Paige, who had halted and half turned. He patted the boy's shoulder awkwardly. "I, uh, just wanted to say so long."

Vaughn dropped his gaze uneasily. "Yeah. Okay. See ya." He started to turn away.

"And," Grady added abruptly, "i-if you should need anything…" The thought drifted away while he wondered what he was doing.

Self-consciously, he slid a hand into his coat pocket, his fingertips encountering a single card. He had no idea how it had come to be there, but after slipping it free he saw that it was a card with his private number on it. He watched as his hand reached out and tucked the card into Vaughn's shirt pocket.

"Call me," he said, dropping his voice. "Any time."

The boy stared up at Grady for a moment, then he shrugged and turned away, trudging toward his mother. Paige lifted an arm as Vaughn drew near and draped it around his shoulders.

Grady leaned against the doorjamb and watched them walk away, his heart heavy. He imagined what it would be like for her, returning her only child to the man who had stolen him away from her. Abruptly, he made a decision.

She'd forbidden him to go with them, but she hadn't said anything about going on his own. Striding back into his office, he went to the telephone. It wasn't necessary to dog her all the way to Greenville, but he could meet her in Atlanta, make sure she got home okay, offer a shoulder for her to cry on.

It was a lot less than he wanted to do, but at least it was something, and for now it was enough.

Chapter Eleven

They laughed a lot those last few days, and it grieved Paige that they hadn't been able to do so from the beginning. Perhaps if she had been wiser or Vaughn had not been so angry and resentful, they might have managed it. Instead, it was only as he was leaving her that Paige and her son had found a sense of fun between them. That knowledge haunted her in quiet moments.

If he had known from the beginning that she would let him go, would it have made a difference in his attitude? Or would it have simply hastened his departure? It ceased to matter when she loaded his bags, several more than the two with which he'd arrived, into the back of her truck on that first Wednesday morning in April.

Because she had tried to make the most of every moment with him, she was sending him back to South Carolina with dirty clothes and mismatched luggage, including her cheap, flowered overnighter and a decrepit old thing of Matthias's that was held together with duct tape. They'd made a game out of packing, and she'd managed to keep her eyes dry, at least when she was around Vaughn. Now that the dreaded moment had arrived, however, she had to fight just to keep moving forward when she truly felt like crumpling into a sodden mass of grief.

Thankfully, the journey itself had been stripped of its most tiring part, the long drive to and from Tulsa. The special fare she'd found took them from the local regional airport, through Dallas and on to Greenville via Atlanta. Having to change flights twice lengthened the trip, but that just gave her more time with her son.

Paige tried to believe that Nolan would not simply take Vaughn and disappear with him again as soon as her return airplane lifted off the tarmac in Greenville. God knew she'd done everything in her power to minimize the risk, and she took a good deal of comfort in knowing that Vaughn hadn't run when he'd had the chance. Still, the fear would not entirely leave her, and reminding herself that she was building Vaughn's confidence in her by giving him up was small comfort.

The greater fear, however, was that Nolan would continue to poison the boy against her. She prayed that Vaughn would be less susceptible to his father's propaganda after having spent this time with her, but if not, she was powerless to do anything about it. That, like so much else, could only be left in God's capable hands, but despite the strength of her faith, surrendering her son was undoubtedly the most difficult thing she'd ever done.

They made it through the short flight to Dallas, even maintained the fragile air of adventure during their race through the sprawling DFW airport to catch the next plane, but her spirits flagged during the leg to Atlanta and bottomed out completely even before they boarded the final flight. Paige fought tears throughout that last hour. Hiding behind a magazine, she prayed for composure. When the aircraft touched down in South Carolina, she bullied the tears into submission, or as near as she could manage, and moved out into the aisle ahead of Vaughn so he wouldn't see her struggle for control.

Her arrangement with Nolan, made through their attorneys, called for her to walk Vaughn to the baggage claim area, where his father would be waiting. Then she'd simply go back through security and catch the next plane home without ever meeting Nolan face-to-face. She thought it a shame that they could not, even now, put aside their differences and just agree on what was best for their son, but Nolan apparently wasn't ready for that. He'd have to come to it eventually, though, because she was not going away. Just the opposite, in fact, if all went as planned.

Vaughn walked beside her in silence down the broad concourse, flashing her wary, worried glances. She told herself that he knew she was hurting and cared about her feelings, and she so wanted to be brave for him, but despite her best intentions, she lost it on the escalator, just managing to turn away before the tears began streaming. Then, try as she might, she couldn't beat them back again. All she could do was swipe at her face ineffectually and force a smile.

She spotted Nolan across the baggage carousel at the same time that Vaughn did. He seemed shorter than she remembered, slighter somehow, though he'd obviously put on some extra pounds.

His stare burned triumphantly across the distance. It was hard to remember that they had once been in love, once planned a future together. Then Vaughn turned to face her, and it became much easier to think of Nolan with kindness, pity even.

Whatever else he had done, whatever he had destroyed, he had given her this son, and even if this should be the last moment she ever beheld Vaughn's face, she would be eternally grateful.

Despite the determined campaign of sarcastic animosity that he'd waged, Vaughn was a caring boy beneath that hard shell. His attitude and actions had been dictated by fierce loyalty, and she couldn't fault him for that. He was only doing what seemed right and best to his eleven-year-old mind. If that conflicted with her determination to forge a healthy relationship with him, well, he was not to blame.

It was all in God's hands now, anyway.

Vaughn said uncertainly, "So I guess I'll see you soon."

She smoothed his hair one more time. "Absolutely."

He smiled as if looking forward to her visit. Had

the fun in which they'd indulged these last few days made a difference then? She tried to take comfort in the idea, to believe that somehow she would again be part of his daily life.

"Do you know when?" he asked.

"Not yet, but I'll call you as soon as I make the flight reservations."

"Okay."

He hitched a shoulder, casting a nervous glance behind him. Then suddenly he threw his arms around her.

She managed not to sob as she held him close, whispering brokenly, "I love you, Vaughn, and I want you to be happy. Nothing will ever change that."

He mumbled something that might have been, "You, too." The next instant he tore away, calling out, "Dad!"

She watched as he ran to his father and was greeted with a hug and a pat. She thought he might have waved to her, but she didn't wait to see. Reeling away, she found the nearest ladies' room, stumbled blindly into a stall and clapped both hands over her mouth, letting the agony begin.

Soon, she promised herself, just as soon as Vaughn was ready, they would be together again, even if she had to move to Greenville to make it happen.

No sacrifice was too great if only her son could learn to let her love him.

Grady jingled the change in his pocket, pacing from trash can to pillar and back again.

Paige's plane had landed in Atlanta five or six minutes ago, but thanks to current airport security rules he was the only one waiting at the gate to greet it, a feat accomplished simply by not leaving the concourse after his own flight had gotten in some two hours earlier.

He knew it was foolish to fly all this way at the last minute, paying top dollar for the privilege, just to hold her hand, but he couldn't help feeling that she needed him. Besides, he'd have gone mad at home, waiting to hear from her, knowing she was alone and in pain.

A uniformed airline employee unlocked a door across the way and folded it back to secure it against a wall. Grady yanked his hands from his pockets, dried his palms on his shirt and sucked in a deep breath, well aware that she might not be happy to see him, especially since it was not the attorney who stood here today. It was the man who cared for her more than was probably wise at this time, a man desperate to help. He'd wanted no mistake about that, which was why he'd worn jeans, brown boots and a simple navy-blue T-shirt beneath a khaki-colored windbreaker with upturned collar.

People straggled up the narrow, sloping hallway and out into the gate area, most of them lugging carry-on baggage. Paige was one of the first to appear. Looking haggard and disheveled, eyes red and swollen, she carried nothing more than her handbag with the strap slung over one shoulder.

Grady thought she was at once the most pathetic and the most beautiful thing he'd ever seen. One look at him stopped her dead in her tracks, but sorrow seemed to dull any surprise.

Uncertain what to do next, Grady simply stood there. Then her chin quivered, and he opened his arms. She hit his chest sobbing, and he could do nothing but hold her.

"It's okay, sweetheart. I'm here now."

"But y-you *shouldn't* be h-here," Paige finally managed.

"Neither should you," he replied, "but if you have to be here, then so do I."

"I'm g-glad you came."

He let out a silent breath of relief and gathered her against his side. "Let's find something to eat before we head home."

"I'm not hungry," she mumbled, but she wrapped her arm around his waist and let him lead her toward one of the better restaurants on the concourse.

By the time they were seated, she was more composed, but she ordered a side of fries and nibbled at them after they arrived only because he insisted. He didn't have much appetite himself, but he waded through his club sandwich mechanically, figuring that at least one of them ought to keep up their strength.

After a while, he asked how it had gone, getting a desultory shrug and a few whispered words out of her before she picked up a fry. She dipped it in the tiny cup of ketchup on her plate and lifted it listlessly to her mouth, only to abruptly drop it again and turn a stricken gaze on him.

"We forgot to say grace!"

It seemed a completely understandable lapse to Grady, all things considered, but she was clearly horrified by the omission. He quickly laid aside his sandwich, wiped his fingers on the paper napkin draped across one thigh and reached across the table. She placed her hands in his and bowed her head.

After a moment he realized that she was waiting for *him* to speak. Grady licked his lips and tried to think what to say.

"Lord, this is a tough time…but thank You for the food. And…keep Vaughn safe. And, um…she's done her best for him. That's got to be worth something, so somehow just…help. Amen."

He figured that had to be about the most miserable prayer anyone had ever voiced, but then she squeezed his fingers and whispered, "Amen."

Afterward, she started to cry once more.

"Honey, don't," he begged. "Try to eat."

She picked up the French fry again, but when she swallowed, it was with tears streaming from her eyes. Grady vowed then that he would give her and Vaughn whatever they needed to be happy.

If it took fine houses and cars, he would get them fine houses and cars. He would be friend, protector, guide and provider. Anything. Everything.

Just to see her smile.

* * *

She couldn't stop crying. It was weak, and it was silly, and she hated the attention that it garnered, the pitying, sidelong glances, the uncomfortable silences and appalled stares, but she couldn't help herself.

After years of being strong, sure, determined to find and be reunited with her son, Paige discovered that at the core she was mush, after all, as helpless as a newborn babe. If not for Grady, she couldn't imagine how she would have managed to get herself from gate to gate, onto the right plane and into the right seat, so she let him take care of everything, too sick at heart to care just then about right or fair.

He had their seating assignments switched, upgrading them both to First Class so they could sit together and have some semblance of privacy. It must have cost him a fortune, but she made no protest. Deeply grateful, she sat in the curve of his arm, her head on his shoulder, and concentrated on breathing steadily while tears dripped off her chin.

It was shockingly easy to ignore the whispered exchanges between him and the flight attendant. On occasion she managed to open her eyes and look at him. She could tell then that he was worried, but she couldn't seem to reassure him. It was as if all the grief and fear and failures that she'd stored up over the years had suddenly erupted and now flowed like lava, searing her heart and soul. She couldn't pray but kept recalling over and over again snatches of the eighth chapter of Romans.

"…but the Spirit Himself intercedes for us with groanings too deep for words…according to the will of God."

She tried to make herself focus on the following verses, the promise that all would be worked for the benefit of those who loved the Lord, but at the moment her own groaning went too deep for comfort. Without Grady to anchor her, she feared that she might simply float away on a tide of despair, so although it was unfair, she clung to him.

He'd thought of everything, it seemed. Having arranged to have himself dropped off at the airport earlier, he'd left his vehicle at her house so he could drive her SUV home. Bleary and blessedly numb by the time they reached Arkansas, she handed over her car keys, then let him buckle her into the passenger seat like an overgrown child. She closed her eyes, making not even a token protest, as he paid the parking fee and guided the truck out of the lot and onto the road toward her house.

Once there, she somehow managed to get herself out of the vehicle and onto the porch, though climbing Everest couldn't have been much more arduous than those few steps. Howler greeted her with a whine, but she pushed him away, visions of Vaughn assailing her.

She pushed away Matthias, too, not physically but emotionally. In truth, it had begun days before, almost as soon as she'd made her decision to let Vaughn go back to South Carolina and then follow him. Provided, of course, that he did not again disappear like vapor.

If that happened her son would forever be lost to her; she felt it to the marrow of her bones. Sick with fear, grieving the loss of her son and soon the loss of her home and business and even more that she dared not now contemplate, she felt a gathering anger.

For so long she had held such emotions at bay. For so long she had turned the other cheek. Now she felt a viciousness building. It threatened to overwhelm all she knew and believed until it lashed against the innocents in her life. How much longer she could hold it in, she didn't know, so when Grady suggested that they sit down on the couch, she shook her head vehemently.

"I'm not fit company right now."

She caught the glide of a worried glance between him and Matthias and folded her arms over the howl building in her chest.

"Maybe I should stay a little while, anyway," Grady said, "in case you need something."

"What I need," she retorted, feeling brittle enough to shatter, "is for you both to stop worrying about me."

"Paige, honey," Matthias began mournfully, "I can't help feeling that this is all my fault. If I hadn't—"

"Please!" she interrupted sharply, putting a hand to her head. "I can't talk about this. Not now. I just need to be by myself for a while."

"Paige," Grady said softly, cupping his big, hot

hand around the nape of her neck, "I don't think you should be alone now."

"But without my son I *am* alone," she cried bleakly. "If he disappears, I always will be alone."

"Girl, you know better than that," Matthias rasped.

"Neither of you have ever had a child! You don't know what it's like to give up your only son!"

"God does," Grady reminded her. "You told me so yourself."

"Yes, and what if He requires the same thing of me? What then?"

"Then you do what everyone else who's ever lost someone does," Matthias said brokenly. "You accept, and you go on."

"You hold on to your faith," Grady added softly. "You trust God to do what's best for everyone."

She stared at him for a long moment, lost in desolation, but then she gulped and nodded. "You're right. I'm sorry. My grasp on reason just now is tenuous at best. As I said, I'm not fit company. I—I think I just need to sleep."

Grady still looked worried, but he finally nodded. She didn't wait for more, simply turned and walked out, hurrying down the hall to her room, that lonely place where she had for so long nursed her hope. She would find only fear—and recrimination—there now, for it had suddenly become crystal clear to her that, even if everything worked out as she prayed it would, she was going to lose someone dear.

Worse, what she was planning was nothing short

of a betrayal of those two good men, each of whom cared about her in his own way. Yet, she could find no other way.

Her son had to come first. If Vaughn would not, could not, live here, then she had to be a part of his life some other way. That didn't make what she had to do any easier. It was, in fact, almost as difficult as letting Vaughn go—and that was only if everything went according to plan!

Everything could still fall apart. The sale of her business might not go through. Vaughn might not want her any closer than she was now. Nolan could defy all reason and vanish into the ether with their child.

Meanwhile, all she could do was pray and try for a few hours of oblivion.

Grady sighed and hung up the phone, having reached the limit of his patience. He was mighty tired of speaking to Matthias when what he really wanted was to talk to Paige.

For days she had held herself apart, apparently even from Matthias, who reported to Grady that she had not even joined him at the table for meals, moving wraith-like from her room to the office, on occasion even locking herself away and refusing to answer the door. Even more troubling, she hadn't attended church the Sunday following Vaughn's departure.

On that Sunday, Grady himself had gone with his father and his brother's family to services, and for the first time he hadn't felt like a complete and utter stranger, but neither had he felt as if he quite belonged. He found no fault with the large, enthusiastic congregation or the sumptuous building with its state-of-the-art technologies, but he couldn't help wondering what worship would be like in the little church in Nobb with Pastor Haynes speaking kindly from the pulpit and Paige sitting at his side.

Perhaps it was as well that he not suffer that distraction just now. When she was around, he couldn't seem to concentrate on anything or anyone but Paige.

On the other hand, she was never far from his mind, never completely out of his thoughts. Or his prayers.

Funny how a thing like that so quickly got to be a habit. Funny, too, how he'd learned to make room for it in his life.

If someone had asked him just a few months earlier, Grady would have said that, even had he believed it efficacious, he didn't have time to devote to prayer. Now he found himself in what seemed to be an ongoing conversation with his Maker.

Most of it had to do with Paige and what was best for her. Finally he understood not only why she had done what she had for her son but how she had managed to always think of what was best for Vaughn.

He understood, too, that someone had to shake her out of her depression, and Matthias wasn't getting anywhere. It was Tuesday. Time to rattle her cage.

It only took a few minutes to cancel his next appointment and rearrange the rest of his afternoon.

Then he got into the car and headed out on a drive that had become as familiar to him as the way home.

Along the way construction rerouted traffic through the countryside south of Bentonville. Grady chafed at the delay, but then he noticed the uncommon beauty of the area. He noted something else, as well.

He was driving by the great stone walls and artistically crafted wrought iron gates of what promised to be a truly fine new housing development. Mentally committing the telephone number to memory, he decided to give the builder a call later.

Putting that out of mind for the moment, he hurried on to Paige's place, parked in his usual spot and climbed the steps to the porch, stooping to give Howler a scratch as he moved to the door. It opened just as he got to it, and Matthias stood there glowering at him.

"Well, it's about time," he grumbled. "I was starting to think I was going to have to beat down that door myself."

That felt like permission to Grady. Glad for it, he queried baldly, "Where is she?"

"In her bedroom, where she's been just about every minute since you was last here." He lifted a gnarled hand and pointed to the hallway. "Second door. I'm gonna heat up something for her to eat. See she does."

As Matthias limped off toward the kitchen, Grady moved into the hallway, trying to decide just what tack to take with her. He felt out of his depth on the one hand and that he was doing the right thing on the other. Stationing himself in front of her door, he lifted his hand, but then he paused to arm himself with prayer before letting his fist fall.

"Open this door, Paige, or I'll open it myself," Grady warned, his tone leaving no doubt that he would do just that. "I'll take the casing off and pull out the framing if I have to."

Exasperated, Paige got up off the bed and stomped to the door. Why couldn't everyone just leave her alone? Wasn't it enough that they were right and she was wrong? Even the psychologist had warned her that she was taking the risk of never seeing her son again, but she'd truly believed that, as difficult as it was, letting him go had been the best thing, the *only* thing, she could do.

After five days without a single word from Vaughn, five days of a ringing telephone that had gone unanswered, she knew that she had gambled and lost. The last twenty-four hours were a blur of tears. Now suddenly her misery had once again become the one emotion with which she had least acquaintance, anger. The thing about anger was that it tended to go off in the wrong direction, usually just striking at the closest target.

Grady was the closest target this time. How dare he come pounding on her door like this? Fully prepared to inform him that he wasn't going to bully her, she wrenched the door open.

A moment passed before she fully grasped the fact that he had swept her off her feet and was literally carrying her down the hallway in his arms. Her emotions surged, threatening to swamp her; she grasped at the anger defensively.

"What do you think you're doing?"

Grady neither slowed nor blinked, his profile a study in granite. "I could ask you the same thing."

What *was* she doing?

The answer was at once starkly apparent. She was wallowing in self-recrimination, but she clamped her jaw and refused to say so. If anyone deserved to indulge in a little self-pity, surely it was her.

Grady turned the corner into the living room with her, dipping to make certain that her head made it around without cracking against the plaster and again so that her feet followed safely after. Curiously touched despite her lingering petulance, she let her arm slide across his shoulders, feeling the strength in them. He carried her into the kitchen, where Matthias placed a bowl on the table and hastily pulled out a chair.

Soon she was sitting down, her chair pushed up to the table as if she were a toddler. Matthias plunked a spoon into a bowl of what appeared to be chicken noodle soup.

"Eat," Grady ordered, dropping down into the chair at her side, "or we'll feed you."

"Don't you even…" she began, only to find herself with a mouthful of noodles. She glared at Grady over the spoon, then swallowed of pure necessity. "…think about."

The second time soup dribbled down her chin. A paper napkin appeared. Snatching it, she wiped her face.

"There, that's better," Matthias said complacently, limping around the table to help himself into a chair.

She opened her mouth to tell them both what she thought of them—only to swallow again a moment later. When Grady went after the next, dripping spoonful, she reached for the utensil, muttering, "Okay, okay, I'll do it."

He relinquished the spoon after only a minor tussle. She began to eat, finding, to her surprise, that she was actually quite famished.

"Okay," Grady said as soon as she had slurped up the last mouthful, "talk."

She thought of several scathingly witty remarks, but then her chin began to wobble, and the enormity of her loss came rushing back.

"They've gone," she whispered, and then she wailed, "They've disappeared again!"

Instantly Grady enveloped her, his long, thick arms pulling her close to his side, so close that she found her head on his shoulder. "Sweetheart, I'm so sorry."

"When?" Matthias demanded. "When did they leave?"

"I don't know. Probably right away. I—I didn't call until Friday. I thought I'd give them a day or so. They didn't answer the phone, so I called again on Saturday. And *again* on Sunday, early, late." She shook her head. "Nothing."

"Oh, no," Matthias muttered.

"I told myself they'd taken the weekend, gone camping or fishing or something. Then yesterday I called again, in the morning and in the afternoon, late into the night. No answer, not even an answering machine." She looked at Grady through her tears. "You were right. Nolan took my son and ran!"

"You don't know that," Grady said reasonably.

"Then why don't they answer the phone?"

"Could be any number of reasons. Maybe it's out of order."

"I checked. It's not. This is exactly what he did before, left all the utilities on and just disappeared!"

"Have you called the school?"

"Yesterday. Vaughn hasn't been enrolled."

Grady took out his cell phone and laid it in front of her. "Call again."

The number was on her bedside table, so Matthias hurried out to retrieve it.

"What happens if he's still not there?" she said anxiously.

"I call the cops," he told her calmly. "Then we drop everything and go after them." He tapped her on the end of the nose. "And we don't stop until we find them."

She took a deep breath, feeling considerably more hopeful, until Matthias returned with the telephone number of the school that Vaughn had last attended in South Carolina. Suddenly gripped by fear, she couldn't make herself dial.

Grady picked up the phone and punched in the

number. Within moments he was speaking in his best lawyer's voice, explaining that he was an attorney in Arkansas whose client's son should be enrolled in the school.

"The custody agreement between my client and her ex-husband stipulates that their son attend your school, and we're just checking for compliance," he went on. He spelled Vaughn's full name and gave his birth date, then looked to Paige. "Social security number?"

She closed her eyes, brought the recently memorized number to mind and repeated it. Grady transferred the information to whomever was on the other end of the phone and smiled.

"Excellent," he said pointedly, looking at Paige. "Tell you what I'm going to do, I'm going to send you a copy of the court order validating the agreement, so you'll know how and when to contact us. In fact, I'm sure that Vaughn's mother would be delighted to hear from you in the future for any reason whatsoever. She's very concerned about her son's welfare, and that includes his performance and attendance in school. Thank you so much for your time."

He ended the call and dropped the phone into his pocket, addressing her. "Nolan enrolled Vaughn in school this morning."

She nearly collapsed with relief. Somehow she found herself sitting with her head on his shoulder again.

"Thank God! Thank God."

"I expect the school will be calling you over every

unexplained absence and missing piece of home-work," Grady informed her kindly, patting her back.

"Wonderful!" she sighed, purely delighted.

"Eh. Never thought I'd be grateful for lawyers," Matthias said, limping out of the room.

"Everyone is, sooner or later," Grady remarked drily, and Paige laughed.

She gasped in fresh air, feeling as if she'd just gotten her first breath after days of oxygen depriva-tion. It wasn't long before she was feeling pretty stupid.

"Oh, my. Oh, my." She dropped her head into her hands, elbows braced against the tabletop. "I can't believe how easily I accepted defeat." She lifted her head and looked at Grady. "Or how easily you took care of it."

"Everybody stumbles and falls sometimes, Paige."

"Don't I know it. Lately it seems that every time I do, you're there to pick me up again."

He smiled and cupped her chin with one large, capable hand, his blue eyes shining. "Paige," he said softly, "don't you know yet that I'd do anything for you?"

A feeling of warmth and security flooded her, and it was then that she knew without any doubt that she was going to break both their hearts.

Chapter Twelve

Paige's sigh gusted through the telephone and into Grady's ear, eliciting a frown from him.

"Oh, Grady, I'm sorry," she said, "but I just can't spare the time to go out for dinner. Everything's crazy here. I'm still trying to establish contact with my son and catch up on my work."

Grady pressed the telephone receiver to his ear with his left hand and drew another curlicue on the doodle that he was making with his right. Her excuse was legitimate, but he couldn't escape the notion that she was putting distance between them, and he couldn't figure out why.

Only a couple days ago he'd thought that their relationship had reached a new stage. The worst had seemed behind them when they'd established that Vaughn was where he should be, but she still had not been able to speak with the boy. Now, she no longer seemed to fear that her ex would steal her son away again; instead she feared that Nolan wouldn't have to, that Vaughn had rejected her completely.

Grady blamed himself in a way. He should have mandated in the custody agreement when and how often Vaughn was to call his mother. It would have been unusual and might not have succeeded, but he couldn't help feeling that he should have tried—or wondering if Paige blamed him for not doing so.

"They're still not answering the phone then?" Grady asked, working to keep his tone even.

"Nolan is, but he says Vaughn doesn't want to talk to me."

Grady winced at the angst in her voice, the confusion. "Surely you don't believe that."

"I don't know what to believe."

Her abject distress pierced his heart. "You left a message for Vaughn at the school, as I suggested?"

"Yes, and they say he got it, but he still hasn't called."

"We could ask the police to pay them a courtesy visit, remind Vaughn that you're waiting to hear from him and Nolan that you do have rights."

"I can just imagine how Nolan would spin that," Paige said bitterly.

Grady laid aside his pen and pinched the bridge of his nose. Short of actually making a trip to South Carolina, throwing a headlock on Nolan Ellis and grabbing Vaughn by the ear to haul him in front of a telephone, Grady didn't know what to do.

"If only I could go down there this weekend as

planned," she lamented, proving that their minds were working in similar fashion. "It's my own fault, I know. I should've made the reservation before I even let him go. Now it'll be another week before I can make the trip."

"Paige, I can get you there this weekend," he pointed out. "There are first-class seats left. Let me take care of it."

"No. I can't take money and gifts from you anymore, Grady."

"You could when it was for Vaughn."

"That's different. Besides, if I can't get in touch with him beforehand, I have no guarantee I'll be able to see him when I arrive. Nolan could simply claim they didn't know to expect me."

Grady put a hand to his temple. "Let me think about this, see what I can come up with."

She didn't sound very hopeful when she hung up. Grady turned the page on his legal pad and began to jot down possible actions, weighing pros against cons. No easy answers presented themselves, only disadvantages. He had to find a way to do this without giving Nolan ammunition to use against Paige. By evening he was no closer to finding a solution to this situation.

Worn out from straining his brain, Grady dragged himself home, picking up a burger and scarfing it down on the way. He turned on the television in his bedroom, intending to listen to the early news broadcast. Instead he found himself sitting on the side of his bed, head bowed in prayer.

I don't know what to do, he admitted. *She needs to hear from her son and know that he loves her, that he wants her in his life. Please make him realize how blessed he is to have her for a mom, and don't let Nolan keep on hurting her.*

He went on and on, pleading with God, and finally rose to move into the bathroom, still wearing his clothes. Maybe a hot shower would loosen some of the tension knotting his muscles. He reached to turn the shower on, but the muted buzz of his cell phone stopped him.

The phone was usually the first thing to go on his bedside table once he got home. Otherwise, it wound up hanging in his closet inside a coat pocket instead of accompanying him to work the next day. The fact that he hadn't automatically placed it in its customary place atop his bedside table was indicative of his state of mind. Yet, had he done so, he'd likely have missed this call. Bemused, he removed the small device from his pocket and flipped it open, reading the words on the screen.

Who on earth was C. D. Bishop? Must be a wrong number. Shrugging, he almost closed the phone and put it away, but something prodded him to answer. Even as he watched his thumb press the right button, he shook his head, but then he put the phone to his ear and rumbled a greeting.

"Grady Jones."

The voice that answered him sounded tentative and edgy. "Hi. It's me."

He nearly dropped the phone. Instead, he tightened his grip on it, rolled his eyes heavenward and exclaimed, "Thank you!" confident that he wasn't talking to the ceiling.

"Huh?"

Grady laughed and said, "Good to hear from you, Vaughn."

He'd never meant anything more.

Paige gripped Grady's fingers with one hand and the slip of paper bearing Vaughn's e-mail address with the other. Closing her eyes, she silently thanked God before saying what they both now knew. "It was Nolan all along."

"He takes the phone with him when he leaves the house so Vaughn can't call you," Grady confirmed drily, "but he underestimated his son." He squeezed her hand. "And his son's feelings for you."

She beamed at the thought. "I can't believe Vaughn set up his own e-mail account so we can keep in touch!"

"Everybody knows you can get e-mail free on the Internet," Grady quipped. "Vaughn said so."

Paige laughed. "I have to find a way to thank his hockey coach for letting Vaughn use his cell phone." Sobering, she voiced the one, niggling, little worry that remained. "But why didn't he just call me? Why call you?"

Grady sat back against her couch, maintaining contact with her through their hands. Paige couldn't make herself pull away. She told herself that it was because he'd driven here to bring her this message from her son, but the truth was that she craved his touch.

"Apparently Vaughn found my card in his shirt pocket when he was changing clothes at the ice rink after practice," Grady said. "Nolan was late picking him up, so Vaughn took advantage of that to borrow his coach's phone and make the call. He said he had this number written down at home."

That made sense. "He wouldn't know this number by heart," Paige concluded. "It's not like he's ever called here." Or ever would if his father had anything to do with it. She remembered the day that Grady had tucked that card into Vaughn's shirt pocket and shook her head, marveling anew. "I meant to wash that shirt before he left, but I didn't get around to it."

"Nolan hasn't, either, obviously."

"Thank God."

"Seems to me God's fingerprints are all over this."

She tightened her grip on Grady's fingers. "And yours."

A slow smile spread across Grady's face. Her heart skipped a beat. How did he do it? Every time her world looked its bleakest, here came Grady to the rescue. How was she supposed to resist a man like that?

Because she had to. Because it wasn't fair to him to do otherwise. Chances were that she would be leaving here, after all. And him. She knew that she should tell him, but she didn't know how. Not now. Not after this.

But soon. She would have to tell him soon.

Gulping, she fixed her thoughts on something else, something more pleasant. "This'll teach Nolan to be such a skunk."

"At least now Vaughn knows which one of his parents is fair and compassionate," Grady said, "and which one *isn't*. This proves that you were right to let Vaughn have contact with his dad while he was here with you, by the way."

She shook her head. "Don't give me too much credit, Grady. Most of the time I'm operating blind, bouncing from one wall to another, never certain of my path."

"You may not always know where you're going, Paige," he refuted gently, "but we both know you're guided by godly beliefs and ethics. That's why eventually you always get where you need to be."

She looked away, thinking that where she needed to be now was in South Carolina, near her son. And far from everyone else she cared about. Troubled, she pulled her hand from his, covering the action by adjusting the hem of her sweatshirt. It was not one of her nicer garments, but she hadn't been expecting company.

"Where I need to be right now is at my desk," she said apologetically. "Sorry to throw you out, but I really have to get back to work."

"It's almost nine," Grady said, sitting forward again and checking his watch. "You work too much."

"I have no choice. I have to get it done."

"You should look into hiring some extra help."

"Oh, no, not now."

"Why not? You obviously have enough work."

Paige bit her lip, knowing that she'd just been presented with an ideal opportunity, even if she was loath to take it. "I'm thinking about selling my business," she said carefully.

Grady straightened in surprise. "Really?" She nodded, and to her surprise, he smiled. "That's wonderful."

"It is?"

"Absolutely. I imagine it's worth quite a lot, and selling would free you to spend time with your son. You could spend the whole summer together."

"Exactly."

But not here. Vaughn looked forward to camping trips with his dad in the summer. If she was going to spend any time with him, she'd have to be there in South Carolina, ideally by the time school let out.

Grady got up, saying, "Well, I won't keep you. I know you'll want to have the business in great shape before you go looking for a buyer."

"Actually," she said, cringing inwardly, "I already have someone who's interested."

"Excellent!" Grady exclaimed. Reaching down, he drew her to her feet. "When you're ready, we'll put together a contract that gives both parties a fair shake."

Guiltily, she managed a nod and let him lead her toward the door, steeling herself to tell all. Before she could, he put his head back and sighed happily.

"I'm so relieved. All afternoon I agonized over

what to do about Vaughn, but there just didn't seem to be a good solution. Then I sat down and really prayed about it, and the next thing I knew some guy I've never heard of before was calling. Can you believe I almost didn't answer?" He shook his head. "Hearing Vaughn's voice, well, it was hearing answered prayer."

With that, Grady dropped a casual parting kiss on her forehead and pulled open the door. Paige swallowed the confession she'd been about to make. She just didn't have the heart to tell him at the moment. He stepped out onto the porch.

"Oh," he said, "Almost forgot. According to Vaughn, all the guys think his new hockey gear is 'juicy.'" He winked, smiling, and moved to the steps, repeating to himself, "Juicy." Chuckling, he took the steps and headed for his car.

Paige wandered out onto the porch, both reluctant and relieved to see him go. Limned by moonlight, he lifted a hand and called out in farewell.

"I'll phone you tomorrow, babe. Since it's Friday maybe we can go out to dinner. Bye." He opened the car door and dropped down behind the wheel.

Babe.

She watched him start up the engine and drive away, whispering sadly, "No, Grady. We aren't going out to dinner. We aren't ever going out on a date. I just can't do that to you."

It was bad enough as it was.

She turned back into the house, looking down at the

paper in her hand. One problem was solved, but others remained. She thought of Matthias sleeping in the other room. She hadn't seen the point in telling him what she was planning before because only now was it really looking like a possibility.

On the other hand, what was the point in upsetting everyone until she knew for sure that the move was going to happen? After the tension and turmoil of the past weeks, didn't they all deserve a little peace before she broke the news? Besides, so much could still go wrong.

She knew that she was looking for excuses to delay, but the last thing she wanted to do was hurt either of the two men who had supported and helped her during the worst times of her life. She'd just have to pray for the right time and words.

And the courage.

"So what do you think?"

Grady glanced at the church secretary standing on the patch of lawn in front of the building. He knew what Paige was asking but teased her by pretending to misunderstand.

"I think Betty's a frustrated paparazzi."

Paige chortled. "She was *very* disappointed that she didn't get to dog those FFROC investigators with a camera, it's true, but I think Richard was glad when they canceled after the suit was dropped. That's not what I meant, though. I meant, what do you think of the church?"

Grady turned to look back at the rambling building. Built partly of brick, partly of cinder block and partly of wood, it had been painted white in an apparent bid to add continuity, the result being a somewhat lumpy-looking structure that could have served any number of purposes. The only thing about it that really resembled a church from the outside was the steeple. Inside, though, the place felt permeated with a welcoming, almost comfortable, very uncommon *holiness*.

While neither grand nor vast, the sanctuary felt more like church than any place Grady had ever been. Pastor Haynes had opened the simple service by welcoming the congregation to "God's house," and that's just what it had felt like to Grady. Maybe sometimes God's house was a palace where only the most formal of reverences was acceptable or a modern hall with all the bells and whistles of a theater, but apparently sometimes God's house could also be as comfortable and casual as, well, home.

"I think," he said to Paige, "that this church is a far drive from the east side of Fayetteville where I'm living."

She looked a little crestfallen. "You didn't like it then?"

"Of course, I liked it." He smiled. "It was a wonderful service, and it's really not all that far from Bentonville."

She cut him a sharp glance from the corner of those big, soft green eyes. "Bentonville? What's that got to do with anything?"

"Haven't I mentioned that I was thinking of moving to Bentonville?"

"No. What's brought that on?"

He looked down. "Well, my dad's not getting any younger. Bentonville's closer to him in Belle Vista but not too far from the office in Fayetteville. Seems like a good place to be."

"But doesn't your brother already live in Bentonville?"

"He does. That doesn't mean I can't, though. Not that I intend to set down roots in the same neighborhood as my brother. Actually, I've been looking at this new development on the south side, rolling hills, little lake, community stables."

"Stables? Sounds expensive."

He shrugged. "Maybe, but I think it might be worth it. One-to two-acre lots, security gates. Of course, I'd have to build a house, but I've always wanted to. Why don't we drive by there on our way to lunch? You can tell me what you think of the site I've got in mind."

He could almost see her shutting down. She'd been doing that a lot lately. Everything would be fine, then she'd start pulling back. She'd done it again that weekend. After Thursday's turnaround, he'd thought for sure that they'd go out on Friday or Saturday night, but she'd continued to plead work. When he'd shown up at church this morning, she'd first seemed thrilled. Later, she'd clearly been uncomfortable. He didn't know what to do except forge on and hope that whatever was bothering her would work itself out.

"Oh, uh, no. Grady," she began, "I can't let you feed me, not after everything else you've done."

"Yeah, you're right," he cut in, squinting up at the sun. "You owe me. So what's for dinner?" He looked down and grinned.

She melted, spluttering laughter. "Get in the car. We'll decide on the way."

"Yes, ma'am."

Unlocking the Mercedes, he dutifully slid in behind the steering wheel. She called out across the lawn to Matthias, who was chatting with another elderly gentleman.

"Matthias, we're going to lunch." With a nod, the old fellow started limping their way. She got into the car. "You don't mind if he comes with us, do you?"

Grady shrugged. "You're buying."

He wasn't stupid. He knew perfectly well that she was using Matthias as a shield of sorts, but he'd take what he could get, happy just to keep his foot in the door. She already wanted to invite him in; surely before long she would. He just had to be patient. Grady was discovering, to his surprise, that he was pretty good at being patient.

Paige linked her hands behind her back and strolled around the shady hillside, looking out over the rolling vista. Neatly bisected with broad, smooth streets, low, split rail fences and narrow, shady riding paths, it looked like the little piece of heaven that it wanted to be. The small lake in the distance reflected sunlight like a sheet of glass, its subtle landscaping managing to look natural and perfectly balanced at the same time. Even the large, low horse barn in the center of the enclosed pasture below the rise upon which they stood appeared to have grown right up out of the ground. The developer had been wise enough to install a couple of sleek, spirited Thoroughbreds in the near paddock to add to the ambience.

She could almost see the large, sumptuous, sprawling homes that would soon begin rising across this place, their rock faces discreetly turned away for privacy's sake. The house that stood atop this hill would be the pinnacle, trading the sometimes icy ascents of winter for neighborhood primacy.

Vaughn would love it here, bless his mercenary little heart. If only... If only.

Paige leaned her shoulder against the rough, twisted trunk of a hickory that the builder had chosen to leave be and tried to decide what to say to Grady.

"So what do you think?" he asked, using almost the same words she'd used with him after the worship service that morning. "Does it feel like home to you?"

She shook her head, then softened that negative response with a positive one. "It's beautiful, though, Grady."

"Too rich for my blood," Matthias announced, turning back to the car. "How come a pretty day like this always makes me sleepy? Musta eaten too much lunch. Sure was good, though, wasn't it? If anyone wants me, I'll be in the backseat."

Paige chuckled as Grady stepped up beside her. "Real subtle, isn't he?"

Grady braced an arm against the tree trunk above her, smiling wryly. "He knows these are the only minutes you'll spend alone with me."

She hung her head. "Grady. Please try to understand. I'm not free to follow my heart in this. I have to put my son first."

"I get that."

She turned her back to the tree, looking up at him. "No, you don't. You can't."

"That again," he said. "Okay, I don't have any kids. Yet. But I will, one day." He tapped her on the end of the nose, grinning, "I'm counting on you to show me the ropes, you know."

Her heartbeat stuttered. "Grady."

"You're such a great mom. You really ought to have a couple more kids some day."

She looked down. "I always thought I'd have three or four by now, but that obviously wasn't a part of God's plan for my life."

"It's not too late," he said lightly, but she heard the very great import behind the comment and shook her head.

"Oh, but it is. I already have a son, Grady. His wants and needs outweigh everything else."

Grady sighed. "I knew he wasn't crazy about me, but lately I thought he was starting to like me, at least a little."

"Oh, sure. You're great buddies. At a distance of several hundred miles."

"No, really, when we talked on the phone the other night he was real friendly, a little defensive where his dad's concerned, but friendly."

"It's that defensiveness that's the problem," she pointed out gently. "He doesn't want anyone to replace his dad in any way, not even me."

Grady nodded and said, "Yeah, I know, but that'll change. You were right to let him go, Paige. I see that now."

"I hope so. He was such a perfect little stinker while he was here, but I miss him so much. Then when he didn't answer the phone, I thought…but my son *does* want me in his life."

"Of course he does. You're his mom. Someday he's going to realize just how blessed he is by that, and I think sooner rather than later. That's what I'm praying for, anyway."

She smiled because he'd said it as if he'd never doubted that a loving God heard and answered prayers. Reaching up, she framed his beloved face with her hands. "You don't know what it means to me to hear you say that."

"I know what it means to me to hear you laugh," he said smoothly.

She caught her breath. "Oh, Grady, don't."

"I can't help it." He turned his face, pressing a kiss into the palm of her hand. "I know you have other things on your mind right now, and I can wait. But don't ask me not to care."

Perhaps it was wrong of her, but she couldn't find

it in her heart to turn away his gentle kiss after that. Neither could she deny that for those few moments she felt whole and strong again. How could she tell him then that if everything worked out as she hoped, she would soon walk out of his life completely?

How could she not?

"Grady," she began, but just then Matthias opened the back door of the car and stuck his head out.

"You kids about done? The sun's coming right through this window and broiling me where I sit."

Grady chuckled. "Okay. Keep your shirt on. Or not."

"We'd better go before he sets up housekeeping in your backseat," she quipped, secretly relieved.

"Actually," Grady commented, as they strolled back toward the sedan, "I expect Matthias to stay right where he is for the rest of his life."

"Oh, I intend to see to it," she said. It was the least she could do, after all. If only she could do as well by Grady.

It was a weary but happy Paige who climbed out of her truck near midnight the following Sunday evening. She hauled her brand-new overnight bag from the backseat, looked at the Mercedes parked in her yard and shook her head. Obviously, having refused to allow Grady to drive her to and from the airport in Tulsa had not discouraged him from waiting for her here at her house.

She almost wished she could be put out with him. It would be easier for both of them if she didn't care so much for the man and vice versa. Yet, how could she regret a relationship that had so often proved to hold the answers to her prayers?

These days much of her prayer life centered on Grady himself. She owed him so much, and the very last thing she wanted to do was hurt him. If only she could figure out how to avoid it.

Doggy nails clicked on the porch as she climbed the steps, but before she could locate the dog so as not to fall over it, her front door opened, spilling light into the darkness and revealing none other than the big man himself. He stepped outside to greet her with a hug.

"You okay?"

"I'm great."

"Went good, then?"

She set down the overnight case and placed her handbag atop it before looking up into his shadowed face. She knew that the light fell full on her own.

"We had a wonderful time. The apartment building where Vaughn lives isn't much, but there's a forest behind it, and we hiked all over the place yesterday. Then today, after church, we had a picnic. I've never seen him so relaxed and happy."

"What about Nolan? He give you any trouble?"

"He didn't seem happy when he opened the door and saw me standing there, but what could he do?"

"Not a thing unless he wants to lose custody permanently."

"I just don't understand why the two of us can't talk like adults, why we can't discuss our son and make decisions according to what is best for him."

"I don't, either," Grady said, "but that's on Nolan, not you, and Vaughn must realize it now."

"Maybe. We didn't discuss it."

"Of course not." He slid his hands around to the nape of her neck and lightly massaged the weary muscles there.

"Mmm. That feels good."

"You must be worn-out."

"Oh, yes, but it's worth it." She could hear the television softly playing inside. "Where's Matthias? He go off to bed and leave you on your own?"

"In a manner of speaking." Grady tossed his head. "He fell asleep in the recliner a couple hours ago."

"Ah. He does that sometimes."

Howler pushed his way between them then, seeking a pat from someone. Grady was the first to oblige, going down on his haunches to give the animal a good rub. Paige bent at the waist, bringing her nose within a hairbreadth of the dog's.

"Someone asked about you, Howler. I think he misses you."

"I'll bet he misses more than this old hound," Grady said, rising to his full height once again. "Vaughn's going to be asking to come home to Arkansas before you know it."

Straightening, she shook her head. "I don't think so. You have to understand, Grady. Vaughn loves both of his parents. I wasn't so sure before. I am now, but I can't ask Vaughn to choose between us. I won't."

"I never expected you to."

"What's going to change is that Nolan's going to have to learn to deal with me," she went on, "because Vaughn won't give him any other choice."

"And we know how determined Vaughn can be," Grady put in.

She laughed. "Exactly." He lifted his arms above his head, locking his hands and twisting to work out the kinks in his back. "You should go home and get some sleep," she told him.

"Yeah, I should," he agreed, dropping his arms and flopping his head from side to side. "I just wanted to be here, you know, in case things didn't go the way we hoped they would. I'm glad to know it went well."

"Thanks."

"You need to get some rest, too, so good night, babe."

He stepped up and would have dropped a kiss in the center of her forehead, but for some absurdly stupid reason that she could never fathom, she tipped her head back and brought her mouth into contact with his. It was like summertime in April. Warmth enveloped her, and then she realized that he'd wrapped his arms around her.

How easy it was to just forget all the reasons she shouldn't be letting it happen, how easy to justify. A simple expression of affection should be permissible between adults, shouldn't it? But nothing was simple about this. Fraught with complexity, the many layers of emotion, needs and desires were doomed never to be fulfilled. They were both breathing roughly when she finally made herself break away.

"I'm so sor—"

He clapped a finger over her lips, whispering, "Don't." An instant later he took his hand away. "For once let me be the one to pull back."

Chapter Thirteen

Grady stopped by unannounced on Wednesday evening with an armload of rolled-up house plans, which he dumped on her kitchen table, declaring that he needed help. After everything he'd done for her, Paige couldn't very well turn him down, but his dropping by was getting to be a dangerous habit that she felt she had to curtail.

"You might have called first. What if I hadn't been home?"

He gave her a knowing look. "And where else would you be since you've dropped out of choir? Pastor Haynes mentioned it on Sunday. What's up with that, anyway?"

She found that she couldn't quite meet his gaze as she muttered, "I no longer need a distraction from my son's nasty attitude, that's all."

"Speaking of needs, I need input from a female perspective," Grady said, waving a hand at the mound of rolled-up sheets of oversize paper. He grinned and announced, "I bought the lot and talked to an architect. He sent these over for me to look at."

Paige tried to be happy for him, but all she could think about was that she wouldn't be here to see the house that he was going to build on that beautiful piece of land. She managed a smile and a muted, "That's wonderful."

"I'm so anxious to get started," he said, rubbing his hands together, "but there's this weird questionnaire he wants filled out." Pulling a folded set of stapled forms from his hip pocket, he tossed that onto the table with the rest. "I knew I was in trouble when I got to a question about laundry rooms. Do I want laundry facilities near the master bedroom, the other bedrooms, the kitchen, the garage, what?"

He looked so perplexed that Paige chuckled, taking pity on him. "I guess it depends on whether you're using a split bedroom plan or—"

He held up a hand. "Let's just start at the top of the list and go through it that way."

She knew it wasn't wise to get caught up in his building plans, but how did she turn down a plea for help from the one person who constantly came to her aid? Taking the questionnaire in hand, she began to read. Soon she was planning a dream home, the likes of which she'd never before allowed herself to imagine. She had to remind herself that it would never be *her* dream home, nor had Grady said outright that he hoped it would be. She prayed he would not.

Only the day before she'd made a counter offer to a company interested in buying her business. As soon as she knew that the sale was going to go through, she told herself, she'd find a way to tell Grady that she was moving to South Carolina. Somehow.

"Take a look at this one," Grady said, unrolling the papers and holding them open with one hand. He scanned the floor plan. "Here." He planted his big, blunt forefinger and reached into his shirt pocket for a pencil. "What if we moved these walls like this?" He began sketching the changes onto the paper. "And offset the sinks like this."

Paige spread the sheet she was holding and framed an area of that floor plan with her hands. "And put this whole section here, right?"

"Right."

She tilted her head, trying to picture the evolving schematic. They'd been going over plans and formulating others for over a week now. "It's everything you've said you want, the master suite opening onto the pool, the master bath easily accessible from there."

"And, Miss Sunshine, we have plenty of windows," he teased.

She didn't know why she'd criticized so vociferously the dearth of windows in one particular plan. It wasn't as if she would ever live in the house that Grady was going to build, after all. Still, she felt the need to defend her opinion.

"You can't have a master suite of this size with just one little window, I don't care how oddly it's shaped."

"You don't put much store in architectural interest, do you?" Grady observed, grinning.

"Livability trumps architectural interest every time in my view," she grumped.

Grady chuckled. "Yeah, me, too. Besides, I like a bright, cheery room. I have another appointment with the architect Monday, by the way. He says once we approve the final plans, construction can start immediately, so we'll probably break ground by the end of June."

"You," she corrected softly. "Once *you* approve the final plans. All I'm doing is offering a female perspective, remember?"

His grin withered, and he began rolling up the papers. "All right, once *I* approve the final plans." He speared her with a direct look. "Happy?"

Paige didn't dignify that with an answer. Instead she quickly rose to go to the refrigerator and refill her glass with iced tea. He muttered something that could have been, "Didn't think so." She ignored that, too.

The truth was that she had never been more unhappy, and it wasn't just because her son no longer lived in her house. Oh, that was part of it, to be sure, but Grady and his expectations were a larger part.

She'd tried to discourage him, turning down his invitations repeatedly, making sure she was never alone with him, constantly reminding him that her son was the focus of her life and that he needed both of his parents in his. Then Grady would drop by with a new plan or a bag of hamburgers and she'd find herself offering an opinion or laughing at something he said, and before she knew what was happening an hour had passed. Afterward she'd berate herself and vow to tell Grady that her plans for the future did not, could not, include him.

Yet, she hadn't even told Vaughn that she intended to move to South Carolina to be near him. She meant to feel him out about the possibility this weekend. Nolan wouldn't like it if she moved down there, of course, but he had no say about it. No more, unfortunately, than Grady did.

If everything worked out as it should, she'd be living in South Carolina before the builder broke ground on Grady's new house, which was a very good reason to keep her distance from Grady now. Why she couldn't seem to do that was a mystery to her. It made no sense. She'd never been a coward, and it was the right thing to do, after all.

Wasn't it?

She closed the refrigerator, turned and found him watching her. He got up out of his chair and moved to stand beside her, one arm braced against the kitchen counter.

"Want to grab a bite to eat?"

She shook her head, glad that she didn't have to lie to him. "I've already eaten."

"How about just coming along to keep me company then?"

She had to look away and steel herself in order to turn him down as firmly as she knew was necessary. "Sorry, no. I have to be up in the wee hours to catch a plane, remember?"

Even two weeks out, most of that weekend's flights had been booked solid, at least as far as Atlanta, so she'd had little choice but to take an early-morning reservation.

Grady leaned a hip against the counter beside her and said matter-of-factly, "Yeah, about that. I'm driving you into Tulsa."

She pushed aside a spurt of yearning and girded herself for a fight. "No."

"Yes."

"I'm not letting you get up at 2:00 a.m. just to drive me to the airport," she insisted.

"I'm not letting you hit the road at 3:00 a.m. all by your lonesome."

"You tell her, counselor," Matthias put in from the living room. Paige rolled her eyes and folded her arms stubbornly.

"I am an adult. I can get myself to and from Tulsa."

"*I* am an adult," Grady retorted calmly, "an adult *male*, and I wouldn't let any *woman* I care about drive alone at that time of the morning. Call it sexist if you want, but I'll be here at three, and you can either ride with me or I'll follow you in my car. Your choice."

She threw up her hands. "Why ask me? You're obviously making all the decisions."

He dropped his chin, staring at her from beneath the

crag of his brow. "You don't even want to know what would be different around here if I was making all the decisions." She gulped and looked away while he went on earnestly. "But that's beside the point. Do you honestly think I could rest knowing that you were on the road by yourself at that hour? Anything could go wrong with that old truck of yours, and your options for assistance in the open countryside are limited. Besides, I'd rather spend ninety minutes driving you to the airport than almost anything else I can think of, including sleep."

Paige sighed, knowing when she'd lost an argument, and grumbled, "You're a lousy adversary."

"I am an excellent adversary."

"Exactly."

He chuckled, and crooked a finger beneath her chin, turning her face to receive a kiss dropped casually on to the tip of her nose. "I'll see you at three then."

She didn't answer him, but they both knew she'd be climbing into his car in that black hour of the morning.

As he gathered up his house plans and took his leave, she wondered why it was that she couldn't seem to do what was best in this situation. Her business was all but sold, after all, and the longer she put off telling Grady that she was moving, the worse it was going to be. Still, no matter when she did it, she was going to rip out his great big heart, and she didn't know how either one of them was going to survive that.

Thankfully, he had not declared himself, and she hoped to heaven that he never would. She didn't know how she could bear it if he did, which was all the more reason to tell him her plans before they reached that point.

But surely she should tell Vaughn first. If his reaction was negative, she'd have to put her plans on hold, after all, in which case there was no reason to upset anyone. Which was just another excuse for keeping quiet.

"Oh, Lord in heaven, what am I doing?" she whispered, but for once she found no answers.

All she knew was that she couldn't make herself do what she knew she should. She'd never expected to be so torn between two loves. Yet, what choice was there, really, for a mother with a son who needed both of his parents?

The last time they'd made this trip, Grady would rather have taken a beating than be going to South Carolina. Now he wished he could get on that plane with Paige. He knew better than to suggest it, though. For one thing, Dan was flying down to Georgia tomorrow in order to take a deposition on Monday from a witness to an auto accident, and it was their policy that, if possible, both of them not be out of town at the same time. More importantly, Paige would only have said no.

He wasn't sure, even now, what the problem was. In the beginning he'd assumed that she feared Vaughn would object to her being with any man other than his father. Now he suspected that it was more than that, mostly because the kid definitely seemed to be warming up to him.

The two hadn't actually spoken again, but they had exchanged several e-mails. That Vaughn was clever had never been in doubt, but he'd turned out to be something of a wit, too, which Grady found quite entertaining. Like most eleven-year-olds, Vaughn definitely had a selfish bent. He'd hinted broadly that he wanted something which Grady had taken it upon himself to supply. Now Grady feared that Paige would think he'd overstepped, which was why he waited until they reached Tulsa to bring it up.

"I have something for Vaughn. Will you give it to him?"

She glanced over at him just as he put on his blinker for the airport exit. "What is it?"

"Reach behind your seat."

She frowned as she leaned to one side and groped blindly behind her. They'd come to a halt at a red light on the service road to the highway by the time she got a hand on the box and managed to drag it into her lap.

"A *cell phone?*"

"It's not your usual sort," he told her quickly. "It will only dial 9-1-1 and four preprogrammed numbers. I put in your number, mine, his dad's and his hockey coach."

Her next question was predictable. "What did this cost?"

"Irrelevant."

Her mouth tightened. "What's the monthly charge then?"

He considered stonewalling her, but the look on her face clearly indicated that he'd pushed it as far as it was going to go, so he told her. She seemed pleasantly surprised. Opening the box, she took out the small, sturdy, neon bright phone.

"It has a tether," he pointed out, "and a counter to let him know how many minutes he's got left for the month. That can be tracked online, too."

After a moment, she sighed and conceded, "It's perfect."

Grady relaxed. The light changed, and he drove through the intersection. The airport lay straight ahead.

"I thought so. It may not be what he had in mind when he wrote me that if he had his own cell phone he wouldn't have to wait for his dad to 'loosen up' before he could talk to you whenever he wanted, but it's a pretty fail-safe plan."

She dropped the phone back into its packing slot and closed the box, saying, "He asked me for a cell some time ago, but I didn't know about this option, so I told him no."

"Guess that explains why he tapped me," Grady said. "He probably figured I could afford it, too, and he was right about that."

"Nevertheless, I will pay you for this and take over the monthly plan."

Grady signaled for a right turn. "If you pay for the phone, then it won't be a gift from me, now will it?"

"Grady, you've already given him too much."

"I'll concede on the monthly plan," he said, making the turn, "but he asked *me* for the phone, and I want to give it to him. So let's compromise, okay?"

"And if I don't accept your compromise?"

He moved over a lane, following the sign for departures, and said, "Then I'll mail him the phone. And hope Nolan doesn't get to it first."

She threw up her hands, demanding, "How do you always do this? No matter how hard I try to be fair and smart and reasonable, you always manage to get your way!"

His temper suddenly flared. "*My* way?" he snapped. "Oh, baby, I'm so far from getting *my* way that it's not even funny!"

He swerved the car into the first vacant spot in front of the terminal and threw the transmission into park. Hanging one elbow on the steering wheel, he twisted sideways in his seat to face her. The look of misery on her face stopped him cold. Whatever anger or frustration he'd felt evaporated like a puff of breath on a frosty morning. Instantly contrite, he wrapped a hand around the nape of her neck and pulled her head to his.

"I'm sorry. I didn't mean to shout."

"No, I'm sorry," she said miserably. "So very, very sorry. You have every reason to be upset with me, more than you even know. Oh, Grady, I'm going to br—"

Suddenly panicked, he kissed her just to shut her

up, and a very effective means it was, too, until he tasted her tears. Puzzled, he drew back, holding her face in his hands.

"Paige?" To his shock, she began to sob. He wrapped his arms around her. "Honey, a few sharp words are not worth this."

"It's not that. You d-don't understand."

"Tell me."

A car ahead of them pulled away from the curb, and a passing courtesy bus blew its horn. The place was surprisingly busy for so early in the morning. She glanced at the clock on the dash, scrubbing at her face.

"I can't. I have to g-go." She sucked in a deep breath. "But when I get back, we have to talk."

"Fine," he said, brushing at her tears. "Just don't cry anymore. I can't stand it. Rips me up inside."

She closed her eyes, and when she opened them again, the sorrow that he saw there cut like a knife. He'd have done anything, said anything to banish that look. What he did, what he said, had been coming for a long time. He'd have chosen a different time and place if he could have, and he might have worded it more eloquently, but that wouldn't have changed the truth of it.

"You must know that I love you." Her impossibly wide eyes grew larger still, and her bottom lip trembled, but she slowly nodded. It was an oddly solemn moment, one of the most significant of his life, and every bit of the doubt that had dogged him for weeks fell away. "You love me, too, don't you?"

She didn't deny it. She tried to. He watched her try to pull back, to rein in the wealth of emotion in her eyes. And he watched her fail. He wrapped his arms around her again, and this time she reciprocated, clasping him tightly.

"Try to remember that when I get back, will you?" she whispered brokenly.

As if he could forget!

Suddenly she pulled away and had her car door open before he could react. Grinning like an idiot, he hopped out and unlocked the trunk, hurrying around to lift out her single bag and carry it to the curb. She took it from him and immediately backed away. He stood watching her, one hand lifted in farewell, until she turned and strode swiftly toward the terminal.

She loved him.

He pumped a fist and tilted back his head. "Yesss!" It was the most heartfelt prayer of thanks he'd every uttered.

Despite her eagerness to see her son again, Paige couldn't seem to lift the funk that had settled over her in Tulsa. All through the flight to Atlanta she felt on the verge of despair, and when she tried to pray she found herself alternating between morose confession and angrily demanding that God fix this mess that she had created.

How had it happened? She'd known from the

moment she'd decided to let Vaughn return to his father that she'd have to move to South Carolina herself. It was the only way she could be as much a part of his life as he needed her to be, the only way she could be sure that he was well cared for and safe. Yet she'd let herself grow closer and closer to Grady and vice versa.

Now, not only would she have to tell Grady the truth as soon as she got back to Tulsa, she was going to spend this whole trip dreading it. No doubt it served her right, but it wasn't fair to Vaughn, let alone Grady, who had no inkling of what was coming. Tormented by guilt, she paced the length of the terminal in Atlanta during her layover, but nothing could remove the sound of his words from his ears.

You must know that I love you.

Of course she'd known! How could she not? He'd shown her every way imaginable. Hearing him say it had produced a thrill unlike any other—and shame, deep, horrific shame.

She didn't think she'd ever get past it, nor should she for it was nothing less than she deserved. Grady, on the other hand, deserved only joy and respect and consideration, none of which she had given him.

By the time she reached Greenville, rented a car and found the ice rink where Vaughn was playing hockey, the game was in the middle of the second period. He spotted her when he came off the ice during a line change and waved so she'd know it was him.

Even at a distance she couldn't miss the welcome

in that simple gesture, and neither did Nolan. He was sitting right behind the team bench and turned his head to glare at her when Vaughn waved. She ignored him.

Nolan had done plenty to hurt her, but she hadn't been a perfect wife to him, either. Much of the time she'd been absolutely clueless. Still, she'd have worked at their marriage for the rest of her life if he hadn't walked away. Thinking about it now, though, she knew that at the best of times her feelings for Nolan paled in comparison to what she felt for Grady. But that didn't change anything.

Nolan had cost her three-and-a-half years with her son, and if she worked hard at it, she could even blame him for the hurt she was about to cause Grady. Unfortunately, that wouldn't let her off the hook. She was as guilty of crimes of the heart as Nolan, but all she could do now was fulfill her responsibilities to her son as well as she was able.

Paige sucked in a few deep breaths and concentrated on the hockey game. It wasn't long before Vaughn was back in action. Even before that Paige realized that the general level of play in this league was higher than what she'd seen in Arkansas, but Vaughn stood out here, too. He seemed to be showing off for her benefit, a supposition confirmed as soon as he left the ice at the end of the game.

"Did you see me make the winning goal?"

"I did, honey. Good job!"

Nolan appeared at her elbow and took Vaughn's

helmet, into which Vaughn had dropped his mouthpiece. "Good game there, sport. Guess those new skates were worth the money, after all, huh? But then your mother's always known how to get her money's worth."

Vaughn immediately shuttered his expression and began slipping plastic covers on to the blades of his skates. "I gotta shower and change so we can go, Mom, but I'll be real quick."

"I'll wait right here."

Vaughn looked at his father long and hard before stiffly walking away. Paige stared straight ahead, waiting. Vaughn was barely out of sight before Nolan made his first verbal jab.

"I can't believe you thought you'd win him over with expensive skates and other junk."

"I just wanted him to play hockey, Nolan, because I hoped it would make him happy."

"But it didn't, did it? Because *this* is where he wants to be. With me."

"I know that."

"The two of us do things you never could," Nolan went on smugly, "things that boys like."

"I know that, too."

"Then why are you here? Why punish yourself like this? You could be doing something fun back in Arkansas. You've got friends there, *boy*friends, even." She looked at him then, surprised to see anger in his brown eyes. "Vaughn told me. Did you think he wouldn't?"

She shook her head and said only, "I'm here because I love my son and he needs me."

"For what? He's been just fine without you. We both have. Now that he's getting older we can do even more together, the really good stuff."

"He's not your playmate, Nolan."

That's what Vaughn was to him, she realized suddenly, not a son to be guided and taught and provided for into manhood but a permanent buddy, and Vaughn was so anxious for the love and approval of his father that he found ways to pick up the slack and forgive the failures he probably couldn't even identify but nevertheless felt. She knew because she had once done the same thing: overlooked the slights, ignored the selfishness, pretended that Nolan cared when his every action had demonstrated otherwise. She'd given in, gone along, whatever it had taken to hold on to the illusion that her husband would ultimately love her back.

This insight showed her, as nothing else could have, how much her son needed her. She truly had no choice but to move, no matter what it cost her personally. Already she grieved what she would leave behind in Arkansas, but her responsibility was to her son, and she would not, could not, shirk it.

"Vaughn wants and needs a mother," she told Nolan, "just as he wants and needs a father, and I intend to see to it that he has both from now on. We can be partners in this one area, Nolan, for his sake, or you can fight me. But you have to know that the more you fight me on this, the more you'll suffer in comparison."

"I don't have to 'fight' you," he sneered. "Vaughn's already chosen me. I'm the one he lives with. You're just a temporary distraction, a change of pace, and when you're not around he can't even be bothered with you. How long do you think he's going to get excited about the silly little weekends you cook up? He's almost a teenager. How much longer do you think he's going to want to spend his weekends with his mama?"

"Not long," she admitted.

That seemed to satisfy him immensely. "Better enjoy it while you can. That's all I've got to say."

He turned and strolled away as if he didn't have a care in the world, one hand in his jeans pocket, the other lightly swinging Vaughn's helmet. Paige shook her head. His world was about to change, had already changed, and he didn't even know it.

When Vaughn emerged still wet from his quick shower some moments later, his arms loaded with hockey gear, he glanced around apprehensively. "Dad take off?"

"Uh-huh." She reached for a set of pads, blithely changing the subject. "We have some time to kill. Any ideas?"

His smile stretched from ear to ear. "The guys told me about a cool arcade that's opened up in the old ice-cream shop. Wanna go?"

"Sure. You can wreck some race cars while I make

a few phone calls." They turned together toward the exit, hauling his gear.

"Who you calling?" Vaughn asked offhandedly.

Paige strengthened her smile. "Thought I'd check out a few Realtors around town. Know any good ones?"

Vaughn's steps slowed to a halt. He looked up at her, his face twisted. "Realtors? You mean, like, for houses?"

Paige nodded. Her heart beat slow and hard against the wall of her chest. "I thought it might be nice to have my own place here. What do you think?"

"Really? But how can you afford two places?"

"Well, there's someone back in Fayetteville who wants to buy my business. For quite a lot of money, as it turns out."

"That's great!" She wasn't certain if his enthusiasm was for the money or the idea of her having a house of her own here. Then he dropped his gear and threw his arms around her, declaring, "It'd be almost like you lived here!"

Pleased, she hugged him close. "Would you like that, son?"

He bent to retrieve his stuff. "Are you kidding? That'd be perfect!"

She hadn't intended to tell him all, only to sound him out on the subject of her moving here, but now she saw no point in holding back.

"Can you keep a secret, son? Just for a little while? I think I should move here." His jaw dropped, and then he literally leapt into the air, crowing like a rooster, so obviously pleased that she had to laugh. "You

wouldn't have to live with me, of course, if you don't
want to, but it would be a more normal life for both
of us, I think."

He hugged her so hard, that she thought he'd crack
a rib. She realized with a jolt that he was taller than
her now. Had he really grown so much in a few short
weeks? Trampling her foot in his excitement, he
skipped backward. She laughed again, blinking
rapidly. He was so happy! How could she be both
thrilled and on the verge of tears herself?

"What about Matthias?" he asked, suddenly
going still.

"I don't know. I haven't discussed it with him yet.
He may come with me, but more likely he'll stay in
Arkansas."

"If Matthias comes that means Howler will, too,
and it'll be like having my own dog!"

"You could have your own dog anyway, if you
want," she told him. "We'll just look for a house with
a fenced yard."

He whooped, then he threw an arm across her
shoulders, physically propelling her toward the door.
"Dad and me almost got us a place for a dog once,"
he babbled, "but he decided on the boat instead. I was
mad for a while, but you can't fish from a dog. Oh,
man! I can't believe it!"

They hurried to the car, him laughing and talking.
This was how it should be—except for the ache in her
chest. But she would face that later. Then Vaughn un-
wittingly robbed the moment of much of its joy.

"What happened?" he suddenly asked. "Did you and Grady break up or something?"

Paige froze in the act of unlocking the trunk of the car. "I don't know what you mean. We were never a couple, Vaughn. I told you that."

He seemed confused. "Looked that way to me."

"Well, it wasn't. Not really. Besides, I thought you resented Grady. Except for his car and money, of course."

"Grady's okay," he muttered.

"Yes, he is," Paige agreed softly, "but Grady has his life in Arkansas, and mine's here with you now."

He hugged her again. It was bittersweet balm.

"I'm sorry, Mom, for before," he told her in a small, cracking voice. "I guess I forgot some stuff, but it wasn't ever that I don't love you."

"I know, son."

"It's just that I love Dad, too."

"Of course, you do. I wouldn't want it any other way."

He looked up then, sadness in his eyes. "I know he's a mess. He's not like you. I guess it's all that Christian stuff. It's not so dumb as he says it is. Nothing's ever quite what Dad says it is. But he's still my dad, you know?"

Paige managed a nod and a wobbly smile before hugging him close one more time while she silently thanked God.

Her little boy had finally, at long last, come home. She couldn't ask for more than that.

No matter how much she might want to.

Chapter Fourteen

Grady had never considered himself an impulsive sort of fellow. His ex-wife had often complained about it, calling him unimaginative and inhibited. Now he knew that she'd been correct. But that was before.

This Grady, the *new* Grady, the reborn Grady, the in-love Grady, was startlingly imaginative. He made up entire scenarios in his head, visions of himself and Paige and, oddly enough, Vaughn, living together in that big house on the hill that was already taking shape in his mind. He even imagined other occupants of that dream house: Matthias; his father, Howard. And babies. Little blond babies with big, sea-green eyes.

He had become a daydreamer. His father remarked on it Saturday, the very next morning, after he'd driven Paige to Tulsa. Howard had just made a perfect long drive on the seventeenth hole. Grady missed it entirely, realizing that something noteworthy had taken place only when the group of golfers waiting behind them broke into applause.

Glancing around sheepishly, Grady caught the congratulatory statements of the foursome awaiting their turn at the tee. He dropped the club upon which he'd been leaning into the wheeled bag at his elbow, saying, "Good one, Dad."

"Yessir, the old man's still got it!" Howard crowed, doing a little jig and playfully poking his son in the midsection with the head of his club. "And you, son, have got it bad."

Grady lifted his eyebrows. "I don't know what you're talking about."

Howard winked at the golfer teeing up beside him and threw a companionable arm around his son's shoulders as they started off down the hillock. "I am talking," he said in a conspiratorial tone, "about Paige."

Grady grimaced. "Who told you about her?"

"Who do you think? Dan says she's quite remarkable and about as far from Robin as she can get." He slid his club into the bag that Grady pulled behind him. They were so alike in build and size that they played with the same clubs.

Grady should've realized his family would be talking about this.

Howard shoved his hands into the pockets of his jacket, matching his steps to his son's, and remarked, "Dan says she reminds him of your mother." He smiled. "What a gal she was, that Bea, wonderful wife and mother. I miss her."

Grady smiled. "Me, too."

"Used to be, when you were daydreaming like that," Howard said, waving a finger at the top of the hill, "I knew you were thinking of her, remembering her. Did my heart good." He sighed, adding, "Been a long time since I caught you daydreaming about your mother, and you know what? This is better."

"Yes, it is." Grady chuckled, remembering how embarrassed he'd been as a teenager because thoughts of his mother could still reduce him to tears on occasion. He was rather proud of that now. Thoughts of Paige brought all sorts of other emotions to the surface, and he couldn't be ashamed about those, either.

"After you're settled," Howard was saying, "I may have to think about getting married again myself."

Grady barked laughter, completely shocked that his father was talking about marriage. He was even more shocked at his own reaction. With sudden clarity he realized that not too long ago he'd have been angry and hurt if his father had dared to mention remarriage. It had been thirty-three years since his mother's death, and only now was he somehow able to let her go. And he'd thought Vaughn was pigheaded! All the kid had ever done was try to hang on somehow to those he loved.

"What?" Howard asked, glancing over at him, "you don't think this old rooster could talk some old hen into building a nest with him?" He didn't wait for a reply but admitted baldly, "I'm tired of being alone. I'll never love again like I loved your mother, but once like that is enough in any lifetime."

That, too, Grady understood. Such love was rare and to be treasured. It should be grasped with both hands and held close. This time it was Grady who slung an arm across his father's shoulders in a grateful, affectionate hug. Then he simply left the bag standing in the pathway on its little wheeled cart and strode off across the green toward the parking lot.

"Where are you going?" his father demanded.

"Jewelry store," Grady called over his shoulder.

"This means I'm the winner, you know!" Howard crowed.

"We're both winners, Dad," Grady replied.

Actually, they were blessed. So blessed.

Paige waited until just before she left town to give Vaughn the cell phone. Thrilled, he saw instantly that it did much more than she'd realized.

"Games. Cool."

"Really?"

"Sure. See? It even downloads ring tones. Can I get one?"

"Uh, okay."

"I guess Grady told you to buy it, huh?"

"Actually, Grady is entirely responsible for this," Paige told him. "Grady bought the phone. I'm paying the monthly charge. Four hundred and fifty minutes a month, Vaughn, and not a minute more. All right?"

He dropped the tether over his head. "That's like fifteen minutes a day."

"Your math is still good, I see." He chuckled and

scuffed a toe in the dirt, his hockey gear piled on the apartment landing behind him. "Do me a favor will you?" she asked. "Call Grady and thank him, but not until tomorrow. Okay?" She didn't want Vaughn breaking the news to Grady before she could.

"Sure. Okay."

She smiled and ruffled his hair. "Be responsible with this, and we'll see about getting you a regular cell phone later. Deal?"

"Deal." He looped his arms around her neck, and she kissed his cheek. "See you soon." Dropping his arms, he backed away and slapped a hand over the phone hanging against his chest, saying, "Thanks, Mom. For everything."

She smiled. "You're welcome. For everything. Gotta go." She moved toward the car. "You better be calling me," she tossed over one shoulder.

"I will."

She drove off toward Greenville and left him standing there in front of the apartment building, smiling happily. Everything was going to be fine now, she told herself, setting her sights on the airport. Everything was going to be just fine. Once she got through tonight, all would be just as it should be. She swallowed down dread and prayed for strength.

Grady prowled the arrival area at the airport like a cabby looking for a fare. A little red velvet box burned a hole in his jean jacket pocket. He pictured the ring inside and suddenly worried that it was too big and gaudy. Then he saw Paige emerge from the terminal onto the sidewalk and all at once that two-carat center diamond didn't seem nearly big enough, let alone the pair of smaller ones set deeply into the smooth platinum band. They could always take it back, he reminded himself, maneuvering his way to the curb a little way past her. The sales manager had said so. He killed the engine and got out, lifting a hand in greeting.

"Hey, beautiful, need a ride?" Looking serious, she hurried toward him, her little bag rolling behind her. He popped the trunk and tossed the overnight case inside, asking, "You hungry?"

"Yes, uh, no. Grady, we need to talk."

"My thought exactly." He winked at her, refusing the impulse to drop a kiss on those sweet lips. She'd realize how badly he was trembling! He hurried around and opened the door for her. "Get in. I know a quiet little place where we can go and talk privately."

"Oh, I'm not really dressed to go out." She looked down at the neat, slender khaki slacks that she wore with a simple moss-green sweater set and backless flats.

"It's casual," he assured her, standing there in blue jeans and a polo shirt, "and you look great."

She got into the car, murmuring, "Thanks."

He jogged around and slid behind the wheel. "Vaughn like the phone?"

"Oh, boy, did he ever. He'll call you tomorrow."

"Excellent. Everything go okay then?"

"Very much so."

"Terrific. How was the hockey game?" He felt her relax.

"I'm no expert, as you know, but from what I saw, Jason Lowery would love to get his hands on that whole team. Either one, actually."

They talked hockey all the way downtown. He dropped the car with the valet at the lot across the street from the restaurant and took Paige by the hand, somewhat surprised when she pulled back.

"Grady, I'm not so certain this is a good idea."

"No, it is," he assured her. "Trust me on this. I checked the place out."

She gulped, pulled the sides of her little cardigan together and nodded, stepping off the curb. He slipped his hand around the bend of her elbow and escorted her.

The foyer of the restaurant was small and dark. Music played softly in the background, accented perfectly by the gentle clink of flatware against china. The fortyish man behind the reservation stand wore pleated slacks and a dress shirt with an open collar. Grady breathed a silent sigh of relief as he showed them to their table, which was in a quiet corner, just as Grady had requested. He had never been big on potted ferns, but the enormous one that separated the table from the rest of the room got an approving smile from him. Menus were placed in front of them. They both decided on the stuffed pasta shells, beef medallions and house salads.

"This is a nice place," Paige commented, looking through the greenery at the room beyond.

Grady nodded, aware of a waterfall pattering softly somewhere out of sight. He hoped this little restaurant would be a special place, a very special place. They discussed its merits until the food came, the consensus being that it was comfortable but not pretentious, relaxing but not boring, old-school but not old-fashioned. The place was busy in a quiet, familiar fashion.

The quality of the food gave them something else to talk about. By tacit agreement, they said grace silently, bowing their heads in unison, each with his or her own personal entreaty. They didn't hold hands. Paige kept hers in her lap, and in a way Grady was glad. Nerves made his hands quiver, and he didn't want to give himself away until the right moment.

The moment came as they waited for dessert, which they had been warned could take some time but would be worth the wait as the chocolate soufflé with fresh berries and sweetened cream was the house specialty and best served straight from the oven.

"Maybe I'll have room for it by the time it arrives," Paige mused. "I don't know what possessed me to agree to dessert. It just sounds so good."

"I'm glad you like this place," Grady told her, reaching for the hand that she'd briefly rested beside her tea glass. He slipped the other into his pocket. "I spent hours yesterday researching the Internet until I found just the right place for this."

She blinked at him, going very still.

His heart was pounding like a big brass drum as he placed the small velvet-covered box in the center of the table and softly asked, "Will you marry me, sweetheart? Say yes. I promise I'll—"

She pulled her hand from his and pressed it to her mouth. Even then he didn't realize that the whole world had come crashing down, not until she closed her eyes, fisted both hands against the edge of the table and whispered, "Grady, I can't marry you. I'm moving to South Carolina at the end of the month."

She never looked at the ring, never even opened the box. She couldn't. It hurt too much just to have it sitting there, a reproach in red velvet, a dream never to be realized, a promise never to be spoken. This was a sacrifice that she made unwillingly and perhaps not even graciously when all was said and done, but for the life of her, she could do nothing else.

The rushed, apologetic explanations and whispered recriminations did nothing to take the ache from her heart or the glazed, wooden disappointment from his face. Even that proved preferable to the silent, shattering pain that seemed to envelop each of them individually. Regret too deep to be imagined kept tears trembling on the rims of her eyes, but she couldn't shed them. She didn't feel she had the right to cry, not after a single glance at his ravaged face. Oh, why hadn't she told him sooner? How had she let this happen?

They left before the dessert came. It was more than an hour later as they drove through the deepening night before he cleared his throat and asked if she was sure.

"It's the only solution I can find, Grady. Vaughn

needs me so much, and he's so thrilled, so happy. I have to do it."

He swallowed and asked what arrangements she'd made. She told him. "I accepted an offer to buy my business before I left. What happens to the house will depend upon Matthias. If he elects to go with me, I'll probably find an agent to lease it. If not, it will remain his home. He doesn't know, by the way."

Grady's mouth twisted wryly at that. "At least I'm not the only one you've kept in the dark."

"I wasn't sure it would happen at first, and then I just didn't know how to tell you. I did try to warn you, though."

"Yes, you did," he admitted.

"I should have told you I was thinking of it."

"Why didn't you?"

"I guess I just kept hoping..." She didn't say what she'd hoped for; he didn't ask.

She thought of a dozen compromises and as many reasons why they wouldn't work. How could she even suggest that he leave his family and business, his career, the dream house he'd just contracted to build? How could she ask him to give up all that in order to be second in her life? She couldn't ask it of him, and he didn't offer.

The silence ate at her like acid, so that by the time they pulled up to her yard she felt raw and prickly, as if she were held together with barbed wire. He grimly got out and walked her to the porch, carrying her bag stiffly in one hand. There in the darkness the tears finally slipped free.

"I guess some things just aren't meant to be," he whispered.

She gulped, keening inside, and said raggedly, "I'm sorry, Grady. So very sorry. You've been good to us, and you can't begin to believe how I'll miss you, but I have to do this for my son."

"My brother says you remind him of our mother," Grady said in a voice that had an otherworldly quality to it, almost an eeriness. "I thought she was the best mother in the world. I guess she was. And that must mean Dan's right."

She felt him step back then. A shudder passed between them, a blackness as despairing as hopelessness and loss could be. It lifted gooseflesh on her arms and neck. Suddenly he seemed to be far away, a great gulf yawning between them.

"Goodbye, Paige."

She almost cried out, knowing that she would not see him again. Still, she couldn't give him the farewell he deserved. The words simply were not in her. She found herself sitting on the step before she even realized that her legs had given out.

Everything was all wrong suddenly. Matthias hadn't come to the door as he usually did. Home wasn't waiting just up these steps anymore. This time she had pushed Grady away and he had not reached out to pull her in again.

When a cold nose pressed tentatively against the back of her neck, she was pathetically grateful. Reaching around, she locked her hands in Howler's collar and buried her face in the dog's thick black neck. With a snuffle and a scrabble the fat old thing flopped down on her lap, crushing her beneath warm, smelly weight. The dog sat patiently while she sobbed, much as Vaughn must have done on that night when she had begun to let him go.

She tried to let go of Grady in the same way, second by second, tear by tear, prayer by prayer. But this time there was nothing to cling to, no great gamble, no half-formed plan, no feverish hope.

This time there was only loss.

Grady sat in the dark, his head in his hands. He'd plopped down onto the cassock that stood in front of the easy chair in his neat-to-the-point-of-stark living room after coming home from work. The day had been interminable, even for a Monday, and he was exhausted. Just moving by rote, which was all he was capable of just now, required enormous effort.

The only saving grace was that Dan had been held over in Georgia another day, so at least he hadn't had to face a family inquisition. Yet. It would come, though. Even if he tried to pretend that his heart hadn't been ripped out, Dan would know. He'd known after Robin had left.

Grady had come home alone for the weekend. Nothing unusual in that. Robin had rarely accompanied him on those visits. It had been surprisingly easy to pretend that she was home doing whatever it was that she did while he was gone. Howard hadn't suspected a thing, but within the first ten minutes Dan had demanded to know what was wrong.

Grady didn't think he could manage a pretense this time. He wasn't even sure he could manage to live. He ought to get up and eat, but he couldn't seem to make himself do it. Instead he sat, trying not to think or feel or even breathe. He didn't even know what he was doing in here. He hardly ever came into this room, preferring instead to watch TV from his bed when he was home.

Home. This house had never been a home. It was just a place to sleep and change his clothes. The house itself was nothing special, certainly not pretentious— three bedrooms, one of which he'd outfitted but never really used as a home office, and two baths—but it was large enough for a small family. Yet, he'd never thought of making a family here.

He'd never thought of making a family at all, really, not even when he was married to Robin. Somehow the subject of children had never come up with them. But Paige, now Paige was all about being a mother, and he had started to think, to believe, that the two of them together would somehow become three or four or five or....

That was a dream which would never be realized. Like the house on the hill that they'd planned, it would simply never take shape. That was a house for a family, and he knew now that he would never have a family of his own. If he couldn't have it with Paige, it just wasn't meant to be. She was the only woman who didn't make him feel alien and awkward and stupid.

That didn't explain why he hadn't seen this coming. The moment she'd said that she was moving to South Carolina, he'd seen all the signs in retrospect. He couldn't understand how he could have gotten it all so wrong. Again. He hadn't understood his life at six years of age or after his divorce, and he didn't understand it now.

What hurt most was that she hadn't asked him to go with her, hadn't even hinted at such a thing. She had to know that he would. Once before he'd moved for a woman, walked away from his family business, established himself in a strange town. Did Paige think he wouldn't do it again? Obviously she hadn't known what sort of fool she was dealing with. Or was there more to it?

The very idea that she might be getting back together with Nolan made Grady queasy, but it had to be considered. He knew to what lengths she would go to please Vaughn, but was that all it was? She hadn't prosecuted Nolan when ninety-nine out of a hundred women would have. She hadn't wanted to cause him pain, hadn't wanted to see him punished, had gone against expert advice to keep the lines of communication open, had sent her son back to him rather than meet him in open court. Yet, not once had Grady considered that Paige might still care for her ex-husband.

Fool didn't quite cover what he was.

The cell phone in the front pocket of his coat

vibrated. Not wanting to be disturbed, he'd set it on vibrate before he'd picked up Paige at the airport yesterday evening, and he'd left it on vibrate because he still didn't want to be disturbed. He didn't want to talk to anyone, see anyone, be with anyone, not now, not when he hurt this badly.

All the way home from Paige's house last night he'd kept looking down, expecting to see a great, bloody, gaping hole in his chest. At first he'd been too stunned to feel much of anything, but it hadn't taken long for the anguish to come, and now it wouldn't go away.

The phone vibrated again. It lay heavily against his ribs, and the vibration sent a sharp tingle deep into his chest. Grady straightened, stretching out his arm to move his jacket away from his body, and then he remembered once before when he'd meant to ignore this phone. If he hadn't answered it then, would Paige be moving to South Carolina?

"Oh, God," he whispered, "what do I do now?"

He didn't expect an answer, but he didn't expect something to crawl up his back, either. In an instant he was on his feet, certain that he was not alone. Whirling around, he expected to see… What?

It was pitch dark, shadows upon shadows. He reached for the lamp on the side table and nearly tipped it over before he got it on. Even before light flooded the room, he knew what he would see. No one. Nothing, at least nothing out of the ordinary. Still, he stood uncertainly for a moment. Was he losing his mind? Or was someone trying to tell him something?

Turning in a slow circle, he took stock. The couch sat against the wall as always. The drapes were drawn. The glass inset in the coffee table gleamed. The house was stuffy, as usual, and sterile, as usual, and empty. As usual.

You are never alone, he thought suddenly. *Perhaps you won't be with Paige, but you will never be alone.*

Sucking in his breath, he pushed his hands over his face, surprised to feel the dampness of tears on his cheeks. That was when he realized that the phone had not vibrated again. Whoever had called had thought better of it.

It could have been Dan, their dad, any of a dozen people, but he knew, even as he tugged the phone from his pocket who had called. Paige had told him to expect it, after all, before she'd destroyed his world. He flipped the phone open and pushed two buttons in succession in order to bring the number on to the tiny screen, and then he pushed another to dial it. The screen told him that he was calling Vaughn and then that Vaughn had answered. Grady put the phone to his ear and cleared his throat.

"Hello?"

"Hey, it does work. I was starting to think you'd bought me a bum phone, big guy."

Big guy. Grady smiled in spite of everything. "I just didn't get to it before."

"That's okay. Mom didn't answer, either, so I thought maybe it wasn't working or I wasn't doing it right or something."

Grady bit his tongue to keep from asking about Paige. "Hard to do anything wrong with that phone from what I understand."

"Yeah, I know, but I thought maybe something got messed up when I downloaded a new ring tone."

"Ah."

"Or, uh, when Dad threw it."

Grady's free hand went to his waist, and a whole lot of anger that he was doing his best to suppress came roaring to life. "Your father *threw* the phone?"

"He's kinda upset," Vaughn mumbled. "He's always upset about something these days."

Grady frowned, unable to imagine what Nolan Ellis would have to be upset about. "What do you mean?"

"I already know he lied to me," Vaughn wailed, "so what difference does it make if I see Mom?" Grady pressed his temples as Vaughn rushed on. "He's the one making everything tough. She's the one doing everything to make it better. I don't know why he's so mad just 'cause I wanna be with them both. What's he care if she buys me a phone? Which she didn't. Thanks, by the way."

"You're welcome," Grady rumbled absently. So Paige *wasn't* going back to Nolan. Sighing with relief, Grady rubbed a hand over his chin, feeling the rasp of the beard that he sometimes had to shave twice a day.

"Did she really keep him from coming to Arkansas?" Vaughn asked in a thin, choked voice.

Grady tried to think. Had Paige kept Nolan out of Arkansas? "Actually," he said, "I did that. She didn't fight me on it, like she did everything else, but I took it upon myself to secure an order barring your father from coming to Arkansas. I was worried, Vaughn. When she wouldn't put him in jail I tried to see to it that he couldn't come here and take you away again."

"But there's no reason she can't move here if she wants to, is there?" Vaughn asked.

Grady gulped. "No. None."

"So he can't keep her from seeing me?"

"He sure can't. Not legally."

"Okay. I didn't think so, but he says stuff when he's mad. You know?"

Gripping the phone a little tighter, Grady asked, "Did he say he'd keep your mom from seeing you, Vaughn?"

"Yeah, but he can't, can he? I told him, I want her to come. If she moves here, it'll be like it used to be when…when I was a real kid and she took care of everything. When she took care of me."

A real kid. Grady swallowed. "I remember when my mom used to take care of me," he said. "I didn't know what a wonderful thing that was until I didn't have it anymore. But after she died, my dad took care of me. He took good care of me, Vaughn. It didn't make up for my mom being gone, but he was a good father. He still is. Doesn't your dad take care of you, Vaughn?"

Vaughn snorted. "No. More like I take care of him. He's in there drinking now, and when he passes out I'm not putting him to bed, and I'm not making him coffee in the morning when he's hung over, either."

Grady shook his head. No wonder Paige was

moving to South Carolina. What else could she do? "I'm sorry, Vaughn," he said. "Does he drink often?"

"Yeah, but he don't get drunk all that much, not at home, anyway. He doesn't really stay home much. He likes to be out doing stuff, you know. He's got the boat and the bike and the bow and arrow and his bowling team and golf and his online games, and he *really* likes to go to the drag races."

"Do you get to go along?"

"Sometimes."

"But mostly you stay home alone, don't you?"

"Yeah," Vaughn admitted in a small voice.

"Well, I tell you what you do, Vaughn," Grady said. "You call me anytime you want, and if I'm not in a courtroom or with a client, we'll talk. Okay?"

"Okay. But Mom says I just get 450 minutes a month. That's like fifteen minutes a day, and she can talk that much without even saying anything."

Grady chuckled. "Well, there's still e-mail. That's almost as good." He closed his eyes, adding softly, "Besides, she'll be down there with you before long, won't she?"

"Yeah. Hey, you don't play games online, do you? Dad's got this headset, and you can, like, talk to your buddies while you're playing. I play all the time when Dad's not home. It don't cost anything once you've got the setup. But you probably don't play."

Grady smiled at himself. *Now* the kid wanted to be buddies. "I do as soon as I get my hands on a system and you tell me what games."

"Cool!"

Vaughn excitedly rattled off everything Grady could ever want to know about operating systems and headsets and half a dozen different games. He gave Grady a list of screen tags he used, his favorite being SCaB, for South Carolina Boy. Grady promised to call as soon as he got set up. The whole thing was going to be a fiasco, of course. Vaughn was going to trounce him. Grady knew beans about video gaming, but what else did he have to do? Paige might be out of his life, but it looked as if he'd made a friend in Vaughn, at least. That was something, and maybe...

No, he wouldn't think about using Vaughn to stay close to Paige. If she wasn't going back to Nolan, then she just didn't want him, Grady, going to South Carolina with her.

After Vaughn got off the phone, Grady took a deep breath, and it still hurt, but it did seem that he was going to live.

And you're never alone, he reminded himself again, looking around. *Even when you're by yourself, you're never alone. You're always with God.*

That was more than he'd had before, and more than enough to get him through this. Who knew? Someday God might bring another woman into his life, and if not, well, one Paige in a lifetime was all any man could ask for.

Chapter Fifteen

"Grady?"

The voice woke him from a deep, exhausted sleep. Only when he cleared his throat in order to reply did Grady realize that he held the phone pressed to his ear. Obviously he'd plucked it off the bedside table in robotic response to its buzz.

Blinking into the darkness, Grady demanded, "Who is this?"

"It's me."

"Vaughn?" Grady sat straight up in the bed, one thing clear in the jumble of his sleep-fogged brain. "Something's wrong."

"Matthias was right, Grady. My dad did steal me from my mom, and he's trying to do it again."

Grady pivoted to drop his legs off the side of the bed, his mind kicking into high gear. "Your dad's going to run. He wants to hide you from your mom again because she's moving to Greenville to be near you." Somehow, he realized, he'd expected this, maybe even counted on it.

"Yes," Vaughn said. "He started packing boxes after I went to sleep, but I woke up, and I saw him. He says we've got to. He says she's gonna try to get money out of him, that I'll go to live with her and then the courts will try to make him pay again. He says..." Grady could hear the confusion in the pause. "He says he's not gonna let her win."

That was some *game* Nolan Ellis was playing, Grady thought darkly. To Vaughn he said, "You can't let him leave with you."

"I know. I went out the window. Could you come get me?"

Grady paused in the act of rubbing a hand over his face. "Are you telling me that you've run away from your father?"

"I had to! He was gonna make me go with him. I had to. Can't you just come get me?"

"Vaughn, I'm a whole day away from you, *provided* I can even get a flight. You've got to call 9-1-1."

"But they'll send me to that home again, and they'll arrest him."

"I can't promise that Nolan won't pay a price this time, but you know your mom won't do anything without talking to you first. And what if he finds you, Vaughn? What then? Do you never want to see your mom again until you're grown?"

"No."

"Listen to me. My brother Dan is in Augusta,

Georgia. I'll get him to you as quick as I can. He's an attorney, too. He can take care of this, but it's going to take some time, so just tell me where you are, and I'll have the authorities come get you."

A pause followed, during which Grady held his breath. Then Vaughn said, "There's a park with a pavilion and basketball courts. It's on Scot's Trace Trail."

"You stay at that park until someone comes for you, Vaughn. Promise me."

"Yeah, okay."

"I mean it. It'll kill your mom if she loses you again. Please, buddy, let me handle this. Will you?"

"That's why I called you."

Grady heaved a sigh. "Thank you, Vaughn. Don't worry, and keep that phone with you. I'll be in touch soon."

"I don't want my dad to be like this," Vaughn wailed in a tiny voice. Grady could tell that he was crying.

"I know. Maybe we can help him be different, Vaughn. We'll ask God to help us with that, okay?"

"Okay." Vaughn sniffed. "Maybe you better call my mom," he said. "I think I've used up my fifteen minutes."

Grady had to swallow his chuckle. "No problem."

The next several minutes were fraught with heart-pounding anxiety. Because his file with all the pertinent Greenville telephone numbers was at the office, he had to race to the computer and get on the Internet to find what he needed. While he was doing that, he called Dan. It was four in the morning on the east coast, but Dan rose without complaint to dress and pack and head to the airport. Grady was already punching the number of the Greenville County Sheriff's office into his home phone when he got off the cell with Dan.

The sheriff's deputy to whom Grady spoke agreed to give the heads-up to the Greenville police, freeing Grady to play two-phone tag with three different airlines until he got Dan booked on a flight to Charlotte and another in to Greenville. That looked like a roundabout way to do things to Grady, but it was apparently the fastest route. He called Vaughn to tell him that Dan should be with him shortly after seven-thirty.

Vaughn did not answer.

In a panic, Grady picked up the phone to finally call Paige. He hit his knees instead, begging God to spare her the agony of losing her son again.

He made every argument he could think of, pointing out what a really good person she was: kind, thoughtful, generous. She'd given Matthias a home and stood by him even when his past had presented problems for her. She'd built a business from scratch, without compromising her ethics even once. She hadn't punished Nolan, hadn't sought any retribution, and she'd done everything, everything, for the sake of her son.

Paige was blameless, even in her dealings with him. He'd known she was holding back, holding him off, and he'd ignored that, worked his way around her, pushed and pushed a little more, until she'd had no

choice but to hurt him. He would never regret what
had happened between the two of them because, if
nothing else, she'd shown him the reality of God, the
way to a personal relationship with his own Maker.
Now he was making his best case to that Great Judge
on her behalf.

This life was not fair. Grady knew it well. Otherwise,
would his own mother have died in a senseless accident
when he was only six years old? Would Nolan have
stolen Vaughn from his mother in the first place? Would
Matthias have lost everything to a charlatan and a
fraud? Life was not fair, but God would always be God,
with the power to answer prayer and reward right.

"And she's tried so hard to do what's right, Lord,"
he said, *"for everyone, in every situation. You know
her heart. You know how hard she's tried and how
much she's already suffered. I beg You to spare her
this. I don't ask You to punish Nolan, just don't let him
keep Vaughn away from his mother. Please."*

He didn't know how long he implored the
Almighty, but when his cell rang again, he knew that
it was the answer to his prayer, one way or another.
He was entirely correct. It was the Greenville County
Sheriff's office. Vaughn had been picked up by a
police cruiser at the park in Curly and was on his way
to Greenville at that very moment. Nolan Ellis,
however, was nowhere to be found.

Grady couldn't have cared less about Nolan. He
only cared that Vaughn was safe and sound, and he
took time to thank God for that before he decided

how best to tell Paige that her son was once more coming home to her. His first instinct was to pull on clothes and drive to Nobb, but on second thought, he realized that was not the wisest course. For one thing, it would delay the news even longer, and she would want to know as soon as possible. For another, if he saw her he would have to hold her, but he wasn't sure she would welcome that, and he just didn't know if he could bear another rebuff. He picked up the phone.

Paige was sleeping soundly when the call came. It felt like the first time in weeks, which perhaps accounted for the fact that she felt unusually refreshed when she opened her eyes to a surprisingly pitch-dark room. She groped for the phone, got her hand on the receiver of the hopelessly outdated corded telephone on the bedside table and lifted it to her ear. Her voice didn't work quite as expected, sounding raspy and soft.

"Hello?"

Grady's solid baritone greeted her. "Paige? Honey, wake up. I've got something important to tell you. Vaughn called me a few minutes ago."

She sat up. "What's going on?"

He told her in calm, succinct words. For some reason—she didn't know why—she could barely believe it. Nolan was insane to try something like this. What did he have to gain? The only reason for it was to hurt her, but he had succeeded only in punishing himself. Nolan had forced Vaughn to choose, and their son had chosen *her*.

At first she felt that she ought to go to Vaughn straightaway, but Grady counseled her to speak to Vaughn before she did anything, and for once she took his advice to heart. The situation was under control. Vaughn was safe. Dan was already on his way and entirely capable of handling the legalities. God willing, Vaughn could be in Arkansas before bedtime rolled around again. One thing puzzled her.

"Why did he call you with this?"

"You'll have to ask him," Grady answered. "Maybe he figured I could afford to come get him easier than you could. Or maybe he didn't want to worry you. All I know is he's afraid to go over his fifteen-minute-a-day telephone allotment."

Paige shook her head. He was either the most responsible boy she'd ever known or the most mercenary. Maybe both. "That child is a piece of work," she mused aloud.

Grady chuckled. "Yes, he is, and you'd lay down your life for him."

"In a heartbeat," she confirmed.

A moment of silence passed, and then Grady softly asked, "What's going to happen now, Paige?"

She knew what he was asking. Would she and Vaughn stay in Arkansas or move to South Carolina together as they'd planned?

"I don't know, Grady. I just don't know."

Things got a little complicated. It turned out that Vaughn had called his father and warned him that he might be arrested again. Paige couldn't fault him for that. She understood that he didn't want his dad to go to jail. It was enough for her that he had thwarted Nolan's plans to abscond with him. It did, however, delay Vaughn's return.

The sheriff wanted to be sure that Vaughn had no real knowledge of his father's whereabouts, but they couldn't question him until Dan arrived and took stock of the situation. After that all the proper hoops had to be jumped through before Dan could leave the jurisdiction with Vaughn. Child Welfare had to be called in and brought up to date, and this time they had to go before a judge in chambers. They allowed Dan to take Vaughn with him to a local hotel for the night.

It was Wednesday evening before they stepped off the plane at Northwest Regional. Paige was waiting with open arms. She was a little disappointed that Grady was not there, but all things considered, it was probably for the best. She still didn't know what the future held for her and her son.

Vaughn had been through a rough few days and had essentially lost his father. He would need time to calm down and adjust. Then they could discuss the situation and come to some well-reasoned decisions. She was fully prepared to move to Greenville with Vaughn if that was what it was going to take to reconcile him to this new situation, which was why she intended to go ahead with the sale of her business.

She thanked Dan profusely. He was in a hurry to get home, having been gone several days longer than expected, but he was philosophical about the whole thing.

"I figure this was why God had me down in Georgia to begin with. I certainly didn't accomplish what I went there for."

Paige commiserated with him. "I'm so sorry. I guess this means you'll have to go again."

Smiling, he shook his head. "Nope. God had everything under control. The defendant decided to settle. They contacted Grady this morning, and he rushed them into arbitration. They were still at it as of five minutes ago, but I expect we'll have an agreement shortly."

Paige sighed with relief for more than one reason. Was it vain and selfish of her to hope that Grady hadn't yet given up on them? She looked at her son, who appeared tired and sad, and reminded herself that she had much for which to be thankful. Slipping her arms around his shoulders, she shepherded her poor boy to the truck and home.

He rode quietly all the way, answering her careful questions with terse, sad replies. She was gratified that he greeted Howler with a good scratching and Matthias with a quick hug. But then he picked at the supper she had put back for him and glumly asked what was going to happen now. When she told him that it depended on him, he nodded solemnly, said that he was tired and rose from the table to take himself off to bed. Before leaving the room he kissed her cheek and told her that he loved her. She hugged him tight, whispering that she knew he was hurting and how sorry she was about that.

"It's not your fault," he told her, fiercely scrubbing away his tears. "Nothing's been your fault." He looked at Matthias and said, "You were right. I'm sorry for before."

"No, son," Matthias said, looking at Paige. "Your mama is the one who's been right. About everything, and I gave her just about as hard a time as you did."

She shook her head, keeping an arm around her son. "I wish it all wasn't so painful for you, Vaughn."

"How come he has to be this way?" Vaughn cried in a tiny voice, and she knew he was talking about his father.

"I don't know, honey. I wish I did. Then maybe we'd all still be together the way a real family should be."

"We can be a family anyway, can't we?" he asked hopefully, "Just us on our own?"

"Yes, we can. We already are," she assured him. "God will work out everything else."

She would not be greedy enough to ask that He work it out as she wanted Him to. Even if she and Vaughn decided to stay right where they were, it might be too late. A man like Grady could be expected to come in second only so often.

It was the middle of the afternoon when the phone in Grady's office rang. It was Paige's number, but Matthias's voice that greeted Grady. Once again, however, Grady knew immediately that there was trouble, if not catastrophe. The quiver told him as much as the words.

"Grady? You b-better get o-over here. Nolan's showed up."

He was out the door before the connection was broken, leaving a client on hold on the other line and the receptionist gaping. Everything he knew and felt told Grady that Nolan turning up at Paige's house could not be good. Even before he hit the parking lot at a run, he was talking aloud to God.

"Keep them safe, Lord. Keep them safe. I'll do anything. I'll give up anything. Just keep them safe."

Somehow he managed not to get stopped for speeding as he tore through one community after another. He was driving so fast that he dared not even take the time to call and check on them. Instead he just kept handing it off to God, trusting Him to protect them until he could get there. As he sped through the single, timeworn block of downtown Nobb, he noticed that folks were standing out on the side of the road, staring off in the general direction of Paige's house.

He caught the flash of colored lights through the trees as he swung the car onto the drive. Panic seized Grady by the throat. The panic intensified when the cop cars came into view. An ambulance was parked beside a two-tone blue pickup with a creased tailgate. Grady bailed out, stupidly ignored the officer who approached him and was saved a confrontation when Vaughn shot out of the house and threw himself at him. Howler was ripping the sky apart and turning tight circles around everyone in the yard, but the mutt shut up and plopped down on his haunches as Grady caught a sobbing Vaughn against him.

"He hurt her bad! I tried to stop him, but he hurt her!"

Grady nearly dropped. "Where is she?"

He turned instinctively toward the ambulance, only then aware that someone or something was being loaded into it. At the same time, Vaughn pulled him toward the house. Grady left Vaughn behind in two strides, took the steps up onto the porch in one leap and was standing in her living room before the officer guarding the door could even move to block him.

One wild glance around the room showed him Paige sitting calmly on the sofa. A female medical emergency technician was perched next to her, taking her pulse. Grady dropped to his knees beside Paige. She offered him a lopsided smile and a look of such compassion and apology that he sighed. Then she leaned forward and pressed her forehead to his.

"Thank God!" he exclaimed, sliding his arms around her.

She caught her breath, and that's when he realized that she was wearing a sling on her left arm. Before he could even think about it, he was on his feet again, rage unlike anything he'd ever felt tearing through him.

"Where is he?"

A solid hand fell heavily on his shoulder and spun him around. It was the policeman.

"If you're talking about Nolan Ellis," the officer said, "that's him they just loaded into the ambulance."

Grady blinked at that. Nolan was in the ambulance?

"What happened?" he demanded of the room at large. Vaughn, who had entered the house behind him, answered.

"Matthias hit him with his cane."

Grady turned until he found Matthias standing uncertainly against the wall. He looked sick, every bit as shaken as he'd sounded on the phone. "You hit him?"

"Knocked him cold," the policeman confirmed.

"He had to," Vaughn insisted. "I missed him with the lamp."

"Missed *who* with the lamp?"

"Nolan," Paige said softly, reaching out a hand to her son. Vaughn stepped to her side and took her hand in his. "Nolan had some crazy idea that he was going to force Vaughn to go with him," Paige explained softly. "When I intervened, he attacked me. Vaughn threw the lamp in his bedroom to try to stop him from twisting my arm."

"It needs an X-ray," the EMT said, getting to her feet. "The wrist could be broken."

"It doesn't hurt now," Paige put in quickly. "It'll keep until we're done here."

Grady looked at the policeman, slipping easily, almost gratefully, into lawyer mode. It made it easier to tame the riot of his emotions. "What do you need to wrap this up? I'll be representing Mr. Porter, if it comes to that. You should know that Ellis has broken several laws just by entering the state."

The policeman held up his hand. "All right, cool your jets. I've had the story from these three, and we're transporting Ellis under custody. He'll be arrested as soon as he regains consciousness. I'll need statements, but it can wait a day or two. You get her taken care of first." He looked pointedly at Paige. "I wanted to call a second ambulance, but she insisted she'd wait for you."

It was Vaughn who said, "That's 'cause Grady always takes care of us."

"I always want to," Grady said automatically, looking down at Paige, who smiled without meeting his gaze. The bottom fell out of Grady's stomach. He swallowed and forced himself to prioritize. "Let's get you to an emergency room."

Paige nodded and rose shakily to her feet.

"I wanna come, too," Vaughn insisted.

Matthias cleared his throat then and stepped forward. Grady took one look at him and said, "We'll all go." Still looking shaken and pale, the old guy simply nodded. Grady glanced at Vaughn and gave his head a little jerk. "Lend a hand?"

Vaughn went straight to Matthias. Looking up at the old man with something akin to hero worship, he took Matthias's hand and lifted it to his shoulder, saying, "Lean on me. I'll be your cane for a while."

Grady watched Matthias beat back tears, nod and pat the boy's shoulder. "Let's go then."

It took several minutes to get them all in the car and several hours to get Paige seen, treated and released again. Grady made sure that she was looked over from head to toe, but the X-ray showed only a hairline fracture in one of the bones in her left wrist.

Vaughn hovered over his mom as if he was her caretaker instead of the other way around. Grady sensed that it was a role with which he had great familiarity, and that alone would have told him about the boy's relationship with his father if Vaughn himself had not already done so. By tacit agreement, the three adults allowed Vaughn to hover and fuss and generally act like he was in charge, fearing that an emotional storm was yet to come.

Grady secured a report on Nolan and passed the information to Vaughn, who accepted it in silence. Although concussed, Nolan was expected to make a full recovery. Vaughn seemed relieved but subdued after hearing this.

It was dark by the time they left the hospital. Grady called ahead and ordered pizza and salad to be picked up for dinner. Vaughn rode in the backseat with his mother, leaving Matthias to ride up front with Grady. The storm broke while they waited in the drive-through lane for the food.

Paige just held her son against her right side and let him cry, whispering comfort and encouragement, telling him over and over again that nothing was his fault. Every once in a while her tear-drenched eyes would meet Grady's in the rearview mirror. He put everything else aside and did his best to telegraph his strength and love straight to her.

Once they got back to the house, he settled Paige

on the couch and sent Matthias for a blanket while Vaughn carried the food into the kitchen. Grady joined Vaughn, and together they got down plates and poured drinks for everyone.

Finally Vaughn looked up at him, eyes swollen and red, to softly ask, "What's going to happen to my dad now?"

Grady didn't sugarcoat it, but he took no pleasure in saying, "He's going to spend some time in jail, Vaughn, probably a few months. Hopefully it'll be enough to convince him that he never wants to do something this stupid again."

Vaughn bowed his head. Grady looped an arm around his shoulders, thinking what a curious mix of man and child Vaughn was. Grady supposed that came of being torn between two parents, one of whom could not seem to live up to his responsibilities. The other, fortunately, was wise, indeed.

"That doesn't mean you can't see your dad," Grady told the boy, "or that God can't change him."

Vaughn nodded, and asked, "What's gonna happen with us?"

"What do you want to happen?" Paige asked from the doorway.

Grady frowned at her, but he knew how much good it would do to scold her for getting up. Instead, he just pulled a chair out from the table and parked her in it. Then he leaned against the counter and folded his arms. He had just as big a stake in Vaughn's answer as anyone, after all.

Paige called Vaughn to her and smoothed his hair from his forehead with her one good hand. "We don't have to make any decisions now, but what do you want to happen, Vaughn? Do you want to stay here so you can see your dad from time to time, assuming this is where he'll be." She looked to Grady for confirmation of that, and he nodded. "Or do you want to go home to South Carolina? If you want to go home, I'll see to it that you get back here as often as possible to visit your dad."

Vaughn screwed up his face. "I dunno. I like Curly. My friends are all there, and the hockey team's better." Paige nodded and smiled wanly, flashing an apologetic look at Grady, who could only swallow and wait for it. "But we already got our own house here," Vaughn went on, "and what about Matthias and Grady?"

Paige squeezed his hand with hers. "What about them?"

"Well, you said that we could be a real family, just the two of us, but aren't they, like, sort of our family, too."

Paige nodded, tears filling her eyes. "Chosen family," she whispered.

Grady cleared his throat and stuck his big foot in the door. "We could be more than *sort of* family," he said, holding her gaze, "if I could convince your mother to marry me."

Vaughn jerked around. "Ha! I knew it!" Grinning slyly, he asked, "Are you still gonna get that new game system?"

Grady laughed, feeling his worries float away. "We'll see."

"Vaughn," Paige said, forcing his attention back to her, "I thought you were upset with the idea of me and Grady together."

Vaughn shrugged and glumly said, "I guess I thought that if you loved Dad he'd change."

"Honey, I did love your dad."

"I know, and he ruined it," Vaughn stated flatly. "He ruins everything. I don't think he can help it." He looked at Grady and said, "He doesn't know how to take care of anybody like you do, not even himself."

"You know how," Grady said. He looked to Paige, adding, "Must get it from your mom."

Vaughn smiled. "Yeah. She's the best."

"You know what I think?" Grady asked, latching a hand on to the boy's shoulder. "I think you'd be a really good big brother."

Paige gasped at the same time Vaughn declared, "That'd be cool!"

Suddenly Paige began to sob. "I love you both so much!" she wailed.

Grady looked at Vaughn, and they shared what he was sure would not be their last moment of masculine understanding.

"Well, do something," Vaughn instructed.

Grady did the only thing he could think to do, the thing he wanted most to do. He went to Paige and picked her up, cradling her in his arms like a weeping child.

"Bring the pizza," he told Vaughn, carrying her into the living room.

Matthias walked into the room carrying a blanket at the same time Grady walked in carrying Paige. "What's wrong with her now?" he wanted to know.

"She loves us," Grady said, dropping down onto the couch with her in his lap. Paige chortled and spluttered.

Matthias grunted and plopped down into his chair, dropping the blanket beside it. Vaughn appeared and thrust a plate of pizza and salad at Matthias, announcing, "Mom and Grady are getting married."

"'Bout time."

"And I'm gonna be a big brother."

"Well, of course you are, a good one, too."

Paige wiped her eyes on Grady's shoulder and petulantly demanded, "Where's my ring?"

Grady chuckled, the hole in his chest finally closing, and kissed her temple. "On my bedside table." He glanced down at her swollen left hand and added, "You'll get it just as soon as you can wear it."

She sniffed and said, "Are we still building the house?"

"What house?" Vaughn asked, bringing them a plate piled high with pizza enough for two.

"Oh, Vaughn, it's the most amazing thing, stables and a pool and a media room."

"Sweet! Where?"

"Here or there," Grady said, taking the plate that Vaughn offered them. He kissed Paige's nose. "If

Vaughn wants South Carolina, we'll give him South Carolina."

Paige looked at Grady, wonder in her eyes. Foolish woman. "You'd really do that?"

"Sweetheart, I moved once for a woman I didn't care about half as much as I love you. Do you really think I wouldn't move for you and Vaughn?"

"I just couldn't ask it of you," she whispered. "Your family and career are here."

"My family want me to be happy, and they need lawyers in South Carolina, too."

Paige wrapped her arms around his neck and squeezed before turning to Vaughn, who'd taken a seat on the end of the sofa opposite them. "What do you say now, son? Here or there?"

Vaughn shrugged as if it was immaterial to him and bit off a huge chunk of pizza. He looked at Grady and with a full mouth asked, "Suppose Jason will let me back on the team?"

"Don't talk with your mouth full," Grady said mildly, smiling, "and yeah, I think we can get you back on the team."

Vaughn cut his eyes at his mom and swallowed. "Can I get that new cell phone?"

She stared at him and sternly warned, "Don't push it, buster."

Vaughn grinned. "I don't know why we'd go back to South Carolina when everything that matters most is here."

"There you go," Matthias put in. "Kid's got brains. Always said he had brains. Takes after his mother."

Paige laughed, and said to him, "I'm counting on you to walk me down the aisle, you know."

"I'll walk you down the aisle, but I ain't giving you away," Matthias told her. He winked at Grady and added, "I'm keeping the lot of you, and that's that."

They all laughed. And then Paige realized that they hadn't said grace over the pizza. Grady did the honors, finding so much to be thankful for that the words just fell out of him. When he was done, he opened his eyes to find Vaughn gazing at him.

"I guess, in a way, I got my mom and dad in the same place, after all, just not like I thought it would be."

"That's a good way to look at it," Grady said, smiling.

Vaughn nodded and said, "This way is better, I think."

Grady reached out and laid a hand on the nape of the boy's neck. "I hope that one day your dad will say the same thing, Vaughn."

"We'll pray about it," Vaughn said matter-of-factly, going back to his pizza.

Grady looked down at the woman who had made them both understand just how powerful a simple thing like prayer could be.

"We certainly will," he said.

It was the right thing to do, after all, and maybe one day even Nolan would find his way home, home to love and healing and understanding, home to God, where love reigns and we all belong.

* * * * *

Dear Reader,

The very bedrock of Christianity is forgiveness. Through the work of Christ, God forgives our transgressions, and we are admonished to forgive those who harm us, as well. Yet, if we're honest, we could all recognize something that we find nearly impossible to forgive.

In writing Paige's story, I had to imagine what would be truly difficult for her to forgive, which meant imagining what would be truly difficult for *me* to forgive. Didn't take much thought, actually. It's pretty much been a given since the day after Christmas of 1972, when my first son was born. Harm me, I think I can find a way to forgive; harm my child…that's another struggle entirely.

Yet God loved us enough to actually sacrifice His own Son. That greatest of sacrifices should inspire and empower us to do that which may be most difficult, simply because it is right and best. May we all find that strength and know the rewards of truly forgiving.

God bless,

Arlene James

QUESTIONS FOR DISCUSSION

1. Is it ever foolish for a Christian to forgive? Why or why not?

2. Grady feared that Paige's forgiving attitude toward her ex-husband would expose her and her son to danger. Does forgiveness always bring rewards for the Christian or might it actually bring danger?

3. If forgiving a wrong brings danger for a Christian, are biblical commandments to forgive nullified?

4. Paige struggled to "take the high road" and not criticize her ex to their son, even after the boy remained hostile to his being reunited with her. Is it always wise to take the high road in such cases?

5. Parents constantly struggle to do what's best for their children, but it's easy to become confused about what's best and what's simply most indulgent. Do you think that Paige's willingness to move to another state and share her son with his father was the right choice or a foolish indulgence?

6. We've all heard it said that love is blind, but sometimes it seems that the need to *be* loved is even more blinding. Does Vaughn's need to be loved by his father make his attitude toward his mother reasonable or understandable? Why or why not?

7. Grady's awkwardness made his personal relationships with women difficult. How much of this might be personality and how much of it could be attributed to losing his mother at such an early age?

8. How did Paige's example help Grady deal with his unresolved grief and confusion concerning his mother's death?

9. Did Matthias's rescue of Paige from the physical menace of her ex-husband provide a satisfying closure for the characters? For the reader? Why or why not?

10. In the end, were Paige's attitude and actions—particularly toward her ex, but also concerning her son and Grady—laudable or unwise?